SERPENT
in the
THORNS

The Crispin Guest Novels by Jeri Westerson

Veil of Lies

Serpent in the Thorns

SERPENT
in the
THORNS

A Crispin Guest Medieval Noir

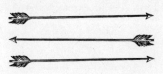

Jeri Westerson

MINOTAUR BOOKS ◪ NEW YORK

This is a work of fiction. All of the characters, organizations, and events
portrayed in this novel are either products of the author's imagination
or are used fictitiously.

SERPENT IN THE THORNS. Copyright © 2009 by Jeri Westerson. All rights
reserved. Printed in the United States of America. For information, address St.
Martin's Press, 175 Fifth Avenue, New York, N.Y. 10010.

www.minotaurbooks.com

The Library of Congress has cataloged the hardcover edition as follows:

Westerson, Jeri.
    Serpent in the thorns / Jeri Westerson. — 1st ed.
       p. cm.
    ISBN 978-0-312-53498-1
    1. Great Britain—History—14th century—Fiction. 2. London
(England)—Fiction. 3. Murder—Investigation—Fiction. I. Title
  PS3623.E8478S47 2009
  813'.6—dc22

                2009012739

ISBN 978-0-312-64944-9 (trade paperback)

First Minotaur Books Paperback Edition: October 2010

10 9 8 7 6 5 4 3 2 1

For Craig and Graham

Acknowledgments

Again, my first thanks go to my ever-patient husband, Craig, my wonderful son, Graham, and my Vicious Circle of Ana Brazil, Bobbie Gosnell, and Laura James. Thanks also to my agent, Joshua Bilmes, for continuing to hold my hand, and a very special thanks goes out to Julia Spencer-Fleming and her husband, Ross, for their kind words and their wonderful help! Another very special thanks also goes to Kevin Cooper and Carl Vitolo of Inland Color Graphics. They have continued to help me with their support and their valuable printing for all my wonderful promotional materials. And thanks also to DiAnne Cooper, my idea person at ICG. (Thanks, guys! I owe you more tequila.) Paige Vignola offered help in the Latin, and there were scores of others who helped with aspects of history and answered many other questions I posed on mediev-l. I've met librarians and booksellers who have been nothing but supportive and kind and I thank you all, wherever you are. Last but not least, I thank Keith Kahla at St. Martin's Press for his excellent editing and advice. Long may you wave!

SERPENT
in the
THORNS

I

London, 1384

PRETTY, LIKE A WINDBLOWN shepherdess. Sweet, but a bit dim. Crispin sensed it from the way she ran her chapped fingers over her right hand and by the care she took pronouncing each word. She lifted her chin and parted her lips even when she wasn't speaking. He leaned forward and focused his blurry eyes on her. "Tell me again about the dead man," he said. "Slowly."

She rubbed her hands, meekly, hurriedly, as if she knew she would be chastised for it.

Crispin watched her busy hands and closed his eyes. His head felt like an eggshell liable to crack, and the merest sound seemed to rake the back of his eyeballs with sharp needles. He glanced at the wine jug on its shelf. Hair of the dog?

She sat on a stool in his lodgings, a small room above a tinker shop on the pungent streets of the Shambles with its meat markets and butchering stalls. One of his broken shutters rattled with an acrid wind that did nothing to sooth the belch of the room's smoky hearth. A table, a chair, another stool, a narrow bed, and a chest. All rented. He owned little more than the clothes on his back, and they made a poor showing.

"There's a dead man in me room," she said, thick with a Southwark accent. She overpronounced her words, letting her lips slip back over her teeth, revealing them often. One bottom tooth was chipped and gray. "Livith wasn't there. I couldn't ask her. She's always there to explain, but she wasn't there."

He passed a hand over his face but his head hurt too much. He slowly sank to the stool. "Who is Livith?"

"She's me sister. She looks after me. I get confused. She always explains."

"I see," he said, barely understanding. Wine might not be a bad idea at that, and he moved to the larder. He poured a bowl, but not for himself, and handed it to her. She stared into the wine and then looked up at him. "Go on," he said. "You look as if you need it."

She tipped the bowl with trembling fingers, sloshing some of the wine onto her faded blue gown and apron-covered lap. She tried to smile. A wine mustache made it pathetic.

Crispin sat on the chest this time and rested his hands on his thighs. He hoped it would keep the room from tilting. "Why did you come to me?"

Her lips twisted. "You're the Tracker, ain't you? I heard of you from the others. You find out things. They say you was once a knight and know all sorts of matters."

He waved his hand and scowled, but that, too, hurt his head. "Never mind that. Past history. It is your difficulty that intrigues me now. You have a problem and I am happy to solve it for you. But . . . I am paid for such a service."

"I couldn't find Livith, so I came to you. Not the sheriffs. They scare me. I heard you was smart like her. Like Livith. You could reckon things out."

"Yes, that is true. But I do so for a fee. Do you understand?"

"Livith won't let me have money."

No surprise there. "Where is the dead man now?"

"In our room. At the King's Head Inn. We're scullions there. He's got an arrow in him, doesn't he?"

An arrow? Crispin sat up straighter. "I haven't yet seen him. Do you know who he is?"

"No. Never saw him before. But he's dead now."

"Never fear. I will do my best to find the man who killed him."

She cocked her head and blinked. "But I already know who killed him."

Crispin made a surprised sound, but before he could respond with a question, the door flung wide. Crispin shot to his feet and blocked the woman from the unknown intruder.

A ginger-haired boy dashed into the room, slammed and bolted the door, and rested against it, panting. He looked up at Crispin through a mane of curled locks. Riotous freckles showed darker against his bone pale skin.

"Jack!" Crispin put a hand to his throbbing head. "What by God's toes are you doing?"

"Master," said the boy. His gaze darted between the girl peering around Crispin's back and then up to Crispin again. "Nought. Nought much."

Crispin glared at his charge. Jack Tucker was more trouble than any servant had a right to be. Certainly more so than had served him in the past. A pitiful servant, was Tucker. Seldom present when needed, almost always an annoyance, and just another mouth to feed. He had not wanted a servant! Not anymore. Not when he didn't deserve one.

Ah, if only seven years ago Crispin had not plotted treason. If only he had not been caught by the king's guards. If only they hadn't stripped him of his knighthood and his lands. If only . . . if only. Then he wouldn't be living on the stinking streets of the Shambles above a tinker's shop with a thief as a servant and a simpleton girl as a client.

"The gods, too, are fond of a joke," he lamented.

Jack was eyeing the wine jug and Crispin was about to berate him for interrupting when the tinker's door below shook with muffled pounding. Crispin crossed to the opposing wall and threw open the shutters to the small window overlooking the street. The stench of butchering and offal rose to his second-story room. A boy lugging chickens in a stick cage hurried next door to the poulterer followed by a man carrying several dead coneys by their feet. He tramped through the mud, the rabbits' long ears dragging with each stride.

Crispin leaned out over the sill. Two men stood at the tinker shop door right below him and beat on it with their fists.

He turned back to the room. "For God's sake, Jack. What have you done?"

Jack shrugged, still looking at the girl. "Begging your pardon, sir, for interrupting."

"Why are those men after you?"

"It's a little disagreement over property, you might say."

"You stole from them."

Jack opened his mouth. His brows widened. "Now why is that the first thing you think about me?" He thrust his fist into his hip. "I get into a little bit of trouble and you think I've gone and cut a purse."

"Well? Did you?"

"Ain't that beside the point?"

Beneath Crispin's window, the men grumbled as they waited, and Crispin peered out again, observing them. Martin Kemp, Crispin's landlord, opened his shop door a crack. The meek tinker made his polite inquiries. And then the men answered. Crispin couldn't hear the words exactly, but their voices rose in volume as each side argued their case. The shrill voice that joined the others could only be Martin's wife, Alice. Crispin winced at the sound filtering up through the timbers. Her appearance only made things worse and, against Martin's protest, the men finally pushed past him. All of them rumbled up Crispin's stairs, still arguing.

Jack sprinted toward the other window facing the back courtyard. "Sorry, Master. Must go. We'll talk later." He quickly pushed opened the shutter and looked back apologetically toward Crispin. Scrambling out the window, Jack leaped down to the next building and minced across the rooftops.

Crispin closed both windows and made a contrite smile to the girl who didn't seem to understand or care what was happening.

His door suddenly shuddered under pounding fists. Steeling himself, he unbolted and yanked open the door, filling the threshold with indignation. "What is the meaning of this?"

The gathering pulled up short. Clearly they did not expect Crispin or his refined accent. Two strangers—one thin and golden-haired and the other short and robust with dark, bushy brows—stood on the landing beside the tinker Martin Kemp and his wife. "We beg your pardon, good sir," said the blond-haired man, making a curt bow, "but we were chasing a thief and have good reason to believe he came this way."

Crispin kicked the door wider so they could see into the sparse room. "Does it look like he's here?"

They stared at the girl—eyes wide, mouth gaping—and then at Crispin. "No sir," said the man with the bushy brows. He scanned the room again, and gave a resigned nod.

The tinker's wife, Alice, pushed forward. "He's here. Mark me."

The bushy-browed man frowned at Alice and then at Crispin. "Sir," he said, "if that boy is here we demand you surrender him to us. He's a thief and we're here to see he gets his just punishment."

"Nonsense. This is my entire lodgings. Do you suggest he is hiding in the walls?"

As one, they all leaned down to look under the pallet bed—the only likely place left.

A solitary chamber pot sat in the shadows.

The bushy-browed man huffed with disappointment and they all straightened again.

Alice postured. "He'll hang from the highest gibbet, if I have my way."

"Hush, dear," said the tinker out of the side of his mouth. His leather cap, snug against his head, trembled with agitation.

The men muttered together until the bushy-browed man finally said, "We'll trouble you no more, sir. Our apologies. God keep you." They bowed to him and the girl, gave Alice a scathing look, and slowly retreated down the stairs.

Martin and Alice remained on the landing.

Crispin glanced back at the girl. Clients were few and far between and the rent—as always—was late. If this girl could name the killer like she said, it could mean a reward from the sheriff. He studied her simpleton's face and clenched his teeth.

If there *was* a body.

He tried to close the door, but Alice Kemp put out a large hand and stopped it. "That is the third time this week that boy has been in trouble," she said, voice rising like a banshee. "I should call the sheriff on him."

"Now my dear," said Martin. His slim frame did not seem a match for Alice's plumpness. Crispin knew the tinker could swing a hammer with all grace and skill, but could not seem to manage his wife. "There's no need for that. Crispin can take care of any difficulty, can't you, Crispin?"

The last was a plea and Crispin nodded. "Yes, Mistress Kemp. I will do my best."

"Your best! Ha! Your best is piss poor." She eyed the girl. "And this had better be a client, Crispin Guest, for I'll have none of your whoring under my roof."

"Madam!" He sputtered and drew up, glaring down his sharp nose at her. "This young woman *is* a client," he said, teeth clenched, "but not for long if you persist. If you want your rent on time—" He jabbed his open hand toward the door, urging her out.

Martin paled and yanked his wife back out of the threshold. Crispin slammed the door and threw the bolt. He breathed through his nostrils at the wood, and listened as their steps disappeared downward. He counted to ten, turned back to the room, and tried to grin, but the throbbing in his head would not allow it. "I apologize," he said tightly. "That was my landlord . . . and his wife." He said the last with bared teeth. He gestured uselessly toward the closed window. "And the boy was Jack Tucker. He insists on calling himself my servant but I'm afraid he is more suited to the vocation of a cutpurse."

The girl did not change expression. She merely lifted her upswept nose. Her eyes were gray like Crispin's but more watery than his slate, and for all her steady gaze, there seemed little sense behind those eyes.

He gave up.

"We were speaking of a dead man," he said quietly. "And his killer. You say you know who it is."

"Livith wasn't there," she repeated.

"No, she wasn't there. You said that." He groaned and slowly blinked. This was going to take all day. "Does anyone else know this man is in your room?"

She shook her head. "I wanted *your* help."

"You have it. Who killed him?"

"I shouldn't say—"

"Are you protecting someone?"

"It ain't like that." She sucked on her dirty index finger.

"If you know who did it then you must tell me."

Her face crumpled and tears spilled down her apple cheeks. She pulled her finger from her mouth and dropped her hand to her lap. In a small voice she said, "*I* did."

2

CRISPIN DID HIS BEST to settle his expression into something bland and unthreatening. He looked her slight frame up and down. She was a hand span shorter than Jack Tucker, who was another hand span shorter than Crispin. "*You* killed him?"

"Aye. I must have, mustn't I? I was the only one there." She wiped her moist nose with her fingers.

He sat on the chair and pulled it up to her, looking her in the eye. "It doesn't necessarily follow that you killed him."

"But I did!" Her wide eyes darted, lighting here and there in the room, never finding a resting place. "I must have."

"Did he attack you?"

"No."

He watched her lip tremble, and a tear rolled with ferocity down her cheek, dragging a dirty trail with it. "I think it best we go to your lodgings and discover what we can. Maybe your sister has returned."

"Aye!" She jumped to her feet and pushed him out of the way to get to the door. "Maybe she's back."

She unbolted the door and scurried over the threshold. Crispin watched her descend the stairs. He settled his cloak over his shoulders, locked the door, and tromped down the steps after her.

The midmorning shadows hatched the lane, leaving some puddles to catch the blue-tinted sky while others reflected a dull gray. A man with a pushcart of bundled sticks heaved his charge over the muddy ruts, swearing colorfully to the saints as he did so. A dog sniffed at his heel at first and then trotted onward to lift his leg at the first rung of Crispin's stair.

"Make haste!" The girl danced near a frost-edged puddle outside the tinker shop. "Livith might be back and she'll be awful cross with me."

"Leaving a dead man in her room," Crispin muttered. "I should think so."

He followed her along the Shambles over muddy lanes and dark alleys stinking of mold. The clouds, so recently parted above, closed in again and made the way dark and threatening with rain. Crispin knew the King's Head, an inn little better than his favorite haunt, the Boar's Tusk on Gutter Lane. Though he considered the latter no fine tavern, his friends Gilbert and Eleanor Langton owned it and made it homey. The King's Head was a rougher place, an inn near the wharves, less inviting except to drown a man's sorrows in watered wine and even smaller beer.

They traveled south. Men with fine garb and fur-trimmed mantles became fewer, replaced by anonymous gray men frowning under rough hoods made of cat skins. Even the horses looked different the closer they came to the Thames. The lustrous coats of good mounts gave way to frail stotts, pulling carts with shuffling gaits, their ribs clearly visible on their dull flanks. The rats, on the other hand, were healthy and sleek and, in some instances, as big as piglets. They shambled along the foundations, foraging unabated.

Once Crispin and the girl passed through a narrow close, the inn slowly emerged out of the gloom of London's choking smoke and the brackish mist rising from the nearby Thames. A big, square building, the inn's dark half-timbers looked like frown lines and its drooping roof tiles like brows. A boy no older than Jack was sweeping the threshold of the inn's entrance with a mended broom in a lazy back and forth motion. The girl did not greet him nor did the boy look up. Instead, the girl took Crispin across the courtyard and behind the building into the stable yard. The air was pungent with its aroma of sweaty horses, moldy hay, and dung. A rat eyed Crispin with a twist of its whiskers, turned, and scurried up the wall before it disappeared beneath a roof tile.

The girl looked back once at Crispin to make sure he still followed, stepped down a short staircase to a lower croft, and opened a door.

The passage lay in darkness except for the slightly brighter outline of a door ahead. The girl opened it and stepped aside. Crispin inhaled old smoke and mildew. The stone walls were streaked brown with moisture. A small half-round window studded with iron bars squinted from above their heads, letting in only strands of blue-tinted light and sprinkling rain. The window sat at street level, and all he could see was the slick street and striding feet.

One lit candle and the hearth—if the small collection of stones and sticks in the center of the floor could be called a hearth—burned halfheartedly. The smoke rose to the low arched ceiling, whirled in eddies between the beams, and meandered toward the open window.

The storeroom, with its stacked barrels and plump sacks, offered barely enough space for a pallet with a pile of straw, a chipped chamber pot, a table, a bench, two bowls, two wooden spoons.

And a dead man in the corner.

No signs of a scuffle or a break-in. Nothing out of place or out of the ordinary. The man simply seemed to have dropped where he was shot. He lay with his back propped against the wall, legs out before him, head lolled to one side. The wooden shaft of an arrow protruded from his chest, just the right place for his heart. A direct hit. Only six inches of shaft and hawk fletching rose out of a houppelande coat soaked with blood. Crispin knelt and touched the man's throat, but the ashen skin and dry staring eyes told him he would find no pulse.

Except for the rusty smell of blood, the man was fragrant with lavender water. Crispin picked up his limp hand and examined it in the sparse light. The nails were clean and trimmed. By his side rested a large bag containing a wooden box.

Not a ruffian out for a bit of fun. His garb of a quartered houppe-lande with its blue and gold fields of fleur-de-lis made Crispin's skin crawl. This man was not merely a Frenchman, but his livery indicated he came from the French court.

Crispin glanced over his shoulder to look back at the girl. "Did you open this bag?"

She shook her head.

He rubbed sweat from his upper lip. A courier, perhaps. A *dead* courier. There was no possible good side to this.

He heard a gasp and turned. A woman stood silhouetted against the open doorway. "What by Saint Cuthbert's bollocks goes on here?" she cried.

The simpleton girl rushed into the woman's arms and fell to loud weeping. The woman's square face twisted into a look of shock, and she dragged the girl into the room trying to shush her. Her shaking hands covered the girl's mouth.

Crispin rose unsteadily. "Are you Livith?"

The woman clutched her sister's head to her breast. The girl visibly calmed and nestled there. The woman's mouth parted, but not in the dull-witted way of her sister. Her shiny lips were ruddy, almost as ruddy as the dark spots on her cheeks. Her angular face—not soft and round like her sister's—played out in planes of shadows and high-lights, touched by long, flailing strands of ash blond hair. And her eyes. Crispin liked those eyes, shaded with hazel instead of the watery gray of the younger woman. There was a cleverness gleaming from them, even with fear shining bright. "Who the hell are you? What have you done here?"

"My name is Crispin Guest. They call me the Tracker."

The arch of her brows showed recognition.

He glanced back at the body. "I did not kill him. Your sister came to fetch me. She believes *she* killed this man."

Livith stared at the crumpled body in the corner, the arrow shaft now gleaming with a passing ray of sun. "Jesus wept!" she hissed. She pushed her sister from her bosom and glared into her face. "You stupid girl! You couldn't have killed him. You know it!"

"But I was the only one here, Livith, and you weren't—" She choked on a sob and hiccupped.

"I'm here now." Clutching the girl, she turned to Crispin. "How could she have possibly *shot* him?"

Crispin cast about the room halfheartedly. He didn't expect to find a bow. "Your sister has somehow twisted the truth. But there is a truth here. And a serious one."

Livith put the girl onto the bench and stood back. "Her name is Grayce."

Crispin made an uneven bow. "I beg your pardon. She never introduced herself—"

"And you never bothered to ask."

He didn't dispute it. Instead he nodded and rubbed his heavy eyes with his knuckles.

"You're drunk. Some sarding help you are." She thrust her hand at her hip, chin high. Even a smudge of dirt on her nose did not diminish her appearance, though Crispin was not endeared by her rough speech.

He straightened his shoulder cape over his cloak. "I am not drunk, wench. Last night I was drunk. Today . . . I am suffering from its venomous aftereffects."

She snorted. "The great 'Tracker.'"

He sighed wearily. "Do you know this dead man?'

She hugged her arms and gave the dead man a cursory glance before shaking her head. "Never saw him before."

"And yet drunk or no, I *do* know that this man is a French courier.

Do you know how much trouble you are in for having such a dead man in your room?"

"I'm beginning to." She bit her fingernail.

He thrust his thumbs into his belt and tapped the leather. "Your sister admitted to killing him."

"But she didn't! Christ!"

"So it would seem. But the sheriff will not be as understanding as I am."

The defiance drained from her sharp features. "Then what are we to do?"

"I'm thinking." He turned back toward the dead man, and then stared up at the window. "Why would he have cause to come down here?"

"He was drunk," Livith offered.

"Or looking for someone, perhaps, and came to the wrong room."

Livith followed his gaze to the window. She pointed. "The window. Someone could have shot him from there."

Crispin examined the angle. "And yet it does not explain what he was doing in here."

Livith turned to Grayce sitting in the bench. She knelt at her feet and placed her hands on Grayce's knees. Her harsh voice gentled. "Now Grayce, you went and fetched this fine gentleman. You must tell us what happened."

Grayce, who had calmed during Livith's arrival, now arched forward with taut shoulders. Her hands curled into claws before her face. "I told him already."

"No, love," cooed Livith. "You didn't tell him. You only made some cockeyed confession. Now you know you couldn't have killed him. Ain't that right?"

Grayce's hands plunged into her hair. She matted it into a bird's nest. "You've got me confused."

"Now, now Grayce. Just tell the gentleman what happened."

"Yes, Grayce." Crispin tried to smile. "Just tell me."

Grayce looked from one face to another. Her eyes rested at last on the body. "I killed him, that's all. I killed him! Stop asking me!"

Livith grasped Grayce's shoulders, opened her mouth, but said nothing. With an expelled breath of frustration, she released her and rose. "She can't say nought. When she gets like this, there's no getting through to her."

Crispin stared at the girl. She clasped her arms and rocked herself, whimpering. *Gracious Jesu.* That wasn't much to tell the sheriff, and Simon Wynchecombe was a man likely to hang them first and ask questions later. Unless he could manage to talk to the other sheriff, John More, first . . . No. The man deferred all unpleasant work to Wynchecombe. There was no getting around it. He sighed and looked at the dead man again. He knelt beside the body, grasped the courier pouch, and unbuckled its leather straps. Inside was a carved wooden box resembling a reliquary. He lifted it from the pouch and set it on the table.

Locked.

Crispin went back to the man and rummaged through his other pouches and purses. He found gold and silver coins, letters of passage in French, and a key. He scanned the letter, but it told him what he already surmised: the man, along with two others, was a courier for the French court and was to be given safe passage across France and England. Their intended destination was London. "Well," he said to the corpse, "you've arrived."

3

CRISPIN TOOK THE KEY to the box, fit it in the lock, and turned it. He lifted the box's lid. Within sat another box made of gold, studded with gems. Livith stepped closer.

"Mary's blessed dugs!" she whispered over his shoulder. "That's solid gold, that!"

"I doubt it is solid gold," said Crispin. But he felt as excited as any thief peering at the royal treasury. With both hands, he lifted the golden casket free of the wooden box and set it on the table.

"Was he killed for this?" she asked.

"If that is so, he was killed in vain." The courier's letter mentioned other companions and Crispin wondered about those men. Where were they? Also dead? Or perhaps simply guilty of murder.

"Could he have been shot outside and made his way in here?"

Crispin glanced along the earthen floor to the entry and saw no blood, no scrapings of staggering steps along the dirt. "The evidence does not bear it out." He grasped the lid and opened. The box was lined in red velvet. In its center indentation sat a wreath made of rushes woven in a decorative pattern of diamonds and zigzags. Large black thorns were thrust here and there within the rush circlet, some three to four inches long. Crispin ran a finger along one of the pronged spikes. "Curious."

"What is it?"

"I have no idea. It looks like some sort of circlet . . . with thorns. Very unpleasant."

"A crown of thorns?"

"Crown of thorns?" He looked at her. "You may be right."

"Not *the* Crown of Thorns?" She took a step back, grasping her patched skirt with chapped fingers.

"No, but possibly *a* crown of thorns, used for feast days." He closed the lid and ran his hand over the gold and gems. He picked it up again, replaced it into the wooden box, put that back into the courier bag, and slung it over his shoulder.

"Here! What are you going to do with that?" Livith's hands gestured toward the pouch, fingers moving, grasping.

That much gold would be a king's ransom to the likes of her. *Come to think of it, the same would be true for me.* "If it's any business of yours, I'm taking it for safekeeping. As for him—" He glanced back at the dead man. "I will have to call in the sheriff."

"But he'll arrest Grayce!"

Grayce leapt up and threw her arms about Livith.

"She is surely innocent," said Crispin. "I can make the sheriff see that."

"But I'm *not*!" she cried between sobs. "I shot him."

Livith glared up at Crispin. "What will the sheriff make of that?"

Crispin sighed. He pictured Wynchecombe's face. "I'm afraid he'll hang her." Grayce wailed and Livith tried to calm her with cooing sounds. She held Grayce's shoulders and rocked her.

Crispin rubbed his stubbled chin and considered. The first priority was to get Grayce the hell out of here, but he couldn't take both women back to his lodgings. His landlord's harridan of a wife would raise the devil.

He thought about his dry throat and decided a trip to the Boar's Tusk was in order.

* * *

CRISPIN LEFT THE WOMEN alone to survey the yard, looking for clues that did not materialize. The women gathered their meager belongings quickly and soon joined him. They set out toward the Shambles in silence, but it didn't last. Livith dragged Grayce behind her. "God's teeth, be still, Grayce! You're wearing me out!" Grayce's cries fell silent except for an occasional sniffle. Livith left Grayce to shuffle along in the mud behind while Livith trotted up to Crispin, boldly appraising him. "Where are we going?"

He didn't like Livith's tone or her constant use of foul language. She was the lowest kind of wench, little better than a whore. "A friend of mine owns a tavern," he said. "He'll hire you both and give you lodgings. It's temporary until all this blows over."

"Just like that. No asking us what we'd sarding like?"

Crispin stopped. Livith ran into him before she could stop herself. He leaned toward her and scowled. "Are you actually ungrateful? You do recall I'm saving your hides, and with very little hope of remuneration for my effort."

She nodded to the parcel slung over his shoulder. "Looks like you got plenty right there."

"The gold box? It does not belong to me. Nor to you, so get those ideas out of your head."

She steadied her gaze on his face and stood so close he felt her fiery breath on his lips. He was angry, but staring at her at such close range made him rethink the situation. Her heavy brows seemed on first glance unattractive, but such bold strokes served to give her face more expression and animation. Her mouth was small but possessed a certain tartness a fuller set of lips lacked—though he feared she would open that mouth again and he'd have to endure a string of unwholesome taunts.

"And I urge you to curb your tongue," he said. "The Boar's Tusk may be on Gutter Lane but *I* do not tolerate gutter language."

"You don't?" Her lips twisted artfully. "Well, I beg his majesty's pardon."

Crispin's frown deepened. "You think this a game? It's your sister's life you gamble with."

Livith dropped her eyes and toed the ground with her muddy wooden shoes. "We've never needed some knight in shining armor rescuing us."

Crispin's frown firmed into a tight line. "Well, I'm no knight."

"Grayce and me have done fine on our own. It ain't our fault some poor bastard got himself killed in our lodgings. What are *we* to do? That was our life back there. And just like that it's snuffed out."

"There is little I can do about the circumstances. And though it may not be your fault a man died in your lodgings, it certainly does not help your cause when your sister keeps confessing to the crime. But if you don't need my help—" He straightened his shoulders and pulled at his patched coat. "I'll be on my way."

He took several steps before she grabbed his arm. She lowered her face and bit her lip. He had a feeling she wasn't used to asking for help. "It's not that I'm ungrateful," she said. This time he sensed her sincerity. "But I—I—"

"Don't know how to *be* grateful?" He snorted a halfhearted chuckle. "Neither do I."

Her face changed when she looked at him. Her demeanor seemed to lighten, finding a kindred spirit, perhaps. How long had she suffered with her dim-witted sister? Grayce did not look more than twenty and Livith maybe a few years older, though the worry line that divided her brow and the dark pouches under her eyes added years to her. She managed a smile. It took those years off again. "Lead on, then," she said and gestured him forward like a noblewoman.

Crispin hid his smile and proceeded on, helping her over the bigger puddles in spite of himself. Grayce followed, carrying the heavy bundle of their goods.

The Boar's Tusk crouched on its corner of Gutter Lane like a great sleeping turtle. Long before Crispin's day, it had boasted the patronage of knights and lords, but the passage of time changed the parish, and now only ruffians made the Boar's Tusk their home. Crispin preferred it that way. Its timber frame was grayed from the weather and the speckled daub had needed refreshing for years, but its great oaken doors were as strong as ever. Needed to be to keep out would-be thieves at night.

He pushed open the door and scanned the low-slung room. Dark, except for a few sputtering oil lamps on the tables and a large hearth burning with decent-sized logs. The heavy beams above seemed as old as Merlin, and Crispin often wondered with their weathered and cracked state if they had the integrity to uphold the roof at all.

Under the uncertain beams, uneven rectangular tables crowded together and were sparsely filled with men hunched over their horn cups, eyes shadowed by hoods or dark deeds.

The tavern's owners, however, were the opposite of its dilapidated plaster and frame. Though they trafficked in the rougher elements of Gutter Lane, Gilbert and Eleanor Langton were kind and generous souls. They somehow did not belong where their sad tavern gripped its foundations, but it would be a poorer place indeed without them.

Crispin spied Eleanor sweeping the floor with a gorse broom and yelling at a servant over a spilled tray.

Crispin approached. "I hope I'm not interrupting."

Eleanor spun. "Oh Crispin! Bless my soul." She grinned and hugged him. The white linen wimple, wrapped about her face in folds and tucks, revealed only her face's smooth contours. An ageless face. Crispin reckoned she might be thirty like himself, but he wasn't certain. "I was just telling this knave," she said, gesturing with the broom toward the servant, "what a wastrel he is, dropping good food onto my floor."

The servant glanced up with hangdog eyes. He scooped a swath of debris onto his tray. "She was 'telling' me awful loud."

Crispin nodded. "I have been under that glare myself, Ned, many a time."

"Make haste, Ned," she barked and smoothed her spotted apron. She looked up and only then noticed Livith and Grayce standing behind Crispin. Her brows drew down and her wimple with it, making her face appear only as a small horizontal oval. "What's this?"

Crispin pulled her aside and said quietly, "Nell, I have a favor to ask."

"Oh no, Crispin. Not again. Why do you use our poor establishment as a dumping ground for your discards?"

Crispin drew himself up. This was the second time this morning a woman accused him of lechery. Not that he wasn't often guilty, but his innocent protestations today seemed to fall on deaf ears. "They are not my 'discards,'" he said in a rumbling tone. "They are my *clients*. They need my help and I need yours."

She rolled her eyes and folded her arms over her chest. "What will Gilbert say? I tell you, Crispin, you take too many liberties."

"That may be so, but this is urgent."

She clutched the broom and made a few conciliatory sweeps. "It always is."

He considered offering money in compensation, but the thought didn't stay long. He had no money at the moment and, indeed, owed Gilbert and Eleanor much already. He softened his tone. "Nell." He smiled. A foul trick, but it usually worked. "The sheriff will be after them, and they need a hiding place. Can you find it in your heart to hire them and keep them here? I would be grateful. It is only temporary until they can return to their lodgings and their situations."

"Aw now, Crispin." She glared at the women. "Well, if it's to grate Wynchecombe. But *only* temporarily, mind. Ned is enough trouble for any establishment. Costs are high and payments—*few*," she said pointedly, rubbing her fingers together.

Crispin bowed formally. "Thank you, Eleanor."

Livith pushed Grayce behind her and raised her sharp chin proudly. "You called us your clients. That means we must needs pay you. What is your fee?"

Crispin thought briefly of declining payment as a chivalrous act. But it had been a long time since he could afford the luxury of chivalry. "Sixpence a day. Plus more for expenses."

She drew in her shoulders and sighed before reaching for the small purse attached to her belt. She poured out its contents into her palm. Four pence, one farthing. She raised her face. "That's all I have." But her eyes traveled back to the bag on Crispin's shoulder.

Crispin scooped up three of the coins to change the direction of her thinking. "I'll take thruppence now. You can pay me later. You'll earn your food and board here, so you will have few expenses." He slipped the coins into his own purse and cleared his throat. "Off with you now. I'll see you here from time to time to let you know the tidings."

"And when can we return to the King's Head?"

"That may not be possible."

The sisters looked at Eleanor.

Crispin made the introductions. "This is your new mistress, Eleanor Langton. Nell, this is Livith and her sister Grayce."

Eleanor frowned. "Very well. Off to the kitchens with you." She gestured with the broom.

The sisters headed toward the kitchen, but Livith looked back at Crispin. "What about that box, then? You can lick more gold off of that than can be had in this place."

Crispin tightened his hold on the strap. "I say again. This is not your property, nor mine. In fact, were either of us to be found with it, it would most certainly mean our deaths. Is that what you want?"

She looked once at the satchel over Crispin's shoulder and shivered. "Aye, I get your meaning at last." She turned and disappeared through the archway.

Eleanor shook her head and clucked her tongue. "Your heart is bigger than your head, sometimes. I know you won't admit it, but you are as soft as dough."

Crispin said nothing. Feeling the small weight of coins in his pouch, he was loath to agree, but knew the truth of it.

"Would you stay, Crispin?" Eleanor set her broom aside and grabbed a drinking jug of wine, wiping its dewy spout with her apron. "Have a cup with me?"

He glanced toward the kitchen archway again and thought staying might be pleasant. But the weight of the courier's bag hanging from his shoulder preyed on him. As did Jack Tucker's hurried appearance and exit this morning. "As much as I would like to," he said, "I fear I have other business to conduct." Possibly the warmth and familiarity of the room enticed him to relax too much, or perhaps it was Eleanor's bright eyes and sincere expression that drew the confession from him. He sniffed the smoky hearth and looked at his favorite spot in the corner with a sigh. "Jack is in trouble. I don't know what to do."

"Again? That boy. He needs a firm hand, Crispin. He's had to care for himself for so long he doesn't know what's right and what's wrong anymore. It's up to you. He is like a son to you. It's time you treat him as such."

"Nonsense. He's twelve. That's old enough to take care of himself. At his age, I had already begun my arms practice and supervised Lancaster's London mills."

"The duke was kind to you and acted as foster father, did he not?"

"Yes." John of Gaunt, duke of Lancaster, was never far from Crispin's thoughts. He barely remembered his own father, who died when he was seven. It was Lancaster's face he saw when he thought of "father," even though Lancaster was now an estranged one.

"Are you saying I should be more solicitous to the boy?"

"I'm saying he needs guidance. And who better?"

He felt an ache in the back of his neck. "I didn't ask for this. I never wanted a servant."

"Yet now you have one." She laid her hand on his shoulder. "But isn't young Jack more than a servant?" Eleanor wore her matronly smile. It had the power to either annoy or mollify him. Today he couldn't tell which it was.

What could he say to her words? He wondered just what his responsibilities to Jack Tucker were. He had met the twelve-year-old only a few months ago when the young thief tried to steal Crispin's purse. It was Jack who had insinuated himself into Crispin's life as his servant, not the other way around. The boy could barely be trusted to keep his hands to himself even after many promises.

He made his thanks to Eleanor but offered no reply to her entreaty. He didn't really want to see the boy hanged, but if Jack didn't curb his ways, that was all that was left to him.

CRISPIN TRUDGED BACK TO the Shambles under a fine spray of drizzle. Up the steps to his lodgings, he unlocked the door and swept the room with a glance. No Jack, as usual. He dropped the bag on the table and poured himself more wine into the bowl that he had offered to Grayce. The wine burned down his throat with a satisfying heat, and he licked his lips. He felt better already.

He looked at the bundle on the table, took his bowl with him, and tossed aside the bag's top flap. He ran his hand over the carved wood, turned the key, and opened the lid. The gold box seemed to glow from its place within the wooden casket. He set the bowl down and pulled out the golden box. Besides the gems that encrusted the casket, there were raised friezes of Christ's journey to the cross encircling it, all crafted in beaten gold. He lifted the lid and stared at the strange object within. "Crown of Thorns," he muttered. A fingertip toyed with a particularly nasty spike before he drew the circlet out of its container and held it aloft. He turned the crown to examine it. Chuckling, he darted his gaze about the obviously empty room, shook his head at his wary suspicions, and placed it on his head.

"The suffering servant," he said without mirth. "That's me." He caught his reflection in the brass mirror pegged to a post above the basin and water jug. The crown had little appeal and did not improve his features. His blurry image suddenly made him feel like a fool, and he lifted the crown from his head. But in the indistinct reflection he noticed something dark on his wide brow and he raised his fingers there. Blood.

He examined the inside of the crown. He hadn't felt any pain when he wore it, but there within were prickly thorns, and what looked like the vestiges of winding stems, all black with age. He placed the crown back within its reliquary and touched his wounds again. "Treacherous little relic." Walking to the window overlooking the street, he pulled open the shutters. He leaned out and took a deep breath. The smell of the Shambles did not overpower today. Perhaps the wind blew in the opposite direction. Whatever the case, he suddenly felt too cooped up in the room. And he did have the task of reporting to the sheriff about the dead man.

Closing the shutters, he threw open the door and trotted down the stairs. He thought about food—he hadn't eaten since last night—but didn't feel hungry. He reached the bottom step and inhaled again, as if the act of filling his lungs and widening his rib cage were a new experience. In fact, the air was unaccountably renewing. So much so that he felt like leaping into the street. He wanted to run up the avenue like a young boy, like he used to do down the long lane from Lancaster's house in the country to its main road. Strange, but exhilarating, this feeling.

And he wanted to forget his troubles—to forget Jack Tucker and his thieving ways, to forget the harsh looks from former peers when he made the odd encounter on the street. He wanted to allow these new sensations to wash over him, to take him like a rushing river far beyond these troubled shoals. His chest felt warm and his limbs bursting with energy. Strange, these feelings. But not unwelcome. Oh no. To feel such a sudden surge of fire in his blood brought him back to his knightly days when his hand curled around a sword hilt and he sped into battle, Lancaster at his side. Yes! It was very like that feeling. He was giddy with it. He hopped down into the street to take it in. He had a bright awareness of the world. The colors of garments were deeper. The smells of the street were stronger but not unpleasant. The men hurrying along, their bundles over their shoulders, seemed infinitely more interesting than before. He took a step into the muddy street . . . and stopped.

Martin Kemp's plump daughter Matilda blocked his progress.

Crispin's abrupt elation was sucked away like water down a gutter, especially when her gaze roved over him, a gaze that might hold more than insolence.

"Going somewhere?" she asked. Her small, piggy eyes blinked with what he thought was an attempt at coquette. On her it was a sloppy interpretation. "You're always off somewhere. Out 'Tracking,' eh?" She giggled. It reminded Crispin of chickens clucking.

"Indeed."

Still her wide hips blocked his path. "Oh. You've hurt yourself." She pointed to the wounds along his forehead. He felt a trickle of blood and wiped it away. "You should put something on that," she said. "It looks painful."

"It isn't, I assure you."

"I could give you something. I could make a poultice."

He gave a brief, insincere smile. "No, thank you."

Once more, he tried to sidestep her but she moved to block him. "Always, you are so busy, so much in haste," she said, twining the end of her apron around her fingers.

"I must work for my keep. As do you and your family."

"Why is it you never take board with us? You've lived here four years and you've never done so."

"I do not pay for board. It makes the rent cheaper." *And I don't have to eat my meals looking at you.* He longed to say it aloud. His tongue tingled with the possibility.

She shrugged, as if money were of little consequence. "You don't always have to eat here. I sometimes sup with my friends. Sometimes at the Rose. And sometimes even at the King's Head, though Mother would hide me good if she knew. You might want to come, too."

"I do not advise your going to the King's Head today. There may be trouble."

She giggled again, an unpleasant rumbling of her throat. "You're always after trouble, aren't you? My father says that you were once a knight, but I don't think that's true."

Crispin rested his hand on his knife hilt. He itched to draw it, but he snipped off the ends of his words instead. "Oh? And what drew you to that conclusion?"

She eyed the street and wrinkled her nose. "No knight would live here, to be sure. And you used to do my father's books. I've never seen any lordly men about here looking for you. Come now. Weren't you a steward and just liked to pretend you were more?" The last was surely her mother's voice. He'd heard that tone too many times before. "It doesn't vex me, of course. You can pretend to be whoever you like."

For a moment, he started his usual reaction to her uncouth comments, which meant a low growl and getting out of her way before he sputtered an inappropriate reply. But a surge of self-assurance swelled his chest again, pushing back the subservient tilt of his head. With a pounding heart, he remembered such a feeling, the very same he felt on the lists just before the charge, lance at the ready, blood rising, horse beneath him toeing the earth.

He loomed over her, his mouth set in a scowl. "Listen, you spoiled whelp. I *was* a knight. Why should I *pretend* I was better than I was? The only reason I haven't slit your throat now is because I like and respect Martin Kemp. But do not try my patience."

Her mouth flopped open. She put her trembling pink fingers to her throat but made no sound.

It felt marvelous. He'd wanted to mouth those words to her for a long time. Something had always curbed his tongue. But not today. He fisted the hilt of his dagger, though it took all his strength not to draw it.

"Now. Are you going to get out of my way, or do I have to throw you aside?"

She shrieked and tumbled after herself to scramble out of the way. Crispin caught a glimpse of a blue stocking before she made her escape back into the Kemp family quarters. He heard her muffled screech to her mother beyond the walls and took this as the perfect moment to leave.

He swaggered onto the muddy street, feeling as proud as a cockerel. There was nothing more satisfying than brutalizing Matilda Kemp, except for, perhaps, Alice Kemp. Poor Martin. The tinker would get the brunt of it. With a disgusted sigh, Crispin knew he would eventually have to apologize with promises of good behavior. He needed these lodgings. They were all he could afford.

He smiled. But he didn't have to apologize just this moment, and causing that horror on her face *was* satisfying.

Pleased with himself, he dug into the street with sure steps, until a large man casually bumped him. The tall, wide-shouldered man continued on but Crispin whirled, grabbed his arm, and spun him. "Here now," he said, pulling his dagger at last. "You did not apologize for jolting me. I think it's owed."

The squared-jawed man stared at Crispin. "Unhand me. I owe you nought."

"This dagger says you do."

"You threaten me?" The man pulled his blade and he looked down at Crispin. His stout arms looked as if they could snap Crispin like a twig, yet Crispin felt no fear of him.

Crispin even smiled. "I have not drawn another's blood in at least a sennight. And my blade is thirsty. Do you apologize?" He showed his teeth. "Say no."

Perhaps it was Crispin's confident posture, or his refined speech that gave the man pause. Whatever the reason, the broad man dropped his dagger to his thigh and inclined his head. "I beg your pardon. I did not see you. I meant no harm."

Crispin took a disappointed breath. With a huff, he saluted with his blade and sheathed it. Without further words, he turned on his heel and proceeded up the avenue. He peered into the shops and stalls he passed, inordinately interested in the commonplace: a butcher drew his knife down the skinned corpse of a pig hanging upside down from a hook; a poulterer held chickens by their feet and waved their struggling bodies to potential customers, wings spread like an angel's; a young apprentice walked carefully to the back of a shop with a tub of blood; a fishmonger briskly scaled a gudgeon, scales flinging into the air like faery dust.

Crispin took it all in, the coppery scent of blood, the sounds of chickens cackling, the slippery rush and splash of a fish in a bucket. This was no fine street of grand houses. These were the shops of laborers, tradesmen. Their many shops along the Shambles were as tired and as worn as their occupants. Narrow structures, shouldering one another in tight proximity. Their stone foundations were speckled with mud; their daub the color of parchment and their timbers a dusky gray from weathering. An autumn sky sputtered beams of sunshine through its cloud cover, recoloring the shop fronts with alternating stripes of sunlight and shadow.

"Master!"

Crispin heard the voice from far off but there were many men called "Master" by their apprentices along any avenue in London. Slapping steps approached from behind and the voice called again, this time more recognizable.

He turned. Jack Tucker approached at a run, his face long with concern. He pulled up short in front of Crispin and panted, hands on knees. "Master Crispin, didn't you hear me?"

Crispin shook his head. "No. I'm afraid I did not." He smiled, thinking of Eleanor's words. Perhaps Jack's stealing could be curbed with more concern. God knows Jack's own parents were long dead. "Jack." He lunged and gathered the boy into his arms in a bear hug.

Jack squirmed like the devil was after him and wriggled out of Crispin's grasp. "God blind me!" He lurched away and positioned as if to run. "Are you drunk?"

Crispin opened his arms to encompass London. "Why does everyone think I'm drunk? I'm just merry."

Jack cringed and studied Crispin. "*Merry?* You're never merry. What vexes you? Are you ill?" He reached up to touch Crispin's forehead and noticed the wounds. "How'd you get those? Now I see. Someone coshed you on the head. Well, never fear, Master. I'll get you home right enough." He took Crispin's arm but Crispin shook him off.

"What nonsense. I am perfectly well. I'm just on my way to the sheriff. Must tell him about a dead body."

"'Strooth! You seem awful cheery about it."

"Well, it isn't an ordinary dead body."

"What's so extraordinary about it that it lightens your mood so? One of your enemies?"

"No." Crispin studied Jack's frowning features and wondered at the lad's sudden concern. He stared at Jack's blue coat, its crisp colors seeming to fade before his eyes. He squeezed his eyes shut and opened them again. No. Jack's coat looked as it always had. His eyes turned to the street, following the rhythmic strides of two Franciscan friars in gray gowns with black hoods, walking side by side. Men stopped and bowed to the clerics before moving on. It was an ordinary scene, something he saw every day. He raised his chin and sniffed the air. Before, the street had smelled like the preparations in a kitchen, warm, inviting, with meat ready for the spit. But now, it smelled more like a charnel house.

The lighthearted feelings glowing in his chest chilled. He found himself wondering why he had challenged a man in the street for no reason but for the desire to do so, and nearly gotten into a knife fight for it.

He looked back toward his own lodgings though he could no longer see them beyond the curve of the road and the uneven magpie colors of shop fronts and houses. He touched the wounds on his forehead, but they no longer bled. His body suddenly felt heavy. He used to feel that way after a battle once his high blood was spent.

Taking a deep breath he could barely find the strength to face Jack. The boy stared at him with mouth gaping. "Why do you look at me like that?" Crispin asked.

Jack clamped his mouth shut and shook his head. His thick ginger hair jostled. "I ain't looking at you with aught. If you must needs go to the sheriff then let us go and get it done with. You know how I dislike Newgate."

Crispin nodded, rolled his shoulders, and shook off the odd feeling. He looked back one last time, and gestured for Jack to follow.

He said nothing as he continued up the lane to where it became Newgate Market. These were the same shops and houses, the same gray faces that greeted him every day. Why had it seemed so different only moments ago?

He looked ahead. Newgate prison lay before him at the end of the row; a gate in the great wall that surrounded most of London. Jack shivered beside him as Crispin nodded to the guard and passed under Newgate's arch with its toothy portcullis.

At Crispin's urging, Jack followed him up the stairs to Sheriff Simon Wynchecombe's tower chamber. Newgate conjured unpleasant memories for both of them, but Crispin had learned over the years to ignore his discomfort.

The sheriff's clerk waved the pair by without looking up, familiar with Crispin's comings and goings. They entered the sheriff's shadowy chamber, and Crispin moved directly in front of the hot fire before Wynchecombe could look up from his table and stop him.

Too late. The sheriff lifted his eyes from his documents and scowled upon resting his gaze on Crispin. "Ha!" he snorted. "I thought I'd see you here ere long. You must have something to do with this dead French courier."

Crispin sighed. Good news traveled fast, and bad news even faster.

4

"FRENCH COURIER, LORD SHERIFF?" Crispin raised his chilled hands to the fire and tried to inhale the toasty aromas from the spitting logs, but all he got was smoke. "I do not know your meaning?"

Jack Tucker made himself scarce in the shadows.

"Don't play thick with me." The sheriff rose. He seemed to enjoy his imposing stature—both in height and rank over Crispin. His dark mustache and beard blended into his dark houppelande with its black fur trim and its long sleeves draping down to the floor.

The sheriff glanced once at the cringing Jack Tucker, dismissed him, and moved to the fire, standing beside Crispin as if comparing his rich garb to Crispin's shabby attire.

"A French courier was found dead this morning at the King's Head Inn on Thames Street. A man was seen stealing away from the vicinity with the two women who lived in the room where the corpse was found. A man of medium height, medium build, clean-shaven, black hair, and wearing a disreputable red cotehardie. Sound familiar?"

"It could be anyone."

The sheriff eyed Crispin's red coat and black hair. "Yes. Anyone."

Crispin stared into the bright flames. "Do you accuse this man, my lord?"

"Of murder? I don't know. But the women certainly have something to do with it. And I would know what that is."

"It seems you must find these women."

The sheriff chuckled. "I shall."

"If I may ask, what was so extraordinary about this courier?"

Wynchecombe sauntered to the sideboard and poured wine into a silver bowl. After a second thought, he poured a splash into another bowl and handed it to Crispin. He gestured toward a chair, inviting Crispin to sit.

Crispin had, by necessity, grown accustomed to wine with a more strident taste, especially the Boar's Tusk's vibrant fare. He drank the sheriff's wine greedily, savoring its refined flavor of dark currants and cherries. He settled into the chair.

The sheriff eyed Crispin like a hawk sizing up a mouse. "Why should I accommodate so readily?" said the sheriff. "Just what might I gain from being so forthcoming?"

Crispin drank, licked his lips, and rested the bowl on his thigh. *The satisfaction of hearing your own voice.* He chuckled, picturing the sheriff's expression if he uttered it aloud. "I have, on occasion, helped you with a puzzle or two, Lord Sheriff. Certainly it can't hurt to divulge a few fragments of information. 'All men by nature desire knowledge.'"

The sheriff made a sound like a growl and settled his arms on the table. He gazed steadily at Crispin. "This Frenchman was transporting a relic from the French court. A loan from the King of France." The sheriff set his wine bowl aside. "You'll never guess what that relic is."

"Don't keep me waiting."

"Bless me, *Jesu,* but it was the Crown of Thorns itself."

"A crown of thorns?"

"Not *a* crown of thorns," said a gleeful Wynchecombe shaking his head. "*The* Crown of Thorns."

"Holy Christ!" Crispin blurted it before he could stop himself. He raised his hand and lightly touched his forehead, but he felt no blood, no scarring.

"Just so," said Wynchecombe. "It was a sort of peace offering from King Charles of France to our King Richard. His Majesty was supposed to take whichever thorn from the Crown he wanted. But now the whole damn thing's missing."

"Oh?" Crispin sat back, consoling himself in his bowl of wine.

"Yes. Whoever killed the courier took the relic. Word has reached court and it is said that Richard thinks the affair a deliberate slight. But the French ambassador thinks Richard stole it."

"It's been a busy morning."

"Yes. And it's going to be a long one as well. I have here a decree from the crown to commence daily archery practice for the kingdom. Immediately."

"But this is already law. 'Every man between the ages of sixteen to sixty is required to practice archery on Sundays and feast days.'" He looked at Jack as if to confirm such a well-known fact. "That was decreed by the king's grandfather King Edward of Windsor. But it isn't Sunday or a feast day."

"This decree"—Wynchecombe glanced at the document—"says that all men must practice *daily*."

Crispin sat up. "Does the king expect an invasion?"

"It's a possibility. Unless that Crown is returned forthwith."

Crispin sat back and tipped his bowl, breathing in the vapors. He stretched out his legs and crossed one ankle over the other. "Do you wish to hire me to find it?"

Wynchecombe laughed. "You are the damnedest man I have ever met, Guest. Is there no opportunity you won't exploit?"

"I merely assumed—"

Wynchecombe stopped laughing. "I didn't summon you. Why did you come?"

Crispin offered a lopsided grin. "I came here to report a dead man. At the King's Head."

Wynchecombe shot to his feet. "I knew it!" He jabbed a long finger at Crispin. "I *knew* you were involved. Tell me you weren't the man stealing away with those women."

Crispin stared at the bottom of the empty wine bowl with a frown and set the cup aside. "Do I need to say it?"

"You are in quite a kettle!" crowed the sheriff. He laughed and slapped his hands together and rubbed them. "Now then. Tell me all you know."

Crispin's gaze rose languidly. "There's not much to tell. The women found the dead man in their room and came to me."

"Why?"

"Because I find things, remember? Murderers, lost items. I am paid for many feats of intellect, my Lord Sheriff. I know you wouldn't understand such."

Crispin expected it, braced for it, and wasn't disappointed when the sheriff grabbed his shoulder cape and hauled him to his feet. Nose to nose, the sheriff glared into Crispin's face, blowing hot breath on him. "I've had about enough of you and your mockery, Guest. You are *my* servant. I am not yours. Remember that." He shook him with each statement then threw him back down into his chair.

Crispin resettled to a sitting position and straightened his clothes.

The sheriff yanked his dagger free and slapped it on the table. "I ask a question. For each wrong answer—you lose something."

Crispin eyed the blade, the brass crosspiece, and the jeweled pommel. "'Something'?"

"An ear, a finger." His lips peeled back. "*Something.*"

Crispin looked back at Jack. "You're not making this conversation very appealing."

"It's not meant to be."

"And here I came to you in good faith telling you of a body—"

"That I already knew about. Come, come, Guest. I await your answer."

"What was the question?"

Wynchecombe snatched the knife and held the side of the blade to Crispin's throat. "Dammit, Guest! Do you mock me?"

The metal felt cool against his neck. "They say 'wit is educated insolence.'"

The sheriff held the blade to Crispin's skin a moment more before withdrawing it. "Your Aristotle again?"

"Yes, my lord." Crispin eased back, but not altogether relaxed. He rubbed his neck. "I commend him to you. He has an aphorism for all occasions."

"Why read him"—Wynchecombe did not sheath the blade, but toyed with the sharp tip instead—"when you are too fond of quoting him to me?"

Crispin closed his eyes and nodded. "Just so."

"But you delay the inevitable." Wynchecombe tapped the flat of the blade into his palm. "Tell me about the women and what you found in that room. And be careful of your answer."

Casually, Crispin wiped sweat from his upper lip. He spared Jack a glance. The boy cringed in the corner. It looked like a good idea. "The women feared they would be blamed for the man's death, so they hired me to discover the murderer."

The blade tapped dully on Wynchecombe's naked palm. Crispin watched it. "So? Where are the women now?" Crispin opened his mouth and took a breath, but Wynchecombe interrupted. He waggled the blade at Crispin's face. "Be careful how you answer."

"As careful as I can be, my lord. They are . . . secured. Somewhere safe."

Wynchecombe leaned forward, the knife pointed at Crispin's nose. "Where?"

Crispin stared at the knife's tip and blew out a sigh, wondering how he'd look without a nose. He swallowed. "That I cannot tell you, my lord. They hired me also for protection."

Wynchecombe rose and sauntered behind Crispin's chair. Crispin felt his presence like a spider crawling up his leg, ready to bite. He dared not move.

"That is not an answer."

"I know, my lord. But what would you have me do? Betray a confidence?"

Wynchecombe's low chuckle raised the hairs on Crispin's neck. "Never that, Master Guest."

The sound of steel sliding back into its leather sheath hissed at his ear. Crispin blew out a sigh.

"Let us go to the place of the crime," said Wynchecombe, "and we can discuss it there."

5

CRISPIN STOOD AGAIN IN the room at the King's Head that the sisters shared, and noted what had changed and what had not. Jack mumbled his complaints about dead bodies and asked Crispin if he could wait outside with the sheriff's men-at-arms. Crispin nodded to him vaguely and Jack looked at the room with a little grimace on his lips before departing like a shadow.

The dead man had been laid out on a straw-covered pallet. Two Frenchmen wearing the same livery as the dead man—a quartered houppelande with the French fleur-de-lis—stood over him.

Crispin eyed their slightly pink complexions and their severely coifed hair. *Where were these two when the man was killed?*

"The French ambassador ordered them to court," Wynchecombe whispered to Crispin, "but no one here speaks French with any facilty." He looked at his clerk standing beside him, but the man shook his head.

"Mes seigneurs, un mot avec vous," said Crispin to the men.

The man with dark hair combed long over his forehead turned. *"Oh oui. Enfin, un anglais qui vaut la peine."*

"You three traveled together?" continued Crispin in French. The men nodded. "Did you see what happened?"

The dark-haired man shrugged. "We were . . . occupied."

"I see. And he did not favor such 'occupation'?"

"We know not. I think he spied his own conquest. Perhaps he followed her here."

"I understand the French ambassador wishes for you to appear at the English court."

The man spit on the floor. "He wants to imprison us for our carelessness. We have no desire to play into his hands."

"If you came to England for the purpose of going to Westminster Palace, then why did you dally here, in this low place?"

He exchanged looks with his fair-haired companion. "We . . . had business here. We were to . . . to prepare for the English court."

"Here?" Crispin asked skeptically.

Wynchecombe elbowed him. "What did he say?"

Crispin held up a hand to the sheriff. "Am I to tell the Lord Sheriff this . . . story?"

The man sneered. "Tell him what you like. We have another companion looking for the relic. We don't need your help."

Crispin turned to an impatient Wynchecombe. "They refuse to go to court. They feel it is a trap."

"Damn these French," muttered Wynchecombe. "Ask them their names."

Crispin turned back to them. "My Lord Sheriff wishes to know your names."

The dark-haired man bowed. "Gautier Le Breton. And this"—he said gesturing to his companion—"is Laurent Lefèvre. Our friend here"—he crossed himself—"is . . . was . . . Michel Girard."

Wynchecombe nodded to his clerk. "Did you get that?" The clerk nodded and busily scribbled on a wax slate with a quill. The sheriff clucked his tongue and turned his attention away from the clerk and the couriers and studied the dead man. The arrow still lay deeply imbedded in his chest. "How about this arrow?" he said to Crispin. "Does it tell you anything?"

Crispin bowed to the couriers and left them in the middle of the room to stand at Wynchecombe's side. "A nobleman's arrow. Hawk fletching is more expensive than the more common goose feather."

"I agree. Where was he when he was shot?"

Crispin strode across the dirt floor and pointed to the spot. There was still a puddle of blood mixed with dirt and now scattered footprints around it. "Here, my lord."

Wynchecombe joined him and stared at the spot. "No struggle?"

"His weapon was still sheathed."

"How about that shot?" He looked up at the window. "It would be an easy effort to shoot from that window to down below."

"Look at the angle of the arrow. The Frenchman would have to have been lying flat on his back to be shot from that window."

"What?" Wynchecombe marched back to the dead man and leaned over him. He fingered the arrow and snorted. "So. The angle is not right."

"As I said, my lord."

"He was shot here, then?"

"It would seem so, Lord Sheriff. At close range."

"For that damned relic."

Crispin paused. What was he to say? He knew the mysterious archer did not kill for the relic, the relic he now possessed. "Possibly. But there may be other motives we know not of."

Wynchecombe's mouth thinned to a straight line. "And why do you say that?"

One of the sheriff's men-at-arms shoved his way through the Frenchmen and bowed to Wynchecombe. "My lord, the king's guards are rousting the men to commence archery practice."

"The king is doing so now?" asked Crispin.

"His decree said immediately, remember?" Wynchecombe nodded to his man. "Very good. See that all is orderly." He turned his glare on Crispin. "Shouldn't you be out there as well?"

Crispin bowed, relieved to get away. "Yes, my lord." Should he say more? Crispin scanned the room—the French couriers eyeing the sheriff's men with suspicion, the dank walls, the muddy mess on the floor—and decided to keep his thoughts to himself. He mulled over the relic in his possession. Yes, the more he kept from the sheriff, the better.

He sidled passed the sheriff's men, enduring their sneers, and joined Jack in the muddy courtyard. He couldn't help but look back into the undercroft and wonder about the couriers. Why would they need to "prepare," as they said, to go to Westminster by lingering at this rough inn? Prepare for what?

They jostled passed the shaggy horses in the inn yard and stood at the yard's edge, looking out on to Thames Street. "What a to-do, Master. Men scrambling out of their houses with their suppers still in their hands."

"You heard the Lord Sheriff. It is the law to practice archery. Archers have saved the day in many a battle. An Englishman brandishing a long bow is feared throughout the continent."

"If it is the law, why have you never gone before?"

He offered a smile. "I do go on occasion. But I must borrow a bow. Even though the law requires it, I do not own one myself. I can't afford it." He raised his head and watched the men moving down the streets, bows in hand. "Let us see what we can."

It was a sight, indeed. Men of all ages and all walks of life were emerging from their houses like bees from a skep, swarming onto the streets, crowding out the shopkeepers. Wayward apprentices hopped nimbly into their shops' doorways to avoid the melee. Arguments broke out as feet were stomped upon and bows smacked the heads of others. It was a cutpurse's dream come true, Crispin supposed; that many men in one place, crowded, unaware of those surrounding them. He'd wager many a man would lose their purse this day. He resolved to keep a sharp eye on Jack Tucker.

Men on horses joined the throng, great destriers and embittered sumpters. Fresh horses, old, worn-out beasts. Dogs followed the stragglers, barking for the sheer novelty of it all. Women leaned out of upper windows, ticking their heads. It was as if a great army were heading out to battle, without the usual cheering and waving that accompanied such an event. Crispin had never seen the like and, by the measure of Jack Tucker's wide-eyed stare, he'd never seen it either.

The dithering lines of men joined their brethren, all under the watchful gaze of the king's guards, sitting on their mounts at every other corner. The would-be archers traveled through alleys and up widening lanes in a northerly direction toward the plains above London.

When an opening in the flood of men presented itself, Crispin and Jack joined them and headed almost all the way back to the Shambles, but turned instead up St. Martin's Street to Aldersgate. Passing under the arch, they traveled with the others up Aldersgate Street.

Jack's eyes were wide as he took in the countryside. "I never been to Islington before."

"We still have quite a walk to go."

The boy looked back toward London and shuddered. "I'm glad to be away from the sheriff. He makes me skin crawl. Why do you bother going to him anyway? He's always beating you or threatening to do so. I say if you've found a dead man, say nought and let the sheriff suffer with it."

"I was fairly confident he would do me no real harm."

"'Fairly confident'? Them's not good enough odds for me. He threatened you with his *knife*! Said he'd cut off something."

Crispin shrugged. "He didn't, as you well know. And I always learn more than I inform. For instance, I know that this relic was the Crown of Thorns to be presented to King Richard. And I know what Wynchecombe does not: where those women are and where the relic is."

"'Slud! How'd you know all that?"

Crispin stopped, whirled, and pushed a surprised Jack up against a short hedgerow. Jack looked down at Crispin's hand pressed into his chest.

"Because while you were on the run from committing larceny, I was out discovering all these matters." Crispin fixed his eyes on Jack's. "Those men who came to my lodgings this morning. I don't want a repeat of that. It soils my good name—such as it is. And it forced an encounter with Madam Kemp. And you know how I feel about that!" The boy's face fell. "Jack, how many times have I told you not to steal?"

"I didn't mean to do it . . . I mean, well, they were rich men. Sure to have more riches at home. What's a few coins to them and, well, it's . . . it's a hard habit to break."

Crispin's hand pressed harder into Jack's chest. "I'll not toy with you further, Jack. If I catch you stealing again, I shall turn you out of my lodgings and return you to the streets where I found you."

"Ah now, Master Crispin—"

"I mean it, Jack. I won't tolerate it. Change your ways or you're out."

Crispin fastened his glare on him, dotting the i's and crossing the t's. He released Jack, turned his back, and strode onward.

Jack followed at some distance, silent and sullen. After a time he trotted up beside Crispin, head hanging, feet dragging. "It ain't like I ain't tryin'," he said quietly.

"Try harder."

"Aye. I will." He said the words like a schoolboy after a brief round with a switch. Crispin almost felt sorry for him. Jack quickly changed the subject.

"Crown o' Thorns," muttered Jack. "If you know where this Crown o' Thorns is why don't you give it to the sheriff? Would you be the cause of war? That's what the sheriff said."

"It won't come to that despite this show," he said, nodding toward the march of men. "I have played the game of politics before, remember?"

"But that was when they called you 'sir.'"

Crispin grumbled. "One never forgets the game, and it hasn't changed. Even after seven years."

"As you say. But I would not see the cursed French set foot in London."

"Never fear that."

Jack was momentarily distracted by the flitting of a chaffinch from hedge to hedge. The houses lining the road soon gave way to open country. Mounds of green rolled into the distance like a verdant sea. "Then why not give the Crown to the sheriff?" said Jack, pulling his cloak about him when the wind swirled up from the low-lying grasslands. "Let him dispatch it."

"Because, Jack, this might be my path back into the king's good graces."

"I thought you didn't give a damn about the king," he said quietly, mindful of others along the rutted path.

Crispin set his jaw. He would be just as happy to see a sword chop King Richard to pieces, or even to watch him die from a lingering disease. "God's blood! I weary of living like this," he growled, not truly meaning to say it aloud, but it was good to give it breath, to snarl it. "If I return the Crown to court, then *I* will be the hero, not Wynchecombe. I weary of scraping to him. I weary of living in one room on a stinking street. And I weary of—"

"Me?"

He glanced at Jack's anxious face, smooth with youth. Crispin took a breath and smiled an easy grin. "No, not of you. But I do weary of your stealing."

Jack's mouth set in a grim line. "I heard you the first time, Master."

They arrived at the butts where the target mounds stood at the other end of the field, some sixty yards away. Some still sported wreath rings as smaller targets on their grassy faces. A low ditch ran before them where broken arrows still resided, like the quills of a hedgehog.

The green plains opened up and spread like a river to the distant darkness of the trees. The target mounds across the field stood mutely, their green turf waiting to be jabbed with arrows. Men and boys took their usual places, though there appeared to be more men than Crispin had seen practice in a long time. Little wonder with the king's soldiers breathing down their necks. The presence of so many people shied a few sheep grazing in the meadow and they scurried off onto a narrow path leading away from the butts.

Jack stood close to Crispin as men gathered at the field's edge, queuing up in a roughly straight line, facing the targets, and either hitching their quivers over their shoulders, or sticking their arrows into the turf at their feet. No one began as yet, making certain that no stragglers strayed onto the field between archer and target. Many began stringing their bows.

With so many men crammed together, Jack dropped to a whisper. "With this relic, do you think the king will forgive and forget, and bring you back to court?"

Crispin sighed. Wind lifted his hair and whipped the ends against his cheeks. "I don't know. But I've got to try."

A layer of autumn mist hovered just over the grass and disappeared into the woods smelling of wet field and sheep dung. Back over his shoulder stood London, reaching into the gray sky with spires and pitched roofs of slate, lead, and red tile. A dull layer of smoke drifted over its uneven landscape, climbing over the rooftops like a thief in the night. His city. His home.

With all these men parading into the field, it reminded Crispin of a fair day, only there was little amusing about it. A man, possibly a baker, taught his son how to hold a long bow. An old man showed a younger how to nock an arrow into a compact hunting bow, the younger man's expression showing his frustration.

Crispin didn't care that he didn't own a bow. It was far down on his list of necessities. And since he could borrow one from his landlord Martin Kemp, the idea of owning the weapon disappeared completely.

Even as he thought it he spied Martin standing at their usual place trying to string the bow. Crispin moved toward him, unconcerned with the activity around him. The back of his mind toyed with the murder of the French courier and why Grayce thought she killed him. What great sin had stolen her mind, forcing her to conclude that she was a murderess?

He waved to Martin Kemp who was thrusting arrows into the soft earth and leaning his unstrung bow awkwardly against his leg. But Martin looked up and frowned upon seeing Crispin, and it was only then that Crispin realized why the tinker's face was so sour. *Jesu mercy. I forgot about Matilda.* He stopped short. "Master Martin," he said in solemn greeting.

"Crispin." Martin Kemp said the one word with a clipped and formal tone, and clamped his lips tight. Martin's expression jumped from anger to disappointment and even slipped into fear. He postured with one foot forward and clenched the weapon. "I must ask you a question I do not wish to ask."

Crispin bent his head. Now that he faced Kemp he felt a wash of shame. "You do not need to speak, Martin. If you refer to my rudeness to your daughter, then I fear it is the truth."

Martin shook his head, his shoulders following suit. "Saint Loy, Crispin! You know how she is; how my *wife* is! You shouldn't have said—"

"I know. And I do apologize. I was out of sorts and—I beg your pardon. Humbly."

"That won't satisfy the wife. Crispin, I don't like reminding you that we took you in when no one would. I do not charge the rent I should for your lodgings. Not as much as my wife would have me do. And then this—" He flailed his bow toward the silent Jack, "You know she does not approve of *him*! Nor do I, should he continue to cause trouble."

"I'm trying to improve m'self, Master Kemp," Jack said. He dragged his torn cloak dramatically over his chest.

Crispin pushed back his pride another notch. "If I must, I shall apologize to Matilda *and* Alice. Will that suffice?"

Martin rocked his head, thinking. Finally, reluctantly, he nodded. He looked behind with the expectation that his wife would swoop down like a harpy from above. "Have better care in the future, Crispin. I know Matilda is no prize, but she's all I have, God help me."

Crispin put on his best contrite expression. Mollified, Martin nodded and settled back into their uneasy alliance.

Martin raised his bow, tucked one end of it in the grass at the arch of his foot, and struggled to string it. He still wore his leather apron and tight-fitting leather cap, whose strings swung in tandem with each bend of the stubborn bow. He looked pitifully out of his element.

Martin managed to string the weapon and watched the others aim toward the targets. Over his shoulder he whispered, "What's all this about anyway, Crispin? Is there to be war?"

"There may be. It's complicated."

"Politics always is. But of course, you would know best."

Crispin made a sound in his throat, one that almost echoed Jack's.

A shout across the field of "Loose arrows!" announced to one and all to commence shooting.

"Well," said Martin, raising his bow. "Here's to it."

He pulled back the string and loosed the arrow. Sloppily, the arrow shot away with a discordant strum and sailed over the target.

"Try again," said Crispin. How a man could practice such a thing for so many years and still prove incompetent, he'd never know. "Pull it farther. Farther! All the way to your ear." Crispin shook his head with a grunt and positioned himself behind Martin. He placed his fingers over Martin's and pulled back the bowstring. Crispin felt the bow tremble in the tinker's hands.

"I can't hold it much longer," Martin whimpered.

"Then let it go," rasped Crispin in his ear.

The arrow whirred forward and tunneled into the ditch below the target. Crispin relaxed and stared at the man.

"It's this bow," said Martin contritely. "It's too powerful."

"Here. Give it to me."

Crispin took the offered bow and gripped it in his left hand. He pulled one of the arrows from the turf and nocked the feathered end in the string, holding the arrow's tip in place with a hooked index finger. With a deep breath he raised the bow. Slowly he pulled back the string until his thumb rested under his cheekbone, took aim, and opened his fingers.

The arrow shushed away and spiraled toward the target, sticking it nearly in the center of a dried wreath.

"God blind me!" exclaimed Jack.

Martin shook his head. "That's a beautiful thing when done correctly."

"It takes practice." Crispin lowered the bow. He looked at the weapon, a fine specimen of yew. He ran his fingers along the waxed linen bowstring and sighed. He turned to Martin and handed it over.

Martin took it and looked at it not with longing but with trepidation. "You don't think we'll ever truly have to defend London, do you?"

Crispin shrugged. "It's always a possibility. Though no one's invaded since William the Conqueror."

"You fought in France with the duke of Lancaster, didn't you?"

Crispin drew an arrow from the ground and handed it to Martin. "Yes. And many other places."

Martin pulled the string back as Crispin taught him and aimed unsteadily. "I'll wager you laid a few low with this," he said.

Crispin flinched but tried to hide it by yanking an arrow from the turf and jamming it back in. He repeated the gesture several times. "I wasn't an archer," he reminded Martin quietly.

The shaft flew into the woods. Martin looked up from over his bow and stammered, "Oh. Of course. You wouldn't have been, would you?"

"No. Indeed." France. France's battlefields, villages, forest-glotted estates. Thank God it wasn't all muddy camps and damp pavilion tents. The duke had estates in France, and there were many similar English holdings where a bed and a grand meal awaited. Crispin circulated in villages aplenty, observing the natives, sampling the food (there was a sweet-tasting bread he especially liked), employing French tailors and French cobblers. French cotehardies were more tapered, more sweeping from the body. Their shoes, particularly the wooden clogs of both peasant and noble, were carved with more flare than the stoically practical English equivalent.

Crispin looked down at the arrow in his hand, rolled the shaft between his fingers. He missed those days. They *seemed* carefree, with that preponderance of time separating those events from these. He had certainly been free with his money. What he wouldn't give for one of those French cotehardies now . . .

He raised his head and scanned the other men practicing with poorly hewn long bows and short bows. Women gathered, too, making an outing of it with food and drink—and why not? The king decreed it, but it didn't mean the people could not make pleasant what the king made a chore.

Martin handed Crispin the bow again and Crispin took his turn with several arrows. The string calloused his fingers, but he didn't care. Fine gloves or leather tabs used to protect his fingers, and a leather brace shielded his bow arm when out hunting with Lancaster on his lands. But Crispin owned no such leather goods now. Still, it felt good to have a weapon in his hands, under his control. To feel the tautness of the string at the folds of his fingers, the arrow's shaft resting on his index finger as he aimed, the breath of wind as the fletching hissed by his ear, and the satisfaction of the faint thud when the point sunk into its target.

"I'd go to war m'self," said Jack, standing just behind Crispin, chin up like a cockerel and keeping a sharp eye on every movement he made.

"Oh?" Crispin pulled back the string again and carefully aimed above the shaft already in the target.

"To see the gonfalons and the banners. And the horses. I'd fight with the best of them and win me ransom. Aye, I'd like to see that."

The arrow whirred away and struck an inch above the first. Jack handed him another and Crispin nocked the arrow in the string. "So you'd like to fight, eh? Ever seen a battle?"

"Only at tournament. The melee. A fine show, that."

Crispin closed his left eye and took aim with the right. "You think so, do you?" He let loose the arrow. It stuck the target above the last shaft. He lowered the bow until one end rested on the ground. He leaned on it and turned to Jack. "Ever see a man dismembered and disemboweled?"

Jack's brows widened. His lips parted and hung open. "No."

"You'd see plenty of it. Swords chopping and arms flung off. Men's entrails spilling out at your feet." Jack looked down at his own feet and stepped back. "Blood spattering your face as you swing your blade. Bits of bone snapping up at your eyes. Men screaming and then drowning in their own blood. That's in the *true* melee, not the spectacle with wooden swords at a tournament." He took the last arrow from the turf and jabbed the point toward Jack's chest. The boy jerked back and stared down his nose at the arrow point. Crispin pursued, jabbing and stepping forward for each of Jack's steps back. "In all probability, you'd be struck down by an arrow before you ever raised a weapon." He jabbed at him again and Jack cringed, his chest caving inward. The boy's fingers covered his breast protectively as if trying to stop a misdirected quarrel.

"Still want to go?" prodded Crispin.

Jack looked at Martin. Both their faces paled with new sobriety. "Well," said Jack, quieter than before, "maybe not."

Crispin turned back to his bow, nocked the arrow, and lifted the weapon.

Jack wiped his hands down his dirty tunic and licked his lips. He sauntered with recovering dignity back beside Crispin and watched him aim. "But what about you, Master? That's what being a knight is, eh? If you were a knight again, would you go to war with the king?"

Crispin drew back the bowstring and pressed his thumb hard against his cheek. He blinked slowly in rhythm to his even breathing. "In a heartbeat," he murmured.

The noise of men and the thump of a heavy horse drew up behind them. "What's all that?" asked Crispin, still taking aim. He couldn't decide whether to hit the target below or above the arrows in the center.

"It's the king's Captain of the Archers," said Martin. "He's a fine-looking gentleman on a splendid horse all frilled out in a colorful trapper."

"All men look like fine gentlemen on a horse," said Crispin. He let the arrow fly. It struck in the middle of his arrows and trembled. Five arrows bristled from the target, all clumped together in the center circle. "But not all *are* gentlemen." He set the bow on one end and turned to look at the Captain of the Archers.

It was a fine horse. Its trapper—the hem reaching down to the horse's fetlocks—swished in the wind and with the horse's skittish gait. A bow hung on the saddle's high pommel as did a quiver with arrows. Crispin looked higher.

A cold hand seemed to close over Crispin's heart and squeezed, holding his breath, his blood, his very life in a suspension of time. Blinding anger overtook the shock and he gritted his teeth to keep from shouting outright. He flung the bow away and stomped up to the man on the horse. Before anyone could say or do anything, Crispin reached up and dragged the man to the ground. He pulled him up to a sitting position, yanked out his blade, and thrust it toward the man's surprised face.

"Throat or gut?" rasped Crispin. "Your choice. Either way, you're a dead man!"

6

"CRISPIN! ARE YOU MAD?" Martin tugged Crispin's arms.

Crispin heard him distantly like a midge buzzing about his head. He did not yield. When the two men-at-arms arrived they did a better job. They swung him to the ground. Crispin sprang to his feet and the men grabbed him again.

"Master!" Jack trotted around them like a sheepdog, trying to get to Crispin.

Crispin spun out of the guards' grip. He kicked one in the gut and slammed his fist in the other's jaw. The first man recovered and pulled his sword. Crispin darted under the blade and grabbed the wrist holding the weapon. With hands firmly on the struggling guard's wrist, he directed the steel toward the other man still groaning on the ground and smacked him in the head with the side of the blade. The man slumped solidly down.

With his fist still ringing the swordsman's wrist, Crispin tried to disarm him, but the man twisted and kneed Crispin's chest, knocking the air out of his lungs. Crispin had no choice but to release his grip and stagger backward. The man raised his sword, but Crispin whirled and landed a blow with the heel of his boot to the man's groin. The man's face squinted and his mouth formed a soundless "O." Crispin threw an uppercut and smiled when the man slammed backward into the mud. The sword flung from his hand.

Crispin spun. Two more men-at-arms came running and Crispin crouched, bloodied fists clenched.

The Captain of the Archers struggled to his feet with Martin's help and called for the men to stop. "I said hold!" he said in a more commanding voice. The men stopped and looked at one another with fists curled. "Leave us!" said the captain.

The men cast questioning looks at a scowling Crispin, and slowly departed, though not too far.

The Captain of the Archers brushed his wheat-colored hair out of his eyes. He straightened his muddied velvet surcote and adjusted his gold-tipped sword pommel. The fawnskin gauntlets, hemmed with fur, dripped with mud. Three gold rings flashed from the gloved fingers on his left hand. He wiped mud from his face and stared at Crispin with a growing smile of recognition. "Crispin Guest. I will be damned. I thought you were dead."

"I might as well have been!" Crispin yanked his fallen dagger from the turf. Jack tried to help Crispin but he shook off the boy. "And you *will* be damned as soon as I kill you."

The Captain's lips drew back in a knife-sharp smile. He examined Crispin and shook his head. He turned toward Jack and Martin as if suddenly remembering them and jerked his head. "Do these two have to be here?"

Crispin swiped the spittle from his mouth with the back of his hand and shook his head.

Without looking at either of them, he said, "Jack. Martin. Would you be so kind as to leave us?"

"Yes, Crispin," muttered Martin. "Come along, Jack." A throng of men nearby also departed under the watchful scowls of the men-at-arms, leaving Crispin and the captain alone.

"I'll be at home, Master." Jack said it loud enough for the Captain of the Archers to clearly hear him. "*Watching* for you."

Crispin ignored Jack and lifted his knife higher. "Now, Miles Aleyn. How do you want to die?"

Miles postured, one foot forward, his gloved hand resting lightly on his sword pommel. His long surcote bore the king's arms—three yellow leopards on a red field—quartered with red arrows on yellow fields. He twisted his rosy lips, too rosy for a man's. His dark eyes followed each of Crispin's moves, hawklike, aware. Crispin knew from experience that those eyes were more alert than Miles's relaxed manner made them appear. "Still so melodramatic," Miles said, one brow raised. "One would think you would have outgrown such theatrics."

"You son of a whore. You misled me. And then like a coward, you tucked and ran."

Miles took a deep breath. He raised his eyes toward the distant men-at-arms. "Treason is still treason, Crispin," he said quietly. "Not even I could have saved you. At any rate, you did only what you wanted to do. As I recall, you were one of the easiest to persuade. Still wet behind the ears."

"I trusted you!"

Miles waved his hand and then let it fall to his side. "Alas."

"You could have spoken up!"

"And had *my* bowels ripped from me? I think not."

"Why did you do it? Why stir up the nobles against King Richard and blame Lancaster?"

"Now, now. Need we be so loud?"

"I'll shout it to the rooftops."

"And get nowhere. Try anything, and I will lay you low before you take a breath."

"If you can."

Miles chuckled. "Crispin, Crispin. Look at you. Alive. Free. I thought you'd be out of London by now. Still festering, I see. Any other man would have given up, found a life elsewhere. Not you. A glutton for punishment. Or a would-be martyr. Which is it? After all, my dear fellow, it was ages ago."

"Ages ago? Like yesterday."

"Not to me." Miles adjusted his right glove, but Crispin could tell he was measuring how far away his men were.

"So why? Why betray us? What had you to gain?"

"I barely remember now. Probably someone paid me to do it."

Crispin's fist knotted over the dagger. "*Who* paid you? What coward would dare?"

"So many questions." Miles glanced back. The men-at-arms talked furtively in a tight knot, hands on sword pommels. They looked toward Miles, awaiting his signal. "You're a very curious fellow, aren't you? You should have been more curious seven years ago. It could have saved your hide."

"Who hired you!"

Miles blinked languidly. "Did I say someone hired me? I do not recall." He looked Crispin up and down. "Why such concern? You thrive, do you not? And Lancaster did speak up for you. 'Begged' for your life, I think the king said. Like a good foster father should."

Crispin snorted. "And the others all under the ax. Except you. But I shall remedy that now."

"Kill a nobleman? They'll put your head on a pike."

"Better that than a coward's life."

"Oh be still, Crispin. You are alive and well. No worse for wear."

"You don't know. You have no idea what I have suffered!"

"So you lost a few shillings—"

"You were there! I lost everything, you bastard! My knighthood, my lands, my title!" Crispin opened his arms, whipping the air with his knife. "This is what the king left me!"

Miles perused Crispin's patched cotehardie, leather hood, threadbare cloak with its tattered hem trailing threads. "And yet you managed to make your way."

"Make my way?" Crispin decided that stabbing him in the gut

would be more pleasing. A knife thrust deep and then jerked upward. Those entrails would nicely cover the shine of Miles's boots and golden spurs.

Crispin gestured with the dagger. His fingers curled tightly around the grip. "You seem to have done very well for yourself. The king's Captain of the Archers?"

"I managed. I went to France and fought in Richard's army and climbed my way into his good graces."

"And you never sought me out, never bothered to discover how I fared?" He couldn't breathe. "You're a dead man."

"I beg to differ." Miles looked down his blunt nose. "Should you attempt to attack me, my men-at-arms would be upon you."

"What do I care if I kill you first?"

"You didn't scrape by all this time just to kill me. You didn't even know I was alive. Surely your life is precious to you. You survived the king's wrath, after all. That is certainly a feat worth note. What have you managed to do all this time? Are you a scribe, perhaps? Or does the Church suit you?"

Crispin looked back over his shoulder. Too many guards. He'd never have the chance to strike a decent blow. Disappointment stabbed at his gut with a long, slow pain, as slow as his knife blade sliding back into its sheath. He raised his chin. "No. I am called the Tracker. I recover lost objects. Find estranged relatives. Investigate for the sheriff."

"God's teeth! That's *you*?" Miles laughed. "I only just heard about this wily fellow yestereve at dinner." He laughed again and hid a guarded expression behind his hand. "Well then. All ends well after all. You defend the indefensible. 'Tis a noble calling."

"Devil take you, Miles!" Crispin looked back at the guards. Maybe one blow would be worth it.

Miles's face drew on a mask of indifference. "Surrender to it, Crispin. It's all in the past. There's truly nothing you can do about it now. Who would believe your word against mine at this point?"

"All the more reason to simply kill you."

"Is that a challenge?" Miles withdrew his sword, inching it from the scabbard.

Crispin stiffened. "I don't have a sword, you turd."

Miles smiled. "So you don't. Keep your little knife where it is then, and there will be no difficulties, eh?"

Miles whipped the air once with the blade and sheathed it. He chuckled. "Good to see you again, Crispin. God keep you." He turned on his heel, reached for his horse, and mounted. He glared down at Crispin and yanked on the reins. The horse arched his neck and Miles turned him, dug in his spurs, and galloped the beast away.

The men-at-arms followed at a trot. They glared back at Crispin but left him alone. Crispin clenched his fists so tight they shook. With a hissing breath through his teeth, he opened his cold fingers and allowed the blood to rush back into them. Pins and needles jabbed his hands until they warmed, warmed as much as a cold September on a London meadow would allow them. He stood a long time, so long the sun burned off the mist, leaving a clear path of trod turf back to town.

He cast a glance toward the grassy butts with his arrows thrust into its center wreath. If only that were Miles's heart. Yet surely the man didn't have one. No wonder he was so difficult to kill.

He snatched the bow from the ground and stomped toward the target. He didn't even bother to watch for flying shafts as he grabbed all five arrows and yanked them free. He hunted for Martin's misspent arrows and found only the two in the ditch in front of the target. The one in the woods was lost.

He turned toward London and strode across the vast field. No question as to where he was going now.

THE DOORS OF THE Boar's Tusk yawned open as if inhaling the first breaths of winter, though winter was still months away. The opened maw welcomed Crispin and he walked through, found his usual seat with his back against the wall, facing the door, and slammed bow and arrows to the table.

A man sitting on the bench beside him gestured toward the weapon. "It ain't right the king should decree a man go forth today. It ain't a Sunday, after all. When's a man to work?"

Crispin never looked at him. "When have you ever done a day's work?"

"That ain't friendly, Master Crispin." He pulled his hood down to his brows.

Crispin rubbed his crusty eyes with the heels of his hands. "It wasn't meant to be."

The man rose, and with an indignant and drunken swagger, departed and nearly bumped into Gilbert.

Gilbert sidestepped the drunk then looked Crispin up and down and motioned for Ned to bring wine and bowls. He sat opposite Crispin with his arms folded over his chest, and after a long, silent pause, Crispin raised his eyes. "What?"

"You're in a sour mood, is all. I was merely waiting for you to tell me."

"Tell you what? That I'm a pauper? That I'm nothing in the eyes of the court? This you already know."

Gilbert eyed the bow and arrows. "What's amiss, Crispin? Is it the archery practice that vexes you?"

Crispin ran his hand over his chin. He felt the spot he missed while shaving. He pictured Miles on the ground and himself above him. Why didn't he slit the bastard's throat when he had the chance? And who, by God, was Miles protecting?

Crispin looked at Gilbert. "I ran in to an old acquaintance today."

"I take it this old acquaintance stirred foul memories."

"He did indeed." Crispin's voice dropped in volume though it wasn't a conscious move. "This man I saw today . . . I have not seen in some seven years. *He* was the instigator of the Plot."

Gilbert hunched forward, cupping their dialogue within his bowed shoulders. There was no need to distinguish which "Plot." "No!"

It was the first time Crispin spoke about Miles to another human being. What did it matter? Miles was right. Who would believe Crispin now after so many years?

Crispin searched over Gilbert's shoulder. Where was Ned with the wine? Such a distasteful subject needed the satisfaction of spirits. "Paid by someone to start the deceit," Crispin went on, "he was the unknown conspirator whom none of us divulged even under torture."

Gilbert's face, so round, so naturally jolly, elongated with horror. "Torture?" he murmured. "I did not know they tortured you, Crispin. You never said. You never spoke much about it at all."

Crispin's belly rumbled uneasily, remembering. The smell of fear made of sweat and piss; the odor of burning flesh. He shut it away again and bolted the memory behind his hate. "It is of no consequence. It turned out to be the least of my worries."

"But Crispin, why wouldn't you say? Why not reveal the scoundrel at the time?"

"I hadn't realized his full guilt then. It was only sometime after it was all over that I knew. Perhaps, even if I had known, I wouldn't have revealed his name."

"For God's sake, why not?"

Crispin looked up, taken aback. "It would not be the honorable thing to do."

Gilbert snorted. "Your honor. It hasn't gotten you very far."

"If I have not that, then what is left to me?"

The wine arrived but not by Ned. Livith faced Crispin and leaned far closer to him than necessary to put the drinking jug on the table. He inhaled the scent of hearth smoke on her clothes and sweat on her skin. When she bent over, he noticed perspiration dotting the tender flesh between her breasts. She put two bowls down, taking longer with Crispin's. "Would you have me pour?" she asked.

Thoughts of torture and Miles Aleyn suddenly receded to a far place in Crispin's mind. A tentative smile wiped away some of the day's rancor. "Yes," he said. She slid the bowl to her, scooped it up to her breast, and poured the wine.

Gilbert squinted at her. "None of your tricks now."

She cast a wearying glance at Gilbert and lowered the cup to the table. She had to push the arrows and bow aside and glanced at it before raising her eyes to Crispin. "Ah now. This brings back memories," she said, sliding her finger suggestively up the curved weapon. "Me dad was an archer in the king's army. Always fiddling with a bow and arrows. Talked of nought but."

Crispin eyed her fingers lightly sliding up the bow. "What happened to him?"

"Died of sickness in his bed. Not the way he would have wanted to go." She sighed and shook out her apron. "And now all this trouble with archery practice. It's a shame, it is." She gave Crispin a smile and sauntered away, looking back over her shoulder in a casual manner, not exactly looking all the way nor catching Crispin's eye, but Crispin knew well what she was about.

"She's trouble." Gilbert shook his head.

"Yes," said Crispin into his bowl. "Maybe the kind I'm looking for."

"Don't get mixed up with her, Crispin. She's got a sly way about her that doesn't sit well with me."

"Never fear, Gilbert. She's not the sort I usually favor." But he watched her disappear behind a curtained alcove and thought long about her slick lips and sweat-misted flesh. Gilbert was talking to him, yet he did not hear his words. He rose with his bowl and walked toward the kitchens when Gilbert grabbed his arm.

"Crispin," he warned.

Crispin merely smiled and when he moved again Gilbert's hand fell away.

He reached the doorway and cast aside the curtain. The alcove led to another door and to the kitchens in a small outbuilding situated too close to the tavern to do much good if it caught fire. He leaned in the open doorway and scanned the tiny space, smaller than his own lodgings. Ned and a female servant were busy roasting and basting meats over a fire burning within the high-arched hearth. Black iron pots, pans, and cooking tools hung on hooks beside the arch, swaying with the smoke rising from the turning meat. A large kettle hung from a rod, its lid rattling from steam.

Grayce sat on a stool by the hearth, peeling turnips. The peels piled in her apron-covered lap like autumn leaves. She did not seem to be looking at her work, but distantly; looking farther than any sane person could, Crispin reckoned. Ned almost tripped over her as he worked, giving her the evil eye.

Livith stood at the worktable that took up the bulk of the floor. She bent over it, kneading a large wad of dough, her sleeves rolled up past her elbows. Flour dusted her breasts. He thought about brushing them off for her, but instead he stood quietly watching, sipping wine from his bowl.

At last she looked up and smiled, a little triumphantly, he thought. "Now what would you be wanting, Master Crispin, that you have to come all this way to the kitchens to get it?"

He sauntered forward two steps, reaching the other end of the table. The woman servant elbowed Ned in the ribs.

"Something I can't get out there in the tavern's hall."

She slapped the dough one last time and planted flour-covered knuckles at her hip. Flour smudged her nose. A wisp of hair dangled from her kerchief and swung before her eyes but it didn't make her blink. Crispin suspected that not much made her blink. "And what would that be?"

He smiled at her audacity. Her angular face was more appealing than on first glance.

"I have a few questions, if you don't mind."

"Questions?" She leaned over and rested her hands on the table, giving Crispin a clear view. "I'd 'a thought you already knew all you needed to know."

He made a point to examine her obvious features before raising his gaze to her's. "You can put those away. I'm not interested."

She straightened abruptly and looked as if she would spit.

Crispin smiled. "I'd like to know where you were during the shooting."

"I was in me place at the inn," she said stiffly.

"On your back?"

She picked up a knife lying on the table. Crispin leaned back to dodge it as it hurled past him out the door.

Grayce popped up, knocking over her stool. "It's the Tracker, Livith. Look, it's him."

"Aye, Grayce. I see him." She narrowed her eyes. "I'm talking to him, ain't I? You go back to your work."

"I'm done with the turnips."

"Then go stir the pot."

A wide smile broke out on Grayce's face. "As you will, Livith. 'Day to you, Tracker."

Crispin gave her a nod and watched her set the stool back on its feet and lean over to stir the pot under Ned's supervision. He wondered how good an idea it was letting her get close to so big a fire, but he supposed Livith knew her business better than he.

Livith wiped her hands on her apron. "You've got a mouth on you, too, *Tracker*." She said the last with oozing sarcasm.

He watched her wipe her apron over her hands. "Why did Grayce admit to killing that man?"

Ned looked up, his face an open question.

Livith shrugged. "She's a simpleton is why. Who knows why she says what she does?"

"Has she always been . . . slow?"

"Aye." Livith glanced at her sister, dreamily stirring the big cauldron. Livith pulled at her apron one more time and let it drop. "She's always been that way. Can teach her a few things and she remembers them, but other things she forgets the moment she's done with it. It's a curse, that."

"Your duties at the King's Head—"

"Don't concern working on me back!"

Crispin raised an unconvinced brow. "Of course. You've been working at the King's Head—how long did you say?"

"I didn't." Her hand at her hip formed the last word on it. Crispin didn't press the matter. Livith seemed to soften. Her weight shifted over one hip. "Any news on that man and who killed him? Can we go back to the King's Head yet?" she added sweetly.

"No, to both. The sheriff is looking for you two."

Her calm manner fled. She crouched forward as if to leap like a spider. "You saw him? You didn't tell him what Grayce said, did you?"

"Of course not. But he knows I am the one who hid you two away."

"Then what are you doing here? Off with you!" She scrambled around the table and shoved him hard in the chest. It barely tilted him.

Crispin chuckled. "The sheriff isn't standing behind me, is he?"

"Get out before he is!"

Crispin smirked and allowed her to turn him and push him toward the open doorway. "Out!" she cried and shoved.

He found himself in the courtyard and chuckled again. He couldn't put his finger on it, but he suspected Livith kept the greater part of the truth from him. Whether it had to do with the murder or something else he was uncertain. *Perhaps she is a thief and lured our courier to his doom—but no. If that were the case, who had the bow? And besides, Livith did not appear to be in the room at the time of the murder and nothing was stolen. And Grayce was not capable of such deception . . .* He had nothing. But murder was murder and someone had to hang for it.

His mind lit on the object that waited for him at his lodgings. "The Crown," he muttered. They didn't get the Crown, if that's what they were after. The courier was murdered and Grayce came to get Crispin. That took half an hour at the most. Another delay while Crispin tried to wrestle the information from Grayce and to return to the King's Head—another half hour and more. That allowed at least an hour for the killer to take what he wished, yet when Crispin examined the dead man, he still possessed his purse, his scrip, and the Crown.

The Crown. He tapped his finger on his lips. He'd better hide it before Wynchecombe decided to pay him a visit.

He entered the Boar's Tusk once more, waved to a frowning Gilbert, and left by the front door. Gutter Lane teemed with people. Not only were men still returning from the butts, but the corn had been newly threshed in the outlying fields and men with scythes or bundles of straw were lumbering down the narrow corridor, laughing and jesting with one another in easy camaraderie. The harvest was nearly done. Crispin had seen its plenty in the stalls of fruit sellers and those merchants selling herbs and vegetables. Soon the plenty would give way to the sparseness of winter and there would be less on his table than there was now.

His lodgings on the Shambles was only a short walk from the Boar's Tusk. He sidestepped a man dragging his goat down the lane, avoiding the beast as the goat whipped its head, pulling on the lead wrapped tight around its horns. But he slowed when he noticed Martin Kemp nervously pacing outside the shop—with Alice beside him.

"God's blood." Crispin moved forward slowly, fingering Martin Kemp's bow and arrows. His apology to Alice Kemp had to be done and in quick order. It wouldn't do to have a raging Alice hovering near his door every moment. He tugged at his wrinkled coat and stiffly approached them. But before he could open his mouth, Alice swooped upon him like a hawk.

"How *dare* you speak to Matilda in that manner! And you *threatened* her! You should be locked up, Crispin Guest! You are not safe to be hard by."

"Mistress Kemp, I offer my sincerest apologies for my lapse in behavior. I was out of sorts and did not know my right mind."

"Out of sorts! So much transpires in that room. I tell you, husband, it is not safe."

"Now dear. He is apologizing."

"Never pays the rent on time—and too little of it there is, I dare say. Strange people coming and going at all hours. And then he threatens the very fruit of your loins."

"He apologized to me, dear. Quite humbly."

"Humble? Him? He hasn't a humble bone in his body."

Crispin rocked on his heels. Impatient to get away, he knew he could not leave until Alice was mollified.

"Ma-til-*da*!" she screeched.

Crispin held his breath. Out of the shadows, the wide specter of Matilda Kemp blocked the light. She posed shyly behind her mother, peered around her, and glared venomously at Crispin.

"You will apologize to my daughter. And further, we will require a service of you to make up for your threats to her."

"A service?" He kept his voice steady, though the effort was supreme.

"Yes. I will decide at a later date what that shall be."

Crispin's glance darted from one woman to the other. Martin Kemp looked worried, but the two women were nothing if not triumphant.

Crispin wished he could use the bow. He swallowed the sour taste in his mouth and inclined his head to Matilda. "Damosel, forgive me for yesterday's outburst. I do apologize for my rudeness and for any distress I might have caused you."

Matilda glanced sideways at her mother and finally curtseyed in return. "I do accept your apology, Master Crispin."

Crispin frowned. *I hope they don't expect me to kiss her hand. I've already kissed her arse.*

The Kemps seemed satisfied. Martin took the weapon and arrows from Crispin and ushered his wife and daughter away. He looked back at Crispin apologetically.

What "service" could Alice want? Perhaps he should offer to look over Martin's books again before Alice could think of something else. Crispin shuddered at the possibilities.

He trotted up the stairs in his relief to get away, pushed opened the door, and felt an immediate prickling on the back of his neck.

The Crown of Thorns sat on the bed out of its casket, and Jack was nowhere to be found.

7

CRISPIN CLOSED THE DOOR and walked toward the bed. He lightly touched the Crown and then went to the rear window. He looked out to the back courtyard, across the many roofs, but saw nothing but doves delicately stepping over the tiles. Slowly he closed the shutters and barred them. He looked at the Crown again. An anxious feeling crept over him.

The door suddenly flung wide behind Crispin. He spun and Jack staggered into the shadowed opening.

"Jack? Where've you been? Did you touch that?" Crispin pointed to the Crown and Jack stared with bulging eyes.

"I fell out the window," he said.

Crispin grabbed Jack by the shoulders, hastily checking for fractured bones. "Are you drunk?"

"I ain't. I fell out the window. After tinkering with that!" His hand shot forward, accusing the Crown.

He pushed Jack back to look at him. "But there isn't a scratch on you."

"I ain't lying, Master. I put it on me head. And the strangest thing. I felt like—" He looked up at the cobwebbed beams. "I felt like I could do anything. I took it off me head, I stood on yonder sill, and then I fell out. I don't remember falling. I was just . . . on the ground. It's bewitched, that's what it is."

"Nonsense." The word soured in Crispin's mouth. He, too, remembered feeling an unnatural elation when he wore the Crown, an elation that almost made him pick a fight. Yes, he, too, could well see—in that state—he might have imagined he could fly out the window. He stared at the Crown. Just coincidence, surely. "Now Jack," he began, soothing himself with his easy words, "you could have imagined it. With a little wine—"

"I tell you true, Master Crispin. I ain't had no wine!"

Crispin turned from Jack to pick up the Crown, running his thumb over the smooth side of a thorn. "There *is* something about this—" The Crown felt substantial in his hands. Not particularly heavy, but thick with the woven rushes and the prickly thorns that did not stab him as he thought they should have done. He glanced at Jack and then carefully placed the Crown within its jeweled casket. He rested his hand on the closed lid and shook his head. "No, I do not believe that God's power can inhabit worldly things. It makes no sense."

"But God was Himself a worldly thing. As Jesus, eh?"

"So now you are a theologian?"

"I don't know what that is, but I know what happened to me. I fell out the sarding window and I didn't feel nought."

Crispin set the jeweled casket within the wooden box and cast about for a place to hide it. His lodgings were particularly bad for hiding large objects—no alcoves, no other rooms. It wouldn't fit in his coffer. The only place was the pile of straw in the corner that Jack used as a bed. He took the box to the straw and dug deep to nestle it there.

"In *my* bed?" cried Jack. "I ain't sleeping with it. God knows what mischief I'd be up to next. Flying off the roof, maybe."

"I've no other place to hide it."

"Why don't you give it over to court if you're so keen to have the king forgive you?"

Crispin pulled the last strands of yellow straw over the box and stepped back to look at the pile. The straw conjured images of the bed he slept on in one of Newgate's cells, little better than this pile of straw, and the cell had been much colder than this room. All had been silent and mostly dark, until they allowed him a candle. Alone had been best, for he knew that when the cell door opened, the questioning and the torture would begin anew. He came to dread the sound of whining hinges and rattling keys. Each time the door yawned he hoped the guards would take him to the executioner. But such relief was not to be. Only the last time. The last time at court.

He thought of Miles. How comfortable life must have been for him the last seven years. All Crispin's comrades executed, and all too brave to name Miles Aleyn. Even Crispin had said nothing. But now Crispin would say. Nothing would stop his tongue. But he must be careful. He must do so with enough evidence. There was still one more unknown conspirator. Someone powerful enough to hire Miles and want either Lancaster or Richard dead. Who at court would dare such a feat? He'd wait to bring the Crown of Thorns so that he could pillory Miles and this other man at the same time. That *would* be a prize.

He looked at Jack. "Not yet," Crispin said. The sneer did not leave his lips. "I have more work to do before I can."

"I would be rid of such a thing. What do you know of it? I mean—" Jack stared at the pile of straw that hid the box. He crushed his arms over his chest. "Is it truly the Crown of Thorns placed on our Lord's head?"

"That is what they say. But for all the answers, I do know someone better to ask. Get your cloak."

THEY SET OFF TOWARD the west end of London. Crispin was grateful Jack didn't ask about Miles. Too much anger bubbled in his gut. It was impossible to discuss the man. But Crispin was puzzled as to why he had not killed Miles outright. Of course, if he had, he'd be in a cell right now truly awaiting the executioner. No axes for him this time, but the strangulation death of the gallows.

He didn't much care for the idea.

"Where are we going, Master?" Jack asked after they passed Charing Cross.

"There." Crispin pointed to the large church. Its rounded apse faced the Thames, as did the long walls of its cloister snuggled next to the church under the crook of the south transept, like a kitten cuddling its mother. The big square tower with the rosette window faced north and jutted upward above the cloister's walls and rooftops. Westminster Abbey.

Over Crispin's shoulder and farther to the east stood Westminster Hall. Court. But he wouldn't go there today. No. He was not yet welcomed at court. The few times he attempted entrance went not well at all. The next time he entered court he intended not a triumphal entrance, perhaps, but a more salutary one.

"Why there?" asked Jack, pulling at his collar.

"I've an old friend at the abbey. He'll be able to tell us about the Crown, if anyone can."

They did not enter by the front entrance, but through a side door that led to the cloister. The barred gate might have discouraged a lesser man, but Crispin expected it and pulled down on the bell chain several times, certain the call of the bell would summon someone. Soon it did. A becassocked monk with a black band of hair across his forehead and a shiny tonsure on his skull turned the corner. He walked with eyes lowered and murmured "Peace be with you" and then raised his head. His face, pallid and frozen in an innocuous expression of passivity, came to life. "Crispin Guest! How good it is to see you!"

"Brother Eric. It is good to see you as well. Is the abbot available? I would take a moment to speak with him."

"Yes, Crispin. For you, there is always time."

Crispin felt Jack's gaze on him as he passed through the opened gate. The lad followed haltingly, eyeing the monk who stared back at him with a full amount of scrutiny.

They strode along the cloister walk, steps echoing into the stone vaulting. The air was cold, particularly in the shadows, and seemed to linger within the windowed arches. Braziers dotted the walkway every few feet, crackling with burning logs, sending smoke up into the sooty ceiling vaults.

The three finally came to a large oak door with ornate hinges. Brother Eric knocked but did not wait for a reply before he opened the door.

One young monk sat at a high desk by the window. He looked up with a quill poised in his hand. The other was older, gray with wisps of hair blowing off his now natural tonsure. He stood before a large Bible lying open on its stand and contemplated the text, a finger pressed to his lips. His triangular nose stretched beaklike over his finger. His gray brows hunched low over hooded eyes. Though the gray hair marked him as old, his face did not seem as lined as perhaps it should be. His cheekbones, set high and pronounced, overshadowed a strong chin. He had a face designed more for a knight's helm than a cowl.

He turned at their step. It took a moment for his eyes to recognize the figures before him but when they did his face dented with smiles. "Crispin Guest!" He opened his arms, strode forward, and enclosed Crispin in a strong embrace. Crispin endured it. The monk pushed him back and held Crispin's arms in muscular hands. "How long has it been? Look at you. You are looking hale." He nodded. "I am pleased."

"And you look no older, my Lord Abbot."

The abbot waved his hand and stood back. "'My Lord Abbot'? I am Nicholas to you." He turned his head and looked down at Jack Tucker, who cringed. "And who is this?"

Crispin laid his hand on Jack's shoulder. The shoulder did not relax. "This is Jack Tucker. He insists on being my servant." Crispin flashed a sideways smile. "Jack, this is the Abbot of Westminster Abbey, Nicholas de Litlyngton."

Jack's wide gaze sped over the abbot and the room with its gold-encased manuscripts, silver candlesticks, and toasty fire. He made an awkward bow. "My lord."

Crispin jerked his head toward the abbot. "I did a minor task for the abbot some years ago—"

"Minor task!" Nicholas guffawed. He patted Crispin heartily on the back. "I was accused of murder and Crispin here uncovered the truth, exonerating me. Minor task indeed!"

"Sweet Christ!" said Jack, and then slammed his hand over his mouth when both monks turned to stare.

Nicholas chuckled and took Crispin by the shoulders, steering him toward the fire. Brother Eric bowed to the abbot, glanced once more at Jack, and departed.

Crispin tolerated the abbot's attention. He knew it was the monk's way. The fire felt good and even smelled good, better than the poor sticks and peat Crispin used for his own hearth.

"Brother Michael," said Nicholas to the other monk at his desk. "Please serve us some wine."

The abbot's room was comfortable, even cozy. Tall arched windows with delicately cut panes of glass cast colored light upon the abbot's desk and stone floor. A hound, ribs showing through the short fur, lay on the floor by the fire undisturbed by all the comings and goings.

Brother Michael offered a goblet of wine to Crispin but not to Jack. The wine was better than good. Smooth, fragrant. Crispin surmised it was probably the abbot's better stock from Spain.

Crispin drank and realized that it had been a year since he last visited the abbot. He cast a glance into a far corner between bookshelves and a prie-dieu, and smiled to see the chessboard still in place. He narrowed his eyes at it and walked forward. If he were not mistaken, none of the pieces had been disturbed since their last meeting.

He looked up at Nicholas. "Our game?"

"Yes," said Nicholas. "And I believe it's your move."

Crispin examined the board. He'd already captured Nicholas's queen and a few other pieces. He picked up the black knight and moved it forward. "Your king is endangered by my knight."

Nicholas frowned and examined the pieces. "Hmm," he said, resting a finger on his lips. He glanced up at Crispin. "So he is. After so many months, I hoped you would not notice. But there is little that escapes your notice, is there, Crispin?" The abbot reached for a piece, paused, and then drew his hand back. "I shall have to mull this over. But in the meantime. . . ." He gestured to the chairs by the fire. The abbot settled in a chair with a blanket made of fox pelts cast across the chair's arms and back. He urged Crispin to take another beside it. Jack positioned himself behind Crispin's chair and grasped its carved back with white fingers. Nicholas bent down to scratch the hound's head. The dog made no move except to raise his tail, thump it a few times on the floor, and drop it again. "Tell me why you are here. I doubt it is purely a social call. As much as that would please me."

"To my regret, Nicholas. I wonder if you could tell me about a particular relic."

"Oh, indeed." He smiled and turned to Brother Michael, who stood by with the flagon. "I have great facility with relics. My chaplain, Brother Michael, has accompanied me on many a quest to see such venerable objects."

"Then you can easily tell me of the Crown of Thorns."

"The Crown of Thorns?" The jovial lines of the abbot's face fell. He shifted forward over his thighs. "Why would you wish to know of that particular relic?"

Crispin made a half smile and ran his finger absently around the lip of the goblet. He did not look up, but studied the glittering amber of the wine swirling in the bowl. "It seems to be on my mind of late."

Nicholas took a deep breath. "The Crown of Thorns." He said it slowly, thoughtfully. "Of course, this was the very same that the cursed Roman soldiers placed on our Lord's head. We do not know its early history—who took it from the place of His glorious death and kept it safe. But I do know from the writings of a monk—who was that?" He rose, went to the bookshelf, and pulled down a large tome. He laid it over the Bible on its stand and thumbed through the pages. "Ah!" He leaned forward and read. "A Brother *Bernard*. Some five hundred years ago. He says the Crown resided in a church on Mount Sion in Jerusalem. And two hundred years after that, it was transferred to Byzantium." He looked up. Crispin at first thought he searched for another book, but the monk was looking farther than that. His eyes glazed as his memory took hold. "'Behold the thorny crown, which was only set upon the head of Our Redeemer in order that all the thorns of the world might be gathered together and broken.'" His lidded eyes looked at Crispin. "The Eastern Holy Emperors presented individual thorns to various Christian monarchs. I know of one such thorn sent to our own ancient King Athelstan—in the old times," he said to Jack, who didn't seem to understand what the old abbot was talking about, "and that very thorn still resides at Malmesbury Abbey." He closed the book, replaced it on the shelf and sat again. He took a sip of his wine and cocked his head thoughtfully but directed his next words back toward Crispin. "As you surely know, one hundred years ago and more, the empire of Constantinople began to crumble, and in a desperate attempt for support—and money— Emperor Baldwin II sought the friendship of King Louis of France. He offered him the Crown of Thorns, though he needed to pay for its return from the pestilent Venetians. They kept it as surety for a loan. Italians!" he muttered. "They certainly understand the business of usury. Disgraceful. At any rate, the Crown of Thorns was soon redeemed and it was sent off to France where Louis built the magnificent Sainte-Chappelle for it. It is there still."

"What does the Crown look like? Can you tell me?"

"Oh yes. I have seen it myself. As you might imagine, there are few thorns left after having been divided amongst the many emperors and kings over the years. It is now a circlet of woven rushes, a weave of decorative design no doubt created by careful fingers. Thrust amongst the rushes are the remaining thorns."

Crispin downed his cup. Before he could object, Brother Michael filled it again. Crispin decided wine was a good idea after all and gulped more. "And what does—" He took another quaff. Nicholas stared at him quizzically. "Does it— Are there qualities it conveys to . . . to anyone who might . . . touch it?"

"Qualities? Oh. You mean the relic's power. Oh yes. It does have power. These thorns pierced our Lord's very brow, drew His precious blood. Of course they are imbued with power. Greater power than other relics, you can be sure."

"But what is that power?"

Nicholas rose. He paced and rolled his goblet's stem between his palms. "I wonder why you are so curious, my friend. You seem to have a personal interest in this." He looked up and his gaze penetrated Crispin's.

Crispin, too, rose to stand close to the old monk. He set his goblet on a side table. "I do have a personal interest in it. But that is all I can say."

Nicholas stared at him another moment and then shrugged. "As you will. Your reasons must be good ones. I trust you," he said with more conviction than was warranted. Was it a warning? "The power of the relic—it is said—makes those who touch it, especially those who wear it, invincible."

"Invincible? In what way?"

"To everything. To fear, to danger. Even to death."

Jack lunged forward and grabbed Crispin's arm. "Master! That's what happened to m—"

"Silence, Jack." Crispin gave the abbot an apologetic smile that did not seem to convince the old monk of a casual exchange. "I think what my Lord Nicholas means to say," he said leaning toward the boy but looking at Nicholas, "is that a man can *feel* a sensation of invincibility."

"No, that is not what I said." Nicholas stared down his hawk nose at Crispin. "The invincibility is real. Perhaps a feeling of euphoria accompanies it, but a man *is* invincible while wearing the Crown. So it is said."

Jack tugged at Crispin's arm. "Master!"

"Be still, for God's sake!" He turned in earnest to Nicholas. "The King of France has loaned the Crown to King Richard as a gesture of peace."

Nicholas pursed his lips and nodded. "I have heard as much."

Crispin drew back. "Have you?"

"I move easily through court, Crispin, as you know. I have kinship in high places. As you also know."

"Yes," said Crispin distractedly. "Why should the King of France wish to give such power to his sworn enemy?"

Nicholas's chuckle turned into a throaty laugh. He looked once at Brother Michael, who didn't get the jest. The abbot laid his hand on Crispin's taut shoulder and said quietly, "Because, my dear friend, this power only falls to those who are pure of heart."

Crispin blinked. "Pure of heart?"

"Yes. Men who desire no ill deeds to the innocent. Men who love God. Men whom the simplest man would trust." He patted Crispin's breast. "Pure of heart."

Crispin almost smiled. "So the king is not capable of summoning such power?"

Nicholas casually looked over his shoulder. No one but Brother Michael stood there. "I shouldn't say so. Perhaps it may even be treason." Brother Michael raised his brows but said nothing. "The king's counterpart in France is equally incapable." He shrugged. "Truth is truth."

Crispin smiled at Jack and winked. "Pure of heart, Jack."

"God blind me," he whispered and put his dirty fingers to his mouth.

"I also hear tell," said Nicholas, "that the Crown is missing. His

Majesty thinks it a French plot to embarrass him. You wouldn't happen to know anything about it, now would you?"

"I, too, hear many things, my Lord Abbot. And I am the Tracker. If it is lost, you can be certain I can find it."

"Oh I am certain of that. If it is lost."

Crispin narrowed his eyes at the shrewd curve of the abbot's mouth, but said nothing.

CRISPIN AND JACK TOOK the rest of the afternoon to walk back to the Shambles. Neither spoke until they turned the corner and the full stench of a day of butchering and burning offal reached their senses.

"Master Crispin." Crispin looked down at the boy, who seemed unusually solemn. Jack bit his nails. "I know you got your own ideas. But wouldn't it be better to be rid of that Crown? Maybe give it over to Abbot Nicholas for safekeeping. We shouldn't be messing about with God's power. We're liable to get ourselves into a foul condition. Maybe even be cast into Hell for it."

"Your thieving is likely to get you into more trouble, Jack."

But Jack truly looked concerned. And Crispin could no longer deny his own discomfort with possession of the Crown.

Pure of heart. He felt far from pure of heart. Especially when he wanted to kill Miles Aleyn. Yet he hadn't killed him. There was plenty of opportunity. The guards be damned. He knew he could have slipped his dagger's blade up between Miles's ribs and gotten away before any of the guards were the wiser. But he didn't. He simply could not kill a man in that manner. Oh, he knew Miles was capable of such dishonorable feats, but not Crispin.

Pure of heart. "It is a curse," he muttered.

"It is, sir, as I was saying," said Jack, but not about the same thing. "We must rid ourselves of the Crown and right quickly."

"Don't be a fool, Jack," Crispin sighed. "There is nothing dangerous about a few rushes and some old thorns—" Crispin's words were cut off by a whoosh and an abrupt flash of hot pain. His shoulder slammed hard against a wall.

Jack screamed.

For a moment, Crispin was perplexed by what happened. But he snapped back to himself and glanced down at his own shoulder. An arrow pinned his coat to the wall, missing the shoulder with only a graze. An arrow with hawk fletching.

8

"CHRIST'S SOUL! MASTER CRISPIN!" Jack jerked forward, but there was little he could do.

Crispin reached up, curled his fingers around the arrow's shaft, and yanked it from the wood. It tore a further hole through his coat and he swore at the ragged cloth. He pressed his hand to his left shoulder, felt a little wetness from blood, and didn't worry further over it. "It is only a graze," he said to Jack and examined the arrow. "More importantly—" He looked up and scanned the rooftops. Nothing but smoke and ravens. "Where did it come from?"

Of course, every man on the street was carrying a bow.

"It couldn't have been no accident," said Jack.

"No, not likely." Crispin pointed to a rooftop across the lane. "He'd have to have been there. Possibly behind that gable." Crispin trotted over the rutted street and looked for handholds on the building. The timbering bowed outward from the daubed wall at differing levels, offering places to put his foot. He did so, grabbing the exposed wood, and hoisted himself up the jettied wall. A windowsill offered more purchase for his foot until his fingers reached the eave and he hung on a corbel for a moment. He tried not to think of loose tiles before he swung his leg up and onto the roof. He pulled himself farther until his entire arm rested on the roof and he managed to roll himself onto the tiles. He stood at the edge and looked down at Jack on the street. "I could use that relic now, eh?"

"Don't jest about it!" cried Jack.

Crispin picked gingerly across the slick tiles until he reached the gable. He grabbed it and looked over every inch of the roof surrounding it. He did not expect to find footprints on the slate, but he hoped for other clues that might lead to finding the culprit. He almost gave up when he spotted a half moon of mud. A heel? No, too small. The ball of a shoe, perhaps? He looked along the edge of the gable and glimpsed something more along the rough edge of its daubed wall. The archer must have leaned there to take his shot. Crispin peered closely and grasped with two fingers. A few hairs—gold-colored—and a few threads. White. Possibly a shirt.

"Find anything?" asked Jack from below. Crispin could not see him from the pitch of the roof.

"Yes, but not much. I'm coming down."

Crispin took one more look over the spine of the roof in the opposite direction, saw nothing, edged down to the eave, lowered himself to the jutting beam, sat on it, and leaped the rest of the way. He showed Jack his spoils.

"That ain't nought but a hair and a thread. What can you make of that?"

Crispin shook his head. He let the items fall to the ground. "I don't know. There was a partial footprint up there, too. It only proves he was where I thought he was." He stood a moment thinking, glancing at Martin Kemp's tinker shop just two doors down.

A queasy feeling rumbled in his gut. "Jack." He slapped Jack in the chest and leaped forward into a run. "The Crown!"

Crispin reached the foot of the stairs first. He took the steps two at a time and fumbled for his key, finally sliding it into the lock. He turned it, left it in the lock, and pulled the door open.

Everything was as he left it. The box lay buried under the straw.

He fell to his knees and dug it out and lifted the golden casket out of the wooden box. He lifted the lid.

Still there.

He sat back on his feet just as Jack slammed into the doorjamb, panting. "Well? Is it gone?"

"No." Crispin slowly closed the lid and replaced the gold casket in the box. He carefully assembled the straw about it again and stood, brushing bits of straw from his knees. "It's untouched. The room is untouched. Surely he knew where I lived. Why didn't he take the Crown?"

"Maybe he wanted to kill you first."

Crispin looked at Jack and noticed the boy clutching the arrow in his fist. Jack raised it. "I thought you'd want it. Evidence."

Crispin smiled. "Very good, Jack. You're learning. You'll be an accomplished Tracker on your own someday."

Jack's brow grew a crop of wrinkles running up into his loose fringe. He handed over the arrow for Crispin's inspection. "What, me? A Tracker? I ain't as smart as you, Master. I could never—"

"You're young. Keep your eyes and ears open and you can be more than a servant."

"God blind me." Jack shook his head and caught sight of Crispin's torn coat. "Oh Master! Let me see to your wound."

He shook off Jack. "It's nothing, I tell you." Crispin was more entranced by the arrow. He knew it was the brother of the one that killed the courier. Hawk fletching, barbed tip. Expensive. Not the kind a man would use for target practice. A hunter's arrow. A nobleman's arrow. The same sort of arrows sitting in the quiver of the Captain of the Archers.

AFTER SHEDDING HIS COAT for Jack to repair and shrugging on his cloak to cover his shirt, Crispin went back outside to look up at the gable across the way. Despite the odd looks from passersby, he climbed the wall again and slid up onto the roof. A light drizzle washed away all sign of the muddy footprint. Not that it could have helped him. Only a shoe left behind would have done that, but Miles would not have been so careless.

Crispin looked up. Was his mind playing tricks, or did he hear Miles's voice?

He stepped to the edge of the roof and looked down. There was Miles, astride his horse and talking to a page. Miles patted the boy on the shoulder and sent him off. He chuckled and fisted the reins.

Crispin noticed the quiver of arrows hanging from the saddle—hawk fletching all.

Miles would be gone in another moment. The horse shook his large head, awaiting his master's instructions.

Crispin scanned the street. The page disappeared around the corner. The street emptied. The drizzle kept them away from the pungent butcher's street. Crispin stared at the top of Miles's head . . . and leaped.

He landed heavily on Miles's back, knocking him off his horse to the mud. Winded, Miles tried to right himself, but Crispin pushed him down. Miles grabbed his ankle and Crispin fell with him. They rolled, each trying to get the upper hand as the horse grunted and stepped out of the way, its trapper swishing.

Crispin shoved Miles down, grinding his face in the sludge. Then he scrambled on top of Miles's shoulder blades, forcing him deeper into the mushy ground. He yanked out his knife and held it to the man's neck.

Miles glared over his shoulder and when he finally got his breath back hissed, "Get the hell off me!"

"I think not. I'd like to have a parley, if you will."

Miles tried to rise but Crispin used his knees to dig into Miles's spine.

Miles twisted to look back. "I don't have a choice, do I?"

"You know," said Crispin calmly, more calmly than he felt, "it's bad enough you manipulated me into committing treason all those years ago, but trying to kill me is quite another matter. I don't like it."

"I never tried to kill you."

Crispin grit his teeth and pressed the blade's tip into Miles's jaw just at the juncture of his ear. Miles grunted when Crispin pressed harder. A pearl of blood oozed up, bulged, and then ran down his neck. "I don't tolerate liars. Let's try this again. Why did you try to kill me?"

"Dammit, let me up! I never tried to kill you, you bastard, but I will now!"

"I am in possession of one of your arrows that just grazed my shoulder not more than a few moments ago. There is another stuck in the flesh of a dead French courier. Care to tell me about these unrelated events?"

Miles stopped struggling. A line of red ran down his neck like a necklace. He blew two bursts from his nostrils and then a third before he turned his head as much as Crispin's blade allowed him. "Let me up and we will talk."

"Why should I do that?"

"I have much to say."

"I rather enjoy my knee in your back." Miles said nothing. Crispin stared at the back of the archer's head, watched his shoulders fall and rise with each labored breath. At last, Crispin leaned back, grabbed Miles's sword from its sheath, and rose. "Get up. No tricks."

Miles pushed up from the mud on his hands and knees and carefully rose. He turned to face Crispin before raising a gloved hand to his bleeding neck. He looked at the blood and mud on his glove and scowled. "Always one for the dramatic, aren't you? Tell me what all this is about."

"I told you. You killed that French courier and you tried to kill me."

"I don't know what the hell you're talking about. What French courier?"

"Must we play this?" Crispin raised the sword. It felt good in his hand. "The French courier that may bring the war with France to our doorstep. The one carrying a particular object from the French court to this one."

Miles's brows rose. "You think I killed him?"

"And tried the same on me. But Miles. With an *arrow*?" He shook his head. "Of course, that is the cowardly way. I'd expect that from you."

The corner of Miles's muddy lip raised in a sneer. "I can assure you, when I choose to kill you, it will be face to face so that you may see it coming."

Crispin tapped the sword point into Miles's chest with each word. "Tell me about the French courier."

"You're repeating yourself. I don't know anything about that or the—" Miles bit down on his cheek. He glared at Crispin and the sword blade at his chest.

"Or the what?" smiled Crispin.

Miles made an unconvincing grin. "The object from the French court. As you said."

"On top of everything else, you're a *bad* liar."

"Oi!"

Crispin turned. Several guards came running up the street, weapons raised. Crispin turned back to Miles and smiled. "Time to go. We'll meet again." He jammed the sword into the mud and leapt for the roof, leaving Miles to react a hairsbreadth too late. Crispin hung on a corbel and swung his legs up to the slate, grabbing hold of the roof's edge. With the strength of his legs, he pulled himself up over the eave the rest of the way and rolled onto the slick tiles, gripping with his fingers so he didn't slip off. Miles stood below him, a shocked look on his face. Crispin saluted him with a grim smile and ran up to the roof's peak and down the other side, leaving the guards and a sputtering Miles behind.

He didn't need Miles or his false testimony. All he needed was the arrow. One he already possessed, but the one that killed the courier would be best. That would convict Miles right well.

He slid on his backside down the roof to the edge and leapt off into a haycart. He rolled out of the hay and righted himself on the ground, brushing the mud and hay off his shirt before he straightened his cloak.

He listened but could not hear anyone following him, neither over the roof nor around the corner. So much for the king's guards and the Captain of the Archers.

He took a deep breath and looked up the lane one side and down the other. Now where would Wynchecombe have put the body?

"IT'S A SIMPLE QUESTION, Lord Sheriff." At least Crispin thought it was.

"I'll make you a bargain, Guest."

Ah. Here it comes.

"I'll tell you where the body is if you tell me where those women are."

"Now my Lord Sheriff, I told you I was protecting them—"

"Do you truly want to be thrown into gaol again?"

Crispin sighed. He stood before the sheriff in his Newgate chamber. Wynchecombe had not offered him a seat, so he stood. "I prefer to remain a free man if given the choice."

"That choice is slipping away."

"I told you I'm protecting them."

"From whom?"

"From you, my lord."

Wynchecombe sat back. His eyes whitened at the edges but the incredulity was not there. "Why should they need protecting from me?"

Should he say? Always difficult to decide how helpful the sheriff would be. Crispin stared at his boots. "The one who found him is dull-witted, my lord, and she, well, she seems to think *she* killed him."

"What!" The sheriff shot to his feet and slammed his hand on the table. His candle wobbled and the flame flickered. "God's teeth, Guest!"

"My Lord Sheriff, with a *bow and arrow*? A kitchen wench?"

Wynchecombe glared. His bushy brows lowered over his eyes until they cast a shadow. "Hmph" was all he said and sat heavily. His sword clanked against the chair.

"I need that arrow from the dead man. I think I know who killed him."

The sheriff recovered and leaned forward. "Who, then?"

Crispin smiled grimly. "I cannot say just yet."

Wynchecombe sat back slowly. "Were you always this annoying, Guest, or did you come by it only after the king dealt with you?"

"'Annoying,' Lord Sheriff?"

"Never mind. Very well. Come with me."

The sheriff rose. He led Crispin down the wooden staircase outside his tower chamber and through several passages, then down another staircase to a dark undercroft lit with a few pitch torches. Ahead, Crispin saw a bier set up with a sheet-covered body. The cloth glowed like pale moonlight in the torches' illumination.

"The French ambassador wanted the body returned to France," said the sheriff gravely, "but the king refuses to release it."

Crispin snorted. Politics.

Once he neared, he noticed the arrow still protruding from the corpse. "No one removed the arrow?"

"Why should we do that?"

Crispin shook his head. "Why indeed." He cast back the sheet. The dead man's dry eyes stared upward. Did he see angels or demons?

Crispin grabbed the arrow's shaft but it stuck solid in the dead flesh. He yanked out his dagger and ripped the dead man's blood-soaked surcote from the neck down to the arrow.

Wynchecombe grabbed Crispin's dagger hand. "Holy Mary! What are you doing? Why do you not simply break it off."

"I want the entire arrow. Do you mind?"

Wynchecombe released him with a rumbled sound in his throat. "Desecrating a corpse? I mind not at all. You're certainly bound for Hell at any rate. Why should I try to stop your progress?"

Crispin continued pulling the blade through the layers of bloody fabric, now stiff and brown. There had been a lot of blood considering the arrow pierced the man's heart. Crispin sawed the blade into the fabric all the way down past his chemise to the man's skin. He used his hands to tear the material away from the arrow wound. The man had not been cleaned and the dried blood rusted his chest and the punctured flesh. The rest of his skin shone white and ashen in the pale light. Crispin tugged on the arrow again but still it would not yield. He glanced once at Wynchecombe. The sheriff shook his head slightly at what he surely knew Crispin was about to do, but Crispin turned back to his task and thrust the tip of his dagger into the wound next to the shaft and worked the blade around, ripping open the flesh. He supposed it was like any other bit of dead meat on his supper table, meat that would not bleed. But knowing it was human flesh made his belly a little uneasy.

He grabbed the arrow again and wiggled it, rocked it, until the arrowhead tore upward. The body rose slightly as Crispin pulled the shaft. The flesh made a distasteful sucking sound until he yanked the arrow free.

He examined the metal broadhead and its glistening blood. He wiped his blade for an extra few seconds on the dead man's surcote and sheathed it.

"What do you plan to do with that?" asked the sheriff. He didn't mask his grimace.

"I know the maker. I wish to have it identified for assurance."

"Isn't that the province of the Lord Sheriff's office?"

Crispin wiped the arrow on the sheet and shoved it through his belt. "Only should you insist."

Wynchecombe looked at the arrow now secured on Crispin's person. He leaned closer and his face dropped into shadow. "What of the Crown of Thorns? Have you found it yet?"

"Not yet. You can be sure that once I have, everyone will know."

"What does that mean? What are you plotting, Guest?"

"Nothing, Lord Sheriff. Do I have your leave to go?"

Wynchecombe glared and inhaled deeply. The exhale through his nostrils ruffled his mustache. "I know you look for trouble, and I'd see you hang yourself. As long as it doesn't drag me in with you."

"No, my lord. If I hang, I will most assuredly hang alone."

"Happy to hear it. Off with you, then."

Crispin knew that wasn't quite the truth. If hang he must, he wanted Miles struggling right beside him.

9

THE DAY HAD CRAWLED on uneventfully. No guards came to his door to haul him away. No sign of that cur Miles. And so the night took hold with a cold dampness that seemed to mourn the day, and Crispin and Jack, resigned to the silence that had enveloped the Shambles, had a meager dinner by a brittle fire, and then settled in for the night.

The following morning was still raw when Crispin awoke with a start. Cold sweat covered his face and body, and he cast off the blanket and threw his naked legs over the side of the bed. He stared at the floor, dark in the absence of moonlight and a dying hearth.

Jack snored nearly beneath Crispin's bed. His body was curled in a tight knot as far away from the Crown's reliquary as he could get.

Crispin ran his hand through his damp hair. He hadn't had that dream in a long time, though it truly wasn't a dream. A memory, then, slipping into the landscape of his dreams.

He sat up and glanced across his dim room, but the half-dream, half-memory lingered. He still felt the rough ropes bite into his wrists, felt the raw wheals from the pressure, from pulling on the bindings so hard. Then the hot pincers, glowing red from the coals. They came closer, so close he could smell the damp, fetid air sizzle on them. "Tell us," they said, over and over. "We won't have these 'meetings' anymore if you just tell us the other names." But he didn't, wouldn't. And so they'd touched the pincers to his flesh. And then it was the sound of skin blistering and steam rising, his own flesh cooking with an acrid odor, smoke wisping skyward.

He rose and staggered to the window. He opened the shutter, stuck his head out, and inhaled the cold, foggy air. Even now he could not fight the nausea, and he spit the sour taste out the window.

He knew why he dreamed it. Miles. Miles brought all those memories back into stinging clarity. Especially that last day. The day they took him from the cell. Crispin thought he was to be executed and even thanked God for it, that it would finally be over. But instead of marching him to the courtyard and the gibbet, he was led instead to Westminster's great hall.

King Richard, ten years old and newly minted as king, sat his gangly frame on his marble throne. His feet did not yet touch the ground and so a cushioned stool rested beneath his long-toed slippers. His smooth face saw neither beard nor scar. Small mouth, small chin, languid lids. But no mere pup. Fire burned in those eyes. Anger. The king knew that the Plot meant his death. The others were gone, every one of them executed in all manner of foul ways. There remained only Crispin on whom to pass judgment.

Crispin staggered toward the king's dais, barely recovered from the torture that had gone on for weeks. The iron shackles pulled his wrists down. Their chains dragged along the floor. His surcote hung torn and bloody on his weakened body.

Stiffly, like a wooden puppet, he lowered to his knees, his last obeisance to the crown at least, if not the one wearing it.

A knight with a conical helm and camail down his chin and chest stood before Crispin. He lifted something. After taking some time to focus his eyes, Crispin recognized it. His sword. The knight pulled it from its sheath and raised it.

What was happening? Was he to be executed with his own sword?

The knight whirled and the sound of steel whistled in the air. But instead of feeling the blade slice through his neck, which Crispin fully expected, he felt the rush of wind as the knight slammed the sword against the stone floor. The shock reverberated throughout the hall. He flinched along with the many lords and ladies from the inharmonious noise and its echo. But the sword remained undamaged. The knight swung it again and even a third time before the tip finally broke off and spun across the floor.

Crispin turned and watched the tip slide until it stopped several paces away. He raised his head and looked with glazed eyes about the crowded hall. Courtiers and ladies, in finery all, men he knew, women he knew better. Even his betrothed—*former* betrothed. The betrothal had been severed as soon as he was arrested.

All present, all staring at him, mouths agape, hands over faces.

What was this if not an execution?

The knight drew forth Crispin's spurs, taken from his boots long before he entered the darkness of Newgate. The knight dropped them to the floor, took a mace, and smashed them to pieces.

Then Crispin understood. They were taking away his knighthood. The accoutrements of his status—his sword and spurs—were removed and destroyed before his eyes, before the eyes of the court.

He expected it then, when the knight took a dagger and stripped his surcote, bright with Crispin's blazon and colors, from his body and tossed the rags to the floor.

So he was a knight no more. And what did it matter if he were to die? His head would join the others on its pike on London Bridge. His body parts would be scattered to the four corners of the realm. In a few years, no one would remember him. No one would speak his name except in the hushed tones of a story told to warn. He would be smashed to pieces like his hapless spurs.

And what was worse, he knew he deserved it. Treason. He hadn't taken it up lightly. He agonized over it for weeks. But he had been loyal to Lancaster, loyal unto death. And now death was knocking.

The king rose, stepped awkwardly over his cushioned stool, and approached only as far as the edge of the dais. His clear young voice rang out. He spoke through a sneer that was all Richard's, not his father, the famed warrior Edward of Woodstock, or his grandfather, the great King Edward of Windsor. "It is *not* at our pleasure that you stand before this court, Crispin Guest."

Crispin squinted and blinked. Candles, rushlights, it was more light than he had seen for five months. Sweat dripped from his grizzled beard. The hall was warm. His cell had been cold. The stink in his nose was his own.

"It was, in fact, our pleasure to see you executed along with the other traitors to the realm. But"—Richard adjusted his belt, hooking his thumbs—"my uncle, my lord of Gaunt, *begged* for your life."

Crispin's jaw slackened at that, and he turned his eyes toward Richard's right. Standing behind the king and almost in the shadows— John of Gaunt, duke of Lancaster. At first glance he appeared to be staring at Crispin, but Crispin soon discovered that Lancaster stared past him, just over his shoulder. He refused to even look Crispin in the eye! That was far worse than this child, this seedling taking from him his sword. Lancaster! He longed to rush to him, to throw himself on the ground before Gaunt. The man's disappointment was palpable. It struck Crispin to the quick.

Of course, the Plot involved Lancaster, or at least Crispin thought it had. The plotters said Gaunt, the fourth son of the old king, was behind a scheme to depose the then Prince Richard and put himself on the throne. Gaunt's brother Edward of Woodstock had been the heir but he had taken sick and died. That put his son Richard in the direct line. But Richard was young. Too young. Lancaster was the better statesmen, more experienced, more power, more wit.

And Crispin, raised in Lancaster's household since he was eight years old, loved the man like a father.

Crispin followed the conspirators, never knowing Lancaster knew nothing of the Plot—until it was far too late.

He came back to himself when they removed the shackles from his wrists and ankles. Then the knight dropped Crispin's belt with his dagger at his feet. Crispin looked down at them without comprehension.

Richard spoke again. His youthful voice broke trying to be loud enough for the immensity of the hall. "It is by our infinite mercy that you live, Crispin Guest, and only by that. Our choice was to let you rot in prison. And if not prison, then to banish you from this realm." He blinked once at his uncle Lancaster. When he turned back to Crispin, his lips curled upward. To call it a smile was to dismiss the grimace of jackals, or the openmouthed anticipation of a buzzard. "But if live you must, then a better punishment is mete. We have decided you shall remain in England. Even London if you like." He snorted a laugh. He looked to his courtiers to join him in his merriment, but their pale faces did not echo his high spirits. The smile soon turned to a sneer. "But not in prison." He nodded to the knight to continue, snapped his ermine-trimmed cloak behind him, and returned to his throne. He climbed into it and settled his rump. He grasped the chair arms with bejeweled fingers and drummed. His eyes looked bored.

The knight stood before Crispin again. "Crispin Guest," he announced. "Stand."

Crispin concentrated on his muscles and forced them into use. He rose, his shoulders last, and he stood unsteadily, eyes taking in the king, the crowd, and the knight when he spoke again.

"By order of his most gracious Majesty King Richard," said the knight, "you are a knight no more. Further: you have no title, you have no lands, no wealth. You are nothing." He stepped forward and pushed Crispin with both hands. Crispin stumbled back. The knight followed him. "Let no man succor you. Let no kinsman support you, or they shall suffer the wrath of the crown." He pushed Crispin again. "By the king's mercy," said the knight, arms dropping to his sides, "you may go in peace."

Crispin raised his head. One by one, across the circle as if in a wave, the crowd turned their backs. All around him, shoulders stiff and taut. Crispin heard it as the sound of skirts rustling, and shoes scraping the floor. Then nothing.

"What?" he heard himself say.

"You are free to go," said the knight, fist at his hip. "Begone."

Then it struck him. The words, all of them, pieced together. *You are a knight no more. No title, no lands. No kinsman may support you.* His heart lurched. He saw the backs of his friends, his companions. He was nothing. His ambitions, his years as Lancaster's protégé, all crumbled like old bones.

He might as well be dead.

He looked at the belt at his feet, the one that once held his sword's scabbard and was now naked of it, holding only the meager dagger. He leaned down and grasped the belt, dragging the dagger's scabbard across the floor. He couldn't quite muster the strength to lift it higher than his thigh. Dispossessed. From everything and everyone. How was he supposed to live? He reckoned that was the point. "But . . . Sire—?" he whispered.

"You *dare* address me, Guest!" Richard leaned forward so far from his throne he looked likely to fall. His smooth face stretched wide; mouth baring uneven teeth, eyes wild. His words spilled from him, rushing forward like a rain of fiery arrows. "You may stay in London, but you will not come to court. You will not communicate with *anyone* of the court. Is that clear? You are an island, Guest. You will remain alone in the sea of London. And if you survive, you may consider yourself lucky. Thus I give you your life and only as a favor to my uncle. But do not *ever* ask of me anything!"

Richard fell back into his chair and wiped the spittle from his lips.

"Such is the king's mercy," said the knight. He drew his sword and raised it. "In the name of the king, begone!"

Miles had been in that crowd. He stared with empty eyes at

Crispin and turned his back dutifully with all the others and said not a word.

And even under the torturers' labors, Crispin, too, had said nothing. Honor bound to hold his tongue, he did. He named no one, knowing nothing of the fate of any of his fellow conspirators. *"Like a lamb led to the slaughterhouse, he opened not his mouth."*

Miles stood there and blended into the crowd and never paid for his part in the Plot.

The memories faded, the echoed voices fell to silence. The reality of his one-room lodgings blurred back into view. Returned to the here and now, a voice at his elbow, soft and timid, still startled him. "Master."

Crispin turned. Jack, his cloak wrapped tight around his shoulders, his hands invisible beneath the ragged material, gazed up at Crispin with wide, moist eyes.

"What troubles you, Master Crispin? Is it your dream again?"

So Jack knew. Little slipped past that boy.

Crispin ran his tongue over his teeth. His mouth tasted bitter. "Go back to bed, Jack."

"I would keep watch, if it's all the same to you, sir."

Crispin sighed. He looked up between the rooftops into the night sky. Woolly clouds unfurled, parted, while stars winked down at him. "I'm just thinking of that day again."

Jack shook his head. No need to explain. Jack knew what day he meant. "I can't say I can ever imagine how you felt when all the world seemed against you. But I know this old town would be a much rougher place without the Tracker on the prowl. And where would I be, eh? In prison, that's what. Maybe even hanged by now." He rubbed his neck. "No, God works his mysterious ways and put you in your place for a reason, and I say God be praised for it."

Crispin smiled a little. "Thank you for that, Jack."

Jack glanced at the two arrows sitting on the table. "Care to tell me now about the Captain of the Archers?"

"Miles Aleyn." Crispin said the name like tar in his mouth. He looked at Jack and put his hand on his shoulder. "What I tell you goes no further than this room. Understand?"

"Aye, Master. Let me tongue be cut out if I breathe a word of it."

He stared at Jack's open innocence. Torture could not drag these words from Crispin's lips, though he had come close. Another few days of torture and who knew what he might have said.

"Miles," he said hoarsely, "was the man who instigated the Plot."

Jack's opinion was swift. "Sarding bastard!"

Crispin agreed. "He never paid for his crime. He brought England's finest young knights together in this conspiracy at the prompting of another, a man still unknown to me. He did not do it for honor or for deep convictions. He did it for greed and vainglory."

"And the other knights—?"

"All dead."

"Did you know he was still at court?"

"No. In fact, I do not think he was. Not until recently. I think he was appointed no more than two months ago. The former captain died in his cups Saint Swithin's day. Fell out of a window. There was talk of a new captain about a month ago but I heard no mention of a name."

"How do you know all that?"

"Because there was no Captain of the Archers evident a month ago at the archery butts. And I asked. You see, Jack, I do practice. Occasionally."

Jack's indignation raised his shoulders and finally his whole body. He paced the brief room, swinging his arms as if to strike an enemy. The sparse hearthlight painted him in the figure of an excitable demon. "And he serves all this time as the high and mighty Captain of the Archers while you live on the Shambles! I'd cut his throat m'self if I could."

"I appreciate the sentiment, Jack, but do me the kindness of sitting. You'll wake the Kemps below."

Jack lighted on the stool. "You're going to get him, aren't you, Master Crispin? You're going to see he gets his."

"Oh yes, Jack. I will. But not merely him. I want to catch the man who hired him."

Jack looked over his shoulder again at the arrows. "Why'd he kill that French courier do you suppose? For the Crown o' Thorns?"

"No. He had ample opportunity to take the Crown. He killed that man as he tried to kill me. But I don't yet know why."

Neither said anything more for a while. And it wasn't until Crispin snuffled awake for the second time—sunlight streaming in his face from the open shutter—that he realized he had slept.

The blanket tucked under his chin fell away when he stirred. He arched his back from his awkward position in the windowsill, but he was otherwise rested. Jack sat on the stool by the fire. Crispin's coat lay across his lap and the boy hunched over it, pulling a threaded needle through the patch at the shoulder. He looked up when Crispin yawned loudly. Jack smiled.

"Good morn, sir. There's porridge on the fire. Shall I get you a bowl?"

Jack stood halfway but Crispin waved him down. "Jack, why didn't you wake me?"

"Didn't know when the last time was you slept so well."

"Neither do I." He went to the hearth with a bowl he dragged from the table—last night's dinner—and knocked its cold contents into the fire. He ladled out the thick porridge of barley, turnips, and peas and stood in nothing but his midthigh chemise, back facing the fire, and spooned the food into his mouth.

Hot, filling, and even tasty.

"It's good," he said, mouth full.

Jack nodded and smiled. Then he raised the repaired coat so Crispin could inspect it. "I think there's more patches than coat left, Master Crispin, but no arrow hole no more."

"Thank you, Jack. You do for me more than I deserve. I truly wish I could pay you a proper wage."

Jack reddened and hid it by brushing out the clotted bloodstain at the repair. "Food and shelter's good enough for my like, never you fear."

Crispin finished eating, dressed in clean braies and stockings, and took the coat Jack offered. He shrugged into the warm cotehardie and buttoned it all the way from the hem to his neck, all twenty-three buttons. There was a time he left the bottom thirteen buttons undone so he could ride his horse. But no more horse.

Jack offered him his belt with its scabbard, and Crispin fitted it around his waist and buckled it in place. He gave his scabbard one slap out of habit and took the arrows from the table and slid them both in his belt.

"Where do you go now, Master?"

"I must go to a fletcher, the man who made these arrows. I would have him identify for whom he made them. That will fix Miles."

"What about archery practice? Did not the king's decree command it daily?"

"Yes, but it will have to wait."

Shouts. Feet running through the early-morning street. Crispin looked at a perplexed Jack. The market bells had not yet rung. Crispin knew the shops must remain shuttered until they did, but this was not a shout to open the markets.

He dashed to the streetside window and cast open the shutters. A young boy ran down the lane below him and then disappeared down another. Butchers slowly emerged from their shops and stood on the muddy avenue.

"Oi!" Crispin cried down to one man standing in the street's filthy gutter spiraling with yesterday's blood. "Master Dickon!"

"Eh?" Dickon looked up and spied Crispin and pointed at him.

"What goes on, Master Dickon? What is the shouting?"

"That boy," said Dickon gesturing after the lad. "He said that all business was to be suspended today."

"Suspended? Why on earth for?"

"He said there's been an attempt on the king's life and his Majesty is in seclusion at Westminster."

10

OPEN OR NOT, THE Boar's Tusk was Crispin's next destination. He knew Gilbert would let him in.

Jack stayed at home, begging off. Crispin knew how he felt. A little frightened, a little at a loss as to what to do. Jack would spend the day cleaning the little room they shared, and that suited Crispin.

The streets were oddly deserted. Merchants stood in their windows staring impotently at the streets. Several philosophers stood over a brazier, shaking their heads, commenting. A short man with a receded hairline hovered just outside their circle. He edged closer as their words became more heated.

"Lenny!" called Crispin to the short man.

Lenny swore an oath with a cloud of breath. The men glanced at him once, but it was enough to break the spell of his anonymity.

He trotted toward Crispin with shaking head. He had the habit of hunching his shoulders and keeping his head below them, much like a buzzard. Crispin supposed he caught the habit from too long a time in low-ceilinged gaol cells.

"What you go and spoil me game for, Master Crispin?"

"You don't want to end up in gaol again, do you, Lenny? You might lose a hand this time for certain."

"You wouldn't put old Lenny back in gaol, would you, good Master? Weren't it enough you done it three times?"

"Let's not make it a fourth. The sheriff is not likely to be cozened again out of taking a limb of yours in punishment. Wasn't the loss of an ear enough?"

Lenny rubbed the scabbed place where his ear had been and where his long, stringy hair covered it. "How's a man like me to make a living, I ask you? I ain't fit for much else, and that's the truth."

"Let my example be yours. *I* have a new profession, after all."

"Well you're you, ain't you?" Lenny rubbed his chin bristling with a three-day beard. His eye twinkled. "There wouldn't be something you want to hire old Lenny for, is there?"

"Not at the moment. You still live near the Thistle Inn?"

"It's a place I can be found."

Crispin considered. "I may have something for you. You know my man Jack, don't you?"

"We met once or twice."

"He may come round and give you a message from me."

"And a farthing?"

"And a farthing. You see? It isn't all that hard to make a decent living."

Lenny smiled and revealed blackened teeth. He trotted off, running along the edge of the gutter.

Crispin watched him disappear into London's grayness. He felt the arrows at his side and thought about the fletcher he needed to talk to. Edward Peale was his name. Crispin had known him well from the old days at court, in the days Crispin used to hunt in the king's deer park with other courtiers. Peale made the finest, straightest arrows. And he made his mark on every one of them, the mark Crispin recognized on both shafts. He also made marks to show the ownership of such arrows. It would be a simple matter, then, for Peale to identify the marks and convict Miles.

But there was the matter of getting into court to talk to Peale. Certainly he was ensconced in the palace grounds as he always had been. Difficult, that. For one, Crispin was forbidden entrance to court. And two, with an attempt on the king's life, Westminster Palace would be shut up tighter than a barrel of French wine.

Thinking of the king he wondered how severe this attempt was. Abbot Nicholas would surely know.

He glanced toward Gutter Lane just ahead and licked his lips. The Boar's Tusk was only a short distance around the corner and it was a long, thirsty walk to Westminster.

"Damn."

Business first. He must find out what happened to the king.

THE STREETS ALONG WESTMINSTER Abbey and Westminster Palace simmered with activity. Soldiers scrambled everywhere like ants, moving just as mindlessly. They stopped Crispin three separate times with a "what's your business?" before he was able to make his way to the abbey's doorstep.

When Crispin rang the bell, it took longer than usual for a monk to appear and open the gate. The monk wasn't a brother Crispin recognized, but he took Crispin to the abbot's empty chamber. The monk served Crispin wine and hurriedly left, leaving him alone to contemplate the stained-glass window raining colors on the abbot's desk.

After a brief interval, the door opened and the abbot rushed in.

"Forgive me, Crispin. As you can imagine, this is a busy time."

"Yes. I came to get information on those very doings."

"Good. I see you have wine. I will pour my own. Please. Sit." Abbot Nicholas fussed with the flagon, lifted the goblet, and pressed the goblet's rim to his dry lips. His throat, peppered with gray stubble from a rushed razor, rolled with a swallow. He moved smoothly to his chair, settled on its cushion, and looked up at Crispin. "A busy morn."

"No doubt."

A pause fell over the room until Nicholas broke it by something between a sigh and a snort. "The king is in good health, God be praised. Thank you for asking." Nicholas's sardonic expression disappeared behind the goblet.

Crispin quaffed his own cup. No, he didn't ask, didn't really care all that much about Richard's health, but as a citizen he was interested to know. "Didn't kill him, eh?"

Nicholas raised a hand. A benediction? A call for silence? "You truly should not speak your treason so loudly."

"Is it treason to wonder if the king is dead?"

His age-yellowed eyes fell kindly on Crispin. "For you, perhaps."

Crispin toyed with his empty goblet. "What happened?"

"His Majesty was taking an early-morning turn in his garden with his counselors when the attempt was made."

"Don't tell me. An arrow?"

The abbot's eyes enlarged twofold. Wine glistened on his parted lips. "How did you know?" he whispered.

Crispin shrugged. He launched from his chair with the goblet, stood at the sideboard, and touched the flagon, but decided against it and left the goblet there. He turned. The abbot's tonsure was a mosaic of color from the window's light. "There is an assassin afoot and he uses a bow. Was anyone hurt?"

"Only a servant. He is well. It hit his arm. It was he who pushed the king aside out of harm's way. He saw a cloaked figure with a bow ready to fire just over the garden wall."

Crispin looked at the flagon and nodded. The innocent. They're always dragged into the king's business with disastrous results. Maybe more wine wasn't such a bad idea. He grabbed the flagon and sloshed wine into the goblet, then snatched up the cup and drank. His sleeve took away the excess from the side of his mouth.

"Did the assassin escape?"

"God help us, but yes. The figure slipped back over the wall. No one else saw a thing, neither guards nor page. He seemed to fade into the shadows of court."

"Hmm. 'Shadows of court.' Interesting."

"Crispin, how do you know of this assassin? Do you know who it is?"

"Yes, I think I do. But there is much I cannot yet reveal."

Crispin noticed the abbot eyeing the arrows in his belt. "You must! Have you told the sheriff?"

Crispin moved his hand over the arrows before he let his fingers drop away. "No. And I won't."

"By God's wounds! Why not?"

The goblet reached his lips again and the deep peach and citrus flavors of the wine smoothed his tongue. "I have my reasons."

Nicholas put his goblet aside and stood. "Is it because you would see the king dead?"

Crispin's eyes narrowed over the rim of his cup and he drank the last of it, licked his lips, and set the goblet down. "Would I see Richard dead at the hands of an assassin? No. He is my king."

Nicholas shook his head. "You have a strange sense of honor."

"Is it strange to protect the crown but not its wearer? If that is so, then . . . well. Perhaps I do have a strange sense of honor. 'It is in justice that the ordering of society is centered.'"

"As always, Aristotle proves wise. Your heart is in the right place, but your philosophy will invariably cause you trouble."

"I do not shy from trouble, my Lord Abbot. 'Trouble' is my patron name."

"Indeed. You know too much about this for my liking."

"Don't you trust me, my lord?"

"Yes." Nicholas said it in a drawn-out tenor that made Crispin doubt.

"I see. Even my friends shy when the possibility of treason lies at the heart of it. Well, I have seen the like before." He strode toward the door in long strides until Nicholas intervened.

"What of your French courier?"

Crispin halted and without turning asked, "What of him?"

"Did you not say he was dispatched by an arrow?"

"Yes. The same sort of arrow, in fact. I do not think it a coincidence."

Nicholas eyed the arrows in Crispin's belt again. "My son, is there . . . is there not something you would confess to me? Something . . . you keep deep in your heart?"

Crispin put his hand involuntarily on the arrows, feeling the stiff fletching under his calloused palm. "No, Lord Abbot. I have no need of shriving today." He turned to go again when the abbot moved forward and laid a strong hand on his arm. Crispin stopped himself from shrugging it off. Nicholas meant well. But then, many had meant well.

Nicholas huffed impatiently. "You would simply leave, Crispin? Surely your path is a dangerous one. Why is it you never ask for a benediction when you depart? Lesser men ask for it. It is so little a gift to give."

"I don't need it."

"Don't need God's blessing? Or is it you don't believe in it?"

"Of course I believe." He bit down on the rest of his words. What he couldn't say was that he didn't believe he deserved it.

Crispin saw the abbot approach and turned his head slightly. The abbot gave his blessing without the asking. The shadow of a cross fell over Crispin, painted in the air by the abbot's sure hand. Crispin accepted it without comment and passed through the threshold, leaving the abbot's lodge.

He did not look back as the door closed on the monk's worried countenance. Instead, he strode purposefully through the familiar colonnade of the cloister, giving the cloister garden a hasty glance, its herbs and greenery slowly browning as summer blooms surrendered to fall. Coming to the end of the colonnade, he met the brother at the gate, thanked him with a bow, and left the abbey's grounds.

Crispin's tongue sang with the abbot's good wine but he still had enough thirst for a bowl of the Boar's Tusk's finest.

AFTER A HALF HOUR of walking back to London he turned the corner at Gutter Lane and caught the sweet sight of the tavern, though the incongruity of men being shoved out the door so early in the day gave rise to a snicker in Crispin's throat.

He watched the spectacle from across the lane. Gilbert himself helped the uncooperative men over the threshold. He clapped his hands together, looked up, and saw Crispin.

"Oi! Crispin!" He waved him over and Crispin trotted across.

"I feared you'd be closing your doors," said Crispin.

"Not to you. Come in."

Crispin was used to the tavern sitting empty, but such a sight was usually reserved for the middle of the night, not noontime. Ned stood in the center of the smoky room, surveying the vacant, worn tables with a sorrowful look on his face. He nodded a greeting to Crispin but couldn't seem to smile it.

Gilbert offered Crispin a seat at his usual spot in the back, farthest from the door, and Crispin took it. "I suppose you know the tidings, then," he said to Crispin.

He nodded and when Ned brought a full jug and two bowls, Crispin felt that he was home.

Gilbert shook his head and poured the wine, scooting the first bowl toward Crispin. "How is the king?"

"He lives," said Crispin. He quaffed the wine then lowered the bowl, grabbed the jug, and splashed more wine in the cup. "I'm becoming concerned that I will not be able to bring the culprit the full attention he deserves."

Gilbert's red nose hovered over his bowl. "You already know who did it?"

"Yes. I have proof right here." He patted the arrows snug against his side.

Ned shuffled forward and laid a round loaf on the table. Crispin felt his belly rumble at the sight and realized he hadn't eaten since Jack's early-morning repast. He tore a hunk from the loaf, clamped a piece in his teeth, and took the bread into his mouth. He chewed and then dipped the edge of a hunk into his wine and sucked up the dripping crumbs.

"Then why don't you go straight to the sheriff with it?"

"That's not the direction I intend to go."

"I don't understand you, Crispin. You've got proof. Let the sheriff do his duty."

"This is my kill," he said quietly. Gilbert stared at him strangely and Crispin realized what he'd said. He tried to smile. "What I mean is, I'd rather do it myself."

Gilbert shook his head and thumbed the rim of his bowl. His lips were slick with wine. "After all you've been through, why do you keep trying?"

Crispin knocked back the bowl. He set it down empty and grabbed the jug. His voice was hard. "I want to win."

"It's a stark game you play."

"It's a never-ending game." He drank and caught Gilbert's sorrowful expression. He patted him on the back until the burly man looked up at him. "Don't worry over me, Gilbert. I can take care of myself."

"Aye, you keep saying that, yet Eleanor and I keep putting you back together. I'm afraid there will come a time when the king gets ahold of you again and they'll be no putting you back together."

Crispin chuckled without mirth. "The king no longer frightens me."

Gilbert opened his mouth to speak but the rest of his words never made it across the table. He rose halfway to his feet with a stunned expression on his face. He looked past Crispin's shoulder.

"Gilbert? What—" Crispin followed Gilbert's gaze and turned to look. He rose abruptly from the bench. The bread dropped from his hand.

Grayce staggered into the tavern's hall. Her face had collapsed into a grimace of anguish.

Gilbert was at her side first though Crispin was on his heels. "What's wrong, girl?"

She looked from Gilbert to Crispin. "Oh help us! Good masters, help. Livith!"

She broke down and dropped her head in her hands. Crispin stood at her other elbow. "What of Livith?"

She lifted her head. Her face was streaked with tears. Her lips parted stickily. "Oh Tracker! You must help her! She's been shot!"

11

"HANDS OFF, IT'S ONLY a light wound!" Livith pushed Crispin's exploring hands away. The arrow had whizzed past the woman's waist, tearing a bit of the flesh and pinning the dress to the worktable. Livith had torn the dress and shift to free herself, revealing a gaping hole. Crispin saw more blood than wound, and though it looked bad, he knew from experience it was not.

"Did anyone see anything?" he asked, looking around the small kitchen.

Livith shrugged. "I think I seen someone at the back courtyard door, but there's always someone coming and going. I can't be sure."

Eleanor knelt at Livith's feet and dabbed the open flesh with a wet cloth. "Now you," she said to Grayce, talking slowly and carefully, "go get me a slice of moldy bread. Find me a good green one now, that's a girl. Your sister'll be right as rain, never you fear."

Grayce chewed on her fingers and rushed away to comply. Eleanor shook her head. She glanced up at Crispin. "Why should anyone want to hurt this girl, Crispin? Didn't that scoundrel get what he wanted?"

Crispin frowned. "A good question. What did he want? I thought it was to kill the king. It certainly wasn't to steal the—" He caught himself and nodded ruefully. His eyes met Livith's. She kept her mouth shut for once. Good. Maybe she was learning. "Why would you be a target?"

"Maybe the bastard thinks we saw something."

Crispin nodded. His hand covered his mouth and he tapped his lips with a finger. "Yes, that could be it. *Did* you see anything?"

"I told you. I wasn't there."

"But Grayce was. We must get her to tell me what happened."

Grayce returned and held out the greenish slab of bread. "What you want this for?"

Eleanor took it. "It's for the wound, dear. It helps it heal." She pressed the oval piece to the open sore. Livith hissed through her teeth.

Grayce shook her fists and stared at her sister. "Oh Livith!"

"I'm well, I tell you. I'll be fine. Sit down."

Grayce rattled her head and sat as ordered. Crispin stood beside her, wondering how to squeeze information from her any more successfully than in their first encounter. He squatted to be at eye level and smiled. "Grayce, Livith will be well, as she said. I need to talk to you about that day. The day you found the dead man."

Grayce sniffed and looked up. Her wet eyes searched his face, stopped a moment on his smile, another on his eyes, and then wandered aimlessly again.

He took her hand lying in her lap. *Jesu mercy!* "Grayce, listen to me. You must tell me everything about that day, from the moment you rose to when you think you killed the Frenchman."

Her wide eyes cracked with red veins. She looked at Livith who looked back at her with unblinking eyes.

"I got up as I usually do, before Livith," she said. She looked down at Crispin's hand clasping hers and brought up a trembling smile. "I washed me face and hands, like Livith always told me to. Then I had a bit of ale and bread. I went to the privy and when I come back Livith was gone."

Crispin turned to Livith. Eleanor patted the bandage she just finished tying around the girl's waist. Livith pulled the remnants of the dress back over it. "Where did you go?" he asked.

"I went to get more ale for the jug. Master lets us get some from the kitchens."

"How long were you gone?"

"My Master was up and he set me to work right away. I didn't come back."

"What sort of work?"

"Not the kind you think."

Crispin made an apologetic smile. "I'm sorry for that. That was out of place."

Livith thrust her shoulders back before she winced from the wound. "That's all well," she said with a dismissive wave of her hand. Eleanor helped her pin the gap in her gown. "The Master had me sweeping out the hearth in the hall. That took some time taking out the ashes and fixing up the fire. I had to scrub m'self good afterwards and that's when I come in."

Crispin nodded and turned back to Grayce. "Once you'd eaten, then what?"

"I was fixin' to go up to the tavern and off to the kitchens before the Master got angry. He was always powerful angry in the mornings, especially if he'd been drinking the night before. Ain't that right, Livith?"

"Aye, he has a right temper, he does."

"Aye," said Grayce. She smoothed out her skirt and cocked her head to look at it. "I didn't want no trouble."

"When did you see the Frenchman? Did you see him come in?"

Grayce's brows wrinkled outward. She lifted her eyes toward Livith. Her lips parted in her dull-witted way, but she said nothing.

"Grayce." Crispin shook her hand but it failed to bring her back. "Grayce! When did you see the man come in?"

She eyed Crispin again, frowned, and pulled her hand from his. "I don't remember!"

"You must! You saw what happened to him."

"I killed him!"

Eleanor gasped and drew back into Gilbert's arms.

Crispin clutched Grayce's shoulders. "You little fool! You didn't! Can't you remember what happened?"

Livith's hand grasped Crispin's shoulder like a hawk's talons and pushed him back. "Stop it! She can't remember. Not anymore."

He expelled a long breath and stood. "No. I see she doesn't." Livith clutched her side but when she noticed Crispin looking she withdrew her hand. "That hurts you more than you like to admit," he said softly.

"It don't."

He took her shoulder. "Let's take you to your bed. Where is it?"

"Crispin," said Gilbert. His brows lowered over worried eyes, eyes that darted toward Grayce who rocked herself and moaned in soothing tones.

"In a moment, Gilbert."

Livith looked over her shoulder at Crispin. "Master Gilbert gave us a bed in the mews. Our things are down there."

"I'll take you, then."

"No you won't." Livith pulled away or tried to, but Crispin's grip tightened.

"No knight in shining armor, but I still remember how to act like a knight," he said.

She cocked her head and smiled, an easy slow one. She leaned into him. He didn't mind the feel of it. "If you will," she conceded and he led her to the stairs.

The mews were dark. Only one candle in a wall sconce burned. Crispin took it and lit the rest of the way down the steps, but at the bottom of the stairs the light fell on something white and misshapen.

"What's that?" she whispered.

"It looks like a blanket."

He pushed the candle forward. A bowl, upturned and near the

casks. A spoon lying in a distant corner. Stockings torn apart and lying flayed on the stone floor darkening from a puddle of wine.

Livith made a noise of surprise in her throat and Crispin instinctively pushed her behind him.

He raised the candle. All of Livith and Grayce's belongings lay scattered, torn, or broken across the cellar floor.

Crispin's lips pressed tight and he flared his nostrils with a breath. "You're not staying here."

12

"I DON'T LIKE THIS, Crispin," said Gilbert, looking back down the darkened stairwell. Crispin left the sisters below to gather what remained of their goods. "This Grayce says she killed a man."

"She's like a child, Gilbert. She doesn't know what she is saying."

"All the same—"

"All the same I must get them someplace safe until I can reckon why the killer wishes to eliminate them."

"What safer place could there be than court?" said Livith, her tone, as always, as mocking as her posture. She stood at the top of the stairs and clutched her shredded bag over her shoulder.

Crispin stared at her. Her expression was filled with scorn, always seemed to be. Determination, too, set her eyes like gray quartz, translucent yet hard and milky. They were eyes that knew how to keep secrets, and for a moment, Crispin allowed himself the luxury of wondering about her, where she came from, what her life had been like caring for a dull-witted sister. He never used to wonder such things when he was a lord. Creatures like her could only be found in the bowels of his manor, never seen, seldom heard, but necessary to the smooth running of a large household. She was like one of many who had cooked his food and cleaned his floors. He never thought twice about them before except in the casual way of a lordling about his people. But Lancaster's household had been different. Crispin had gotten to know the cooks and valets to serve his lord better. Even at Westminster Palace he had made friends in the kitchens, though little help they could offer once he was cast out of the place.

What did Livith think of him when she heard him speak with his court accent and worldly expressions? Did she see him as a lord in rags, or as merely the man who would save her and her sister?

But Livith's words caught up to him at last and he considered their worth. Court, eh? Court was a busy place, like a maze. People milling in all directions. The back stairs was busiest of all. And didn't he have to find a way to see Edward Peale, the king's fletcher? What better excuse to get into court than under the guise of a kitchen worker. If the guards are looking for an assassin, they will not suspect a man and a couple of scullions.

He smiled. "In truth, that is a good idea."

"What?" cried Livith. "I was only jesting. Are you completely mad?" She looked at Gilbert for confirmation.

"Aye," said Gilbert. "He is mad."

"No. It's an excellent idea. The killer would never think to look for you at court. What is more invisible than a couple of scullions?"

He dragged her past the stairs, through the tavern, and over the threshold with one hand and Grayce with the other. He made a backward nod of thanks to Gilbert. "It's closed up secure with extra guards," he assured. "The killer won't be looking for you in the kitchens, not at court, at any rate. He'll be concentrating on the king."

"But if it's closed up so tight how will we get in?"

Crispin stepped into the street. He pulled up short and yanked them both back when a cart rumbled swiftly by, kicking up clods of mud. "I have acquaintances in many places. Perhaps no longer in the finer halls of court, but I do have loyal friends in the scullery."

"Ain't you full of surprises."

He said nothing to that. When the way was clear, he herded the women into the street, thinking about how he was to accomplish the impossible. He chuckled to himself. Impossible feats were his specialty. After all, surviving treason had been an impossible feat and here he was.

He dodged an arrogant-looking man on a fine white stallion. Pulling both women clear of the horse's heavily shod hooves, he bowed low. The man never once looked his way.

Yes, here he was.

They traveled through London's gates without exchanging any words and crossed the Fleet, making the long walk to Temple Barr into a descending fog. Westminster was still a good walk hence, giving him plenty of time to think. Why had Miles run from court just to find the scullions? There must be some greater plan afoot. It was easy enough for Miles to come and go. It made Crispin grind his teeth at the audacity.

He adjusted the arrows in his belt—three now with the one that nearly speared Livith. She must have noticed, for she grabbed one of the arrows and pulled it out. "What you doing with these?"

He stopped, took it out of her hand, and thrust it back in his belt. "They are the arrows the killer used. I know the maker and he can identify for whom he made them by the marks on the shafts."

She whistled. "'Slud! So you don't know who the killer is."

"I'm afraid I do. But I would have solid evidence."

"Who then?"

He looked at her heavy brows, dark near her nose's juncture. They tapered outward, ending in a slight upturn, echoing the angle of her long lashes. They were faeries' eyes, almond-shaped, impish. Her angular cheekbones caught the spilled light from an open shutter and directed his gaze downward toward her small mouth, the top lip with its two sharp points, and its bottom sister, round, pouting, as if some passionate stranger bit it.

"I suppose you have a right to know. It is the king's own Captain of the Archers."

"Christ's bloody hands! Does the king know?"

"Not yet. You see now why I must have absolute proof?" He placed his hand on the three arrows. "That is why I need to take these to Master Edward Peale. He is the king's fletcher. He will know."

"You can't go into court with arrows in your belt. Especially looking like the ones what shot the king."

His fingers teased the hawk feathers. "You may be right." He yanked them from his belt and broke them over his knee. He tossed the pointed ends into the gutter and stuffed the remaining fletched portions into his empty money pouch. "Let us go, then."

Grayce stopped. "You're going to leave them arrowheads in the gutter?"

"Come on, Grayce." Livith grabbed her arm and glanced up at the surrounding rooftops slowly disappearing in the gray-white fog. "Make haste, now, Master Crispin. I don't like being out in the open."

They walked in silence for a time, just another set of travelers along London's streets. Crispin felt Livith looking at him and after her long scrutiny, he turned toward her curious expression. Her face did not exactly inquire but hid more than it told in the slight smile that turned up those appealing lips.

She pushed a strand of blond hair out of her eyes. "What sort of man is a 'Tracker'? It's a strange-sounding profession."

"No more, no less than any other."

"You're like the sheriff but you ain't the sheriff. You're not even the sheriff's man. It don't seem right, you on your own."

"It's the way I like it."

She rubbed the bandage at her side, grunted from pain, and shouldered her bundle again. "You think I don't know who you are, but I do. There's not a soul in this part of London who don't know you—and that you used to be a knight before you committed treason."

"And?" His voice dropped into a threatening tenor, but he didn't care. If she wanted to fish this pond she'd better take the consequences.

"And here you are. Working for *me*. Don't that gall you?"

He eyed her sidelong, but his lids never raised more than half. "Sometimes."

That made her smile, slow and easy. "Ah you're a one, you are. You're hard to reckon. Why not become an outlaw on the highways? Other knights struck by poverty take to it readily enough."

"That is not my way."

"'*That is not my way*,'" she mimicked. "You know there's no chance in hell I'll have your sixpence—and now it's got to a shilling at least. Why do it?"

He had to agree with that. Livith's meager income could never match his fee, and he lived or starved by that fee. He huffed a breath, watching the cloud of cold air wisp up past his sharp nose. "For the challenge," he said at last, surprising himself for uttering it.

Livith laughed, hearty and guttural. The kind of laugh a wench might press against your chest in bed. Crispin nudged his cloak open to get a flush of cold air.

"The challenge?" Livith shook her head. "What stupid nonsense! That's just the sort of rubbish a nobleman might mouth. A man's got to eat and that's that."

"You are clearly not a man."

She laughed that deep laugh again and nudged him with her elbow. "I hoped you'd notice."

Crispin raised a brow. "What I mean is, men need a challenge. They need to feel useful, that they fill an important place in the world."

"And this is yours? Helping poor folk what don't have a pot to piss in? You'll never get rich that way."

"I admit. It isn't the most sensible of professions. But it is mine."

"You're a strange man. But I like you, Crispin Guest."

He sniffed the cold air. The smells of the Shambles lay far behind them now. They neared Lancaster's old palace, the Savoy, at least what was left of it after a peasant rabble burnt it to the ground three years ago. The air smelled of the familiarity of court, his old home.

She smiled. A dimple dented one cheek. A pleasant smile, a smile reminding Crispin to keep his warm cloak open. "There's a lot to you," she said. "I'll wager those cockerels at court don't know the half of it."

"Nor would they care."

"And they'd be fools. But you already know that. No, they don't know what they gave up when they sent you away. I suppose they'll be sorry one day, eh? You'll make 'em sorry."

"I don't see how."

"You'll best 'em, that's what. Somehow, some way, you'll best 'em. And they'll know it. And they'll be sorry."

Her face flushed and her eyes stared ahead determinedly. Crispin wondered if this vehemence came from some recent hurt or one of longer ago. "The only one responsible for sending me from court was his Majesty."

"He just might be sorry, too, someday."

Crispin caught her eye and offered her a lopsided grin. "Now *you're* speaking treason."

"Am I?" She crossed herself. "Well, God preserve me, though I don't know why He would. I blaspheme enough, too."

They spoke no more the rest of the way to Westminster. Nearing the palace, Crispin counted far too many men-at-arms pacing the mouth of the street.

"We'll never get through," hissed Livith in his ear. His sentiments, but he didn't agree aloud.

"Say nothing," he said. He threw his hood up over his head and dragged it low to cover his eyes, and moved ahead of the women toward the palace courtyard. They were immediately stopped by two soldiers in armor and helms, visors up.

"I said clear off the street!" said one, raising his gauntlet-covered hand to Crispin.

Crispin bowed, and in his best imitation of Jack Tucker, said, "Ow m'lord! We was just returning to the kitchens from a long trip to me ailing aunt. What's amiss?"

The soldier snorted. "Do you know nothing? There has been an attempt on the king's life. No one enters here."

Crispin portrayed the appropriate astonishment and turned to the women. "Did you hear that? Then his Majesty will be wanting his favorite dainties for sure."

"These are cooks?"

"Ow no m'lord." Crispin chuckled good-naturedly. "These is scullions. *I'm* one of the cooks. Just ask Onslow Blunt. He's the head cook. Go on. Ask him."

The soldier eyed the women and inspected Crispin with a sneer. For once the absence of a sword served Crispin well. The man stepped aside. "Very well. That way, then. To the kitchens."

Crispin bowed several times and dragged the women with him. "Thank you, good Master. God bless you, good Master. God save the king." Out of earshot Crispin straightened. "He'll need it."

Livith turned a grin at him. "I didn't know you did voices."

He only raised a brow in reply and led them through a long alleyway between the palace walls and the palace itself until he came to another small courtyard where the kitchen outbuildings stood. Standing before a large wooden door, he didn't bother trying the handle, reckoning that it would be barred. He knocked and waited only a few beats when a scullion boy answered. "Whose knocking?" he asked and then looked up. "Oh! It's Sir Crispin! What did I say to Master Onslow? I said, 'This wretched business with the king is just the thing for Crispin Guest. He's that Tracker and I'll wager he can find this man with the bow.' That's what I said."

Crispin smiled a grim smile and pushed over the threshold. "And what did Onslow say?"

"He wagered a farthing you wouldn't come. I've won that, I have!"

"So you have."

Crispin stepped in farther and Livith and Grayce entered. The boy stared at them. "And what is all this, Sir Crispin?"

It was useless to tell the lad not to call him that. "Where is Onslow, Freddy?"

Freddy scratched his mane of brown hair. "He's at the hearths. I'll take you."

Freddy moved ahead but couldn't help look over his shoulder at the silent women. Livith merely stared ahead of her, but Grayce rolled her eyes, looking at all the new sights.

The aromas of roasting meats and savory pottage billowed toward them. It was warmer as they neared the fires. A tall, strapping man with flaming ginger hair and an equally flaming beard flung his arms over the chaos of the kitchens. Staff scrabbled in all directions trying to keep up with his shouted orders. Kettles bubbled over the fire. Three-legged cauldrons shot steam out from under iron lids. Two young boys, no older than four, took turns turning the gears to a great iron spit roasting three pigs and four goats over one of the larger hearths. There were six hearths in all and a few separate braziers with smaller fowl dripping juices from prongs.

Crispin stood behind him, fists at hips.

"And move, you!" Onslow bellowed. A young boy, face dirty with soot, carried several large platters in his outstretched arms. Crispin feared he would drop them and earn a beating, but the boy had obviously been at this for some years, and moved nimbly past his master.

"You, Onslow, are the very picture of an Egyptian taskmaster."

Onslow swiveled. His face screwed up in preparation for a barrage of curses . . . when it all loosened into a jovial slant. "Sir Crispin! Mother of God, what are you doing here? It has been many a day!"

"Yes, in the days when I could rightfully be called 'Sir' Crispin."

"Aw now." Onslow reddened. He grabbed Crispin's shoulders, but thankfully did not enclose him in a hug. His apron looked too greasy for that. "You're not here for what I think you're here for?"

"And what do you think I'm here for?"

He sidled up to Crispin and spoke in low tones. "You know. The king? Someone tried to put him out of his misery."

"I thought you did that every day with your cooking."

He smacked Crispin's shoulder affably, but the wallop nearly sent Crispin reeling. Onslow's hands were as large as some of his platters. He laughed but stopped and drew on a serious expression. "That's not a funny jest, Sir Crispin. I could be dragged into prison for suspicions like that."

"You haven't yet," he said.

"You never said as much when you sampled my food before taking them to his grace the duke."

"No, admittedly, I was better behaved then." Crispin's smile turned grave. "Now I have a favor to ask. These women"—he thumbed behind him—"they need work."

Onslow's face brightened. "You've come to the right place. We always need extra hands."

Crispin spoke in quiet tones. "They need a private place to sleep. Away from the others. No cots in the great hall, nor may they clean in the hall. Let them work only in the kitchens, nowhere else. Understand?"

Onslow didn't, but Crispin had known him a long time and he counted on that. Onslow's eyes worked it out and he gave a final nod in agreement. "I'll get Freddy to show them their place. I suppose you'll tell me all about it over a beaker at the Boar's Tusk."

"Soon. Livith. Grayce. This is Master Onslow, the best royal cook of all time."

"Any friends of Sir Crispin's—" He urged them forward and then gave a whistle for Freddy, who remarkably heard it above the clatter. "Join me in a cup now, Sir Crispin?" Onslow asked over his shoulder.

Crispin shook his head. "That would cheer me greatly, but there's no time now. If I may, I would like to look about."

But Onslow's lighthearted expression turned somber. "Er . . . Sir Crispin." He looked around and motioned Crispin aside. "It has been many a year, true. And for the last four years you have been well known, honest as the day is long. But sir . . . you were cast from court because . . . because . . ."

"I would have seen the king deposed," Crispin said quietly.

"Aye, you see the point. Deposed or . . ." He leaned closer and whispered, "Or dead."

Crispin nodded. "I see the difficulty. Perhaps this is why I am here, eh? To finish the job begun seven years ago?"

"Never jest about it! It could mean our heads." His eyes darted this way and that but no one was close enough within the noise of the kitchens to overhear them. "But I have known you since you were a page in Lancaster's household. Treason or no, you are a man of character. And if you swear to me by our Lady that you will do no harm to the king, then I will believe you."

Crispin steadied his gaze on Onslow's gray eyes. He placed his hand upon his own breast. "I solemnly swear to you, Master Onslow, on the soul of our dear Lady, that I will do the king no harm. I am here to protect him."

Onslow let out a long breath and his cheeks rosied again. "There now. That assures me better than any priest's oath." He gestured toward the stairway leading to the great hall. "You know the way."

Onslow didn't stop to observe Crispin depart. He returned to shouting orders to his army of cooks at the hearths and cooking pots.

Freddy ushered the women away to their third lodgings in two days. Crispin's thoughts could now concentrate on a crowd of images. Miles Aleyn, for one. But he also gave a thought or two to the French couriers. Where were they now? Did they make it to court? Return to France? He'd have to make inquiries.

Miles knew something about the women and pursued them to the Boar's Tusk. If he thought Grayce had seen him, why did he not try to kill Grayce? If only she would speak! If he could only get her to say what she saw. Alas. He'd be just as likely to get a mule to speak, though a mule was bound to be wiser! Poor Grayce. Poor Livith. He gave the sinewy sister an extra thought and turned back to catch a glimpse of her in the clutter and scrambling of Onslow's cooks and scullions, but she was lost amid the rabble and savory steam.

He made the short walk across a courtyard and then up some steps that took him from the kitchens to the great hall. An army of servants hustled there almost as much as they did in the kitchens. There were trestle tables to set up, benches to put in place. The trestles whined as they scraped across the stone floor. Servants with linens were carefully draping them over the tables, smoothing the wrinkles away with clean hands. Men on ladders were fitting large wax candles into candelabras as big as saplings, while their assistants were scrambling about bringing more candles. Still others worked tirelessly with brooms at the perimeters, sweeping away the dust and dirt.

No one took notice of Crispin.

And so. Richard wanted his feast to show the court he was not afraid. "But he should be," Crispin muttered. The killer was not through.

Crispin looked out across the huge room with its high ceilings of open timber arches supported by two rows of pillars. Large, arched windows, with reticulated clear glass, lined both long walls north to south. Raised steps with Richard's marble throne stood at one end and heraldic drapery of banners and tapestries hanging from iron rods ran along both sides down the length of the hall, some flat against the wall and others protruding like banners before a battle.

He wondered where Miles might be. Was he quartered in the palace or with the garrison? He couldn't very well ask. But he still wanted to know. He wanted to know so many things. Why did he wish to kill the king? Was the old plot unfolding all over again? But if killing the king was his only objective, why waste time slaying a French courier?

He looked again at the throne, and like a moth drawn to a flame Crispin walked with slow steps toward the chair.

No guards. Stupid. Reckless. But so was Richard. He was seventeen now. Though no longer considered a child, it would be four more years before he was considered in his full majority. He made decisions for the realm relying at first on his uncle Lancaster. And though Parliament refused to make him regent, Lancaster continued to counsel the boy and hence ruled the realm, though from what Crispin heard, the king's former tutor Simon Burley and Richard's Chancellor, Michael de la Pole, had taken over those duties. That surely did not sit well with the duke. Rumors from court suggested that the nobles felt shut out of the king's decisions. Richard more and more used the counsel of his friends over that of the nobles. That sat well with no one.

Crispin stood at the bottom of the steps to the raised platform. The last time he stood so close was on that day, seven years ago. A presence emanated from the throne like some malevolent creature pitched out of Hell.

Richard. Crispin's ire for him was more marked today than seven years earlier, when all he had wanted was his mentor on the throne. Was Abbot Nicholas right about Crispin? Did Crispin keep tidings of Miles to himself not to appear the hero but to let him kill the king?

He didn't like that feeling creeping into his veins, the feeling of culpability. Was he responsible for setting in motion again the very treason that cast him out of his place at court? A sneer curled his lip. No. That kind of thinking could freeze a man solid. And there was nothing static about Crispin.

He rested his foot on the lowest step and leaned on his thigh. The throne—marble, cushioned. So much more than merely a chair. Some men coveted such a thing. Maybe even some of the men caught up in the conspiracy. Maybe some of them fancied themselves covered in ermine and wearing a crown, and Lancaster was only the tool to get them there.

He made a disgusted snort. What did it really matter now? Few men could change the tide of history. He was certainly not one of them. Might have been once, but not now. But Lancaster was such a man. He headed armies and won and lost the day many a time. The son of a king, he was always destined for greatness and he achieved it. It was on Lancaster's shoulders that the tide of history turned, not on the shoulders of underlings, for though Crispin's rank had been high, his personal ambitions had never achieved the status of such as Lancaster or his ilk, nor was it designed to.

If Richard lived or died, what possible difference would it make to Crispin's life now?

But suppose Richard did die. He'd been married little over a year and the queen was not yet with child. What if she never was? Who then would be the heir? Would it be Lancaster after all?

Crispin closed his eyes and took a deep breath. Such thoughts bordered again on treason. He would not allow himself to dwell. Better to protect the throne, whoever sat atop it.

Two servants scraped a trestle table across the floor and Crispin snapped open his lids. The many tables were arranged around the braziers in the center. Everything, of course, piloted the eyes toward the head table on the other side of the room on its raised platform, to Richard.

Crispin had been a guest at the head table many times before, when Richard's grandfather, Edward of Windsor, was king. He recalled chatting with the ladies and high-ranking men at that table while breaking his meats with them, drinking fine wine, absorbing the entertainments.

No more.

No more because of Miles Aleyn and his seducing lies.

Crispin chuffed a hot breath. He wanted his life back. Killing Miles wouldn't grant that, but the deed would make his suffering a hell of a lot easier.

He felt the weight of the arrows in his pouch. A smile peeled back his lips. He needed to pay a visit to the king's fletcher.

He put his hood up and left the hall. The garrison's courtyard was where the archers congregated. The Master Fletcher would certainly be there.

He headed toward the garrison's yard as if he had made the journey only yesterday. His feet took him without question in the right direction. He passed under an arch, down the steps, and into the open courtyard.

Men walked freely across the gravel quadrangle. Blacksmith stalls, armorers, and carpenter and wheelwright stalls lined the courtyard's walls. He turned when he heard the unmistakable whistle and thud of arrows hitting their targets. Two archers, both wearing green chaperon hoods with short liripipe tails, practiced shooting arrows at straw butts. The men wore leather tunics lined with metal plates, but the broad-shouldered one seemed too big for his tunic, thick arms bursting through the tunic's crenelled cap sleeves. A dark fringe hung below the hood's brim and small dark eyes like a ferret's peered out from under bruised lids.

Long sandy hair draped in lackluster strings over the other archer's brows, and though his eyes were set wide apart in a concentrated stare, he did not look the brighter for it.

Crispin ambled along the wall toward them, leaned his shoulder into a wooden post, and watched the arrows meet the target one after the other. They were fine marksmen, as fine as any of the king's archers. Good enough to shoot a man in an undercroft at close range.

They ran out of arrows and chatted in an easy camaraderie born of longtime service together. Crispin emerged from the shadows. "I beg pardon, good sirs." The men turned. The bigger man's small eyes grew smaller. He clutched his empty bow.

Crispin tried a smile. He wasn't certain if he succeeded. "Would either of you know the whereabouts of the Master Fletcher, Edward Peale?"

The archers exchanged looks. "Sometimes he's at yonder booth," said the sandy-haired one, and gestured with his bow. Crispin turned and examined the empty booth. "But he isn't there today," continued the archer. "Try the armory."

This time Crispin's smile was more sincere. "Yes. I will do that. Much thanks." He turned toward the direction of the armory and wondered why the first burly archer's hand had curled around his arm.

"Say!" said the archer. "Didn't you used to be somebody?"

Crispin's face warmed. The urge to snap his arm out of the man's grasp was strong but he did not move. They recognized him, ruining his plan of stealth. Maybe they wouldn't recall. Maybe he'd get away after all without humiliation.

"I know who he is," said the other. "He's Crispin Guest. The Traitor."

No getting away today. The word was meant to sting, and sting it did. Crispin leveled an icy glare at the sandy-haired one.

"Now, now, Peter," said the other. They let Crispin go and stepped back, but only to assess him as one assesses a horse. "That was a long time ago. I hear tell he's that private sheriff they talk of." His tone mocked. As an archer, he had been lower in rank than Crispin. There seemed to be no end of men who were below Crispin in rank and who relished rubbing his nose in his change of status.

Peter made a doubtful expression and rested his hand on his dagger. "Why do you suppose he's here then, Wat? Traitor and all."

"Maybe he's inquiring about the attempt on his Majesty."

"Or maybe," said Peter, drawing his dagger, "*he's* the one who tried to kill the king."

"Gentlemen." Crispin stared at the dagger pointed at him. Wat also drew his and the two archers maneuvered to block off his escape. Crispin quickly measured the courtyard. Open avenues there and there. He could outrun the big man Wat, but the lanky Peter he doubted he could outmaneuver. Crispin lifted his empty palms and took a step back. He used the only weapon left to him: his inbred nobility. "I *am* here to investigate. But I have an urgent need to speak with Master Peale. If you have a dispute with me—" With two fingers he lifted his dagger from its sheath, flipped it up into his hand, and postured. His smooth and practiced movements were obvious even to the archers, and they hesitated. "Then let us meet our troubles here head on." He took a step forward and smiled when they took a step back. Two against one and they were still frightened of him. He wanted to laugh but didn't want to spoil the mood. Instead, he slammed his knife back into its scabbard. "But if there is nothing more . . ." He backed away, eyeing the men with their bobbing blades. They made no more provocative moves, and when Crispin turned, he heard Wat say, "Peter, you best go find Master Miles."

Crispin decided to hurry.

The armory was left unguarded, possibly because men were constantly entering and leaving it. Crispin blended in and became just one more man among many. He passed row on row of spears, halberds, axes, unstrung bows, and arrows, bundles of them, all piled impossibly high. And seeming to inventory every one of them, an old man bent over a wax slate with a candle attached to it. He was grayer than Crispin remembered. Perhaps a little more unsteady of hand, but there was no mistaking the king's fletcher.

Crispin thought about the reaction of the archers, but there was little to be done. "Master Peale."

The man didn't turn from his work. "Eh? What is it? Can't you see I'm busy?"

"Master Peale. I need your help."

The fletcher stopped and raised his head. "I know that voice." When he turned, his yellowed eyes looked Crispin over. His lids drooped with extra folds; skin leathery as arrow quivers, lips chalky and flat, revealing long, discolored teeth. "Crispin Guest?" He said it slowly, running the unfamiliar syllables off his tongue as if speaking a foreign language. His lips didn't seem to believe his words and they murmured an old man's soundless echo.

Crispin stepped closer into the candle's circle of light. "Yes, it's me."

Peale crossed himself. "Saint Sebastian preserve us." He looked Crispin up and down again and set aside the wax slate. "What brings *you* here to court, Crispin Guest?" His voice slid from faint fear to suspicion. His bushy eyebrows lowered over his eyes.

"I know it has been a long time." Crispin looked at the ground and stood one leg forward, the other back, foot gracefully turned outward. It was a practiced, courtly stance, something Lancaster's tutors had hammered into him over the many years that he lived in the duke's household. "*How do you expect to be a proper courtier, Master Crispin?*" Master Edan would say, correcting Crispin for the thousandth time on his deportment on the dance floor. Master Edan taught Crispin all the dances and courtly courtesy befitting a child of his station, lessons his parents would have shouldered had they lived.

"*By my wits,*" Crispin had answered. A child's voice mouthing a child's youthful sentiments. He didn't, couldn't realize then how true those words would become.

Crispin touched the pouch hanging from his belt. "I have here three fletchings from arrows of your design, Master Peale. And I would have you identify for whom they were made."

"Would you now?" He rubbed his gnarled fingers over his white stubbled chin. His gaze darted past Crispin's shoulder. Crispin, too, looked back. No one was there. "Everyone is very interested in arrows of late."

"No doubt." Crispin produced the arrows from his pouch.

Peale didn't look at them. His gaze centered on Crispin. "It has been many a day since you have been to court, if I am not mistaken. In fact, I am fairly certain the king is still of the same opinion about you, no?"

Crispin said nothing. Let the old man think what he will. It wouldn't matter once he got his proof about Miles.

"Still stubborn, eh? Isn't that what got you into your troubles in the first place?"

"And the sin of pride, Master Peale. But besides my sins, I have been given many gifts. The gift of wit and a keen sense of justice."

"Aye, I remember. So." His lips fumbled with a wry smile before his gaze dropped to the three items in Crispin's hand. "And where did you get these fine specimens, if I may ask?"

"One from a dead man, one from my shoulder—a miss—and the third from a scullion." He handed them to Peale.

"A dead man, eh? Anyone I know?"

"No. No one I knew either."

"Yet one you claim was directed toward you."

"A poor shot when the other was so clean. I wonder if it was meant to merely incapacitate rather than kill me."

"And the scullion? Dead, too, I suppose."

"No, barely wounded."

Peale walked with the fletchings to his candle and turned them over in his hands. He examined the little ridges notched into the shaft near the feathers. "Yes. These are mine right enough."

"Who were they made for?"

"Hmm." Peale rubbed his index finger over his marks and stared at the rafters. "Interesting. I believe—"

"Peale!" A voice shouted from the armory's entrance. Crispin knew that voice and with one wild glance at Peale, Crispin ducked into the shadows. He slid his back along the wall and slipped into the tight space between a stack of broad axes. A blade's sharp edge was mere inches from his nose. He tried not to breathe.

Miles's shadow stretched across the floor. Crispin pressed flatter against the wall.

"Peale," said Miles, "has anyone come to see you about some arrows?"

Peale was an old man, and old men were often excused from a curt tone or an impolite eye. Peale seemed to take full advantage of his maturity and squinted at the Captain of the Archers. "Everyone comes to see me about arrows, young man. I am a *fletcher*." He said the last with careful diction as if speaking to a simpleton.

Miles's brow arched with irritation. "Of course. I know that. What I meant was did anyone you would not expect come to you? Anyone who has no cause to be here?"

"Who am I to judge who has cause to be here and who does not? Verily, Master Aleyn, you make little sense. I must see about *all* arrows. Indeed, I must even see to your arrows, Master."

Crispin threw his hand over his mouth to stifle a laugh.

Miles glowered. "Damn you, Peale. You act like a simpleton when I know you are not!"

"Then don't treat me like one, Master Aleyn. Say what you mean and have done with it."

"Very well. I'm looking for that scoundrel Crispin Guest. Surely you remember him."

"Crispin *Guest*?" The old man scratched his head, causing his white hair to twist into a sunburst. "I haven't seen him in years. What would he be doing at court?"

Miles didn't sound as if he were having any of it. "If he comes to you, inform me immediately. He is trespassing. It should be made known to the king."

"I will do my best to inform you, Master Aleyn," said the fletcher with a dismissive bow.

Miles snorted, looked around for a moment, and then swept out of the room. Crispin heard the door close before he rose from his hiding place.

Peale's eyes seemed to soften when they roved over Crispin again. "He doesn't seem very fond of you, Master Guest."

"He never was. And soon, he shan't be enamored at all. The arrows, Master Peale."

Peale brought his hand forward. He had hidden the arrow pieces behind his back. He nodded over them and handed them back to

Crispin. "These are very special arrows. I made them for my Lord of Gaunt, the duke of Lancaster."

Crispin's elation deflated. He drew closer. "Lancaster? Are you certain?"

Peale pointed to his marks. "These are my marks, young man. And these identify the archer. It is the duke. There is no mistaking."

13

CRISPIN STARED AT THE arrows Peale dropped into his palm. Lancaster.

Peale cocked his head at Crispin. "I take it by your tone that you did not expect that name."

"No, I did not."

It had to be a mistake. The blame was on Miles, not Lancaster. Crispin leaned against a stack of spears, didn't particularly mind when their points dug in his back. "Master Peale, could you be mistaken about this?"

"My mark is my mark, young man."

"So it is," he answered absently. He crushed the arrows tight in his hand. Perhaps if he could crush them altogether he might still the thumping of his heart, the pain throbbing there. Lancaster couldn't be involved in such a plot. Unthinkable. What had Miles to do with Lancaster?

"I thank you, Master Peale." He looked toward the empty doorway. "For *everything*," he added pointedly.

Peale inclined his head and then turned back to his work as if the encounter had never happened.

"Oh. One thing more," asked Crispin. Peale continued his inventory but never looked up. "Did you have the opportunity to examine the arrow that was directed at the king?"

The fletcher shook his head. "No. The fools. They destroyed it. They aren't as clever as you." He turned his head, and Crispin thought he saw him wink.

Crispin thanked him again and left the armory. He dropped the arrow pieces into his pouch and brooded as he walked. Miles was the shooter. Crispin felt it in his bones. When Crispin had examined the roof where the archer had treacherously fired on Crispin, he found light-colored strands of hair—hair that matched the archer's.

Perhaps Miles had used Lancaster's arrows. And this would not be so troubling a thing if it weren't for a rising note of conspiracy. For Miles would have little to gain for killing the king, just as he would have had seven years earlier. Unless he was paid by someone to do it. Someone with enough wealth and influence. Someone who *would* have something to gain.

Crispin looked up and saw Miles turning a corner and striding in his direction. He slipped back and slammed himself against a wall. He didn't want Miles to see him just yet. His clear case against him had suddenly become muddied.

Cautiously, Crispin stole into a side passage. He had to get out of the palace. His mind was not on the task. That kind of carelessness might get him killed.

HE MADE HIS WAY back to the kitchens, keeping his hood low over his face and his head down. When he left the kitchens no one remarked on it. No one remarked his passing through the Great Gate and he was safe to make his way through Westminster and back to London. He arrived at his lodgings by late afternoon.

Walking in the door, he inhaled the heady aromas of two hocks of pork roasting over the fire.

Jack turned from his basting and smiled. "Master, what's the news?"

Crispin took off his cloak and hood, hung them on a peg, and fell into a chair. He sighed. "Much has happened, Jack. I've had to move the wenches again." He related the story.

Jack listened and took one hock. Laying it on a slab of hard bread, he handed it to Crispin and then fetched a bowl from the larder shelf and poured wine into it from the jug. He put the bowl beside Crispin and then prepared his own supper.

Crispin chewed the meat, keeping his eyes on his food.

"So," said Jack, settling beside Crispin. "When are you going to tell me the rest?"

Damn the boy. "The rest?"

"Aye. The rest you're trying so hard not to tell me."

Suddenly the pork didn't taste as good. Crispin tossed the bone into the fire. He rose and went to the water jug and basin, pouring the icy water over his hands and shaking off the wet. "I discovered from whom the arrows came."

Jack gulped his wine and settled expectantly on his stool. "Well?"

Crispin shook his head, tried to chuckle. "It's absurd," he said, returning to the table and sitting. "There is a simple explanation."

"Aye. There could be. If you'd just tell me."

Crispin stared at Jack, at a face that didn't seem to belong to a young boy anymore. Jack's eyes were wise. Well, sympathetic, at any rate. They did not show impatience as they should. They only waited. Who was this boy? As alone in the world as Crispin was. Clever. Resourceful. Just born on the wrong side of the Thames.

Crispin sighed. "Very well, Jack. Master Peale was quite insistent that the arrows were made for . . . the duke of Lancaster."

No protestations, no jumping up with shouts of denial. Jack was calm, even nodded thoughtfully.

It irritated like hell.

"The duke's arrows, eh? That's a sly trick, that. Stealing his arrows so he'd appear to be guilty."

The simplest of explanations. Crispin's gut was so tangled that he had not been able to dredge up such an uncomplicated rationalization.

"So," said Jack, mouth bulging with food. "Whoever stole his grace's arrows is the killer."

Crispin bobbed his head inattentively. "It's as good a conjecture as any."

"So what you're saying is, there ain't no way to trace them to the Captain of the Archers now, is there?"

Crispin gritted his teeth and took a swig. The wine—turning quickly to vinegar—burned down his throat. "In truth, no." He slammed the table with the flat of his hand. "Damn!"

"Then you'll have to catch him in the act."

He looked up at Jack. The boy's face wore all the confidence in Crispin that Crispin did not have for himself. Jack's chin jutted in pride, the same pride he'd seen on the faces of squires watching their masters at tournament or on the battlefield.

Crispin leaned back in his chair. His fingers toyed with the rim of his wine bowl. "There is the possibility that he will not strike again. Not any time soon."

Jack chewed thoughtfully until his jaw slowed and stopped. "You may be right, there. He might lie low for months!" Jack scratched his head. He slowly pivoted his glance toward the buried reliquary. "Master! What are we going to do with that? We can't keep it for months."

They both looked at the unassuming pile of straw.

"The longer we delay giving it back," said Jack, "the worse it will get."

"For 'us'?"

"Well, I deem m'self in your care—and you in mine."

Crispin's smile flattened. "You're right, of course. I've kept it too long already. I suppose I can leave out how I acquired it."

"Will the king accept that?"

"I don't know." He scowled. "God's blood! It's looking more and more like I should surrender it to the sheriff."

"It would take the blame from you."

"And the credit!" He shot from the chair and paced the small room. Finally he lighted in front of the hearth. He leaned forward and pressed his hands against the wall and stared into the short flames. "I have so few opportunities—so few chances to prove myself." He laughed but it came out a bitter sound. "Who am I fooling? No matter what I do—even if I announced the Second Coming myself—Richard would never allow me back to court. Never give me back my—" He made an airless chuckle. "My title and knighthood." He shook his head, a smile still pasted on his mouth. "I am nothing," he said quietly. "That's what they told me, Jack. 'You are nothing.' And only God can make something from nothing."

He hung his head between his outstretched arms and closed his eyes. What foolish pride had made him think he could overcome this Hell with a simple return of goods? His head whipped up and he glared at the straw pile. He stomped toward it and cast the straw aside.

"What are you going to do?" asked Jack's worried voice behind him.

"Why do these things curse me?" Crispin opened the box. He lifted out the golden casket and threw open the lid. He snatched the Crown of Thorns and turned it in his hand. "Look at this. It should be so treasured a thing. But look what it's done to me. It gave me hope. I promised myself I would allow no one and nothing to do so ever again."

Jack stood at his shoulder and looked down at the Crown. His hands fumbled forward as if trying to protect it. "But it touched Jesus' head, Master. I wouldn't— You shouldn't be touching it."

Crispin clenched the Crown in his hand. The dry rushes crackled. He wanted to heave it against the wall. He wanted to see it splinter into a million pieces. And he didn't know why he was so angry at such a thing. It certainly wasn't the Crown's fault he was in this situation. After no choices for so long, he had chosen to become this "Tracker," and it had been his saving grace. He could use the acuity of his mind, his fighting skills, and his knowledge to fight injustice. He was proud of his accomplishments. Miles was evil and had tricked him as he tricked all those other knights, now dead. But it wasn't the Crown's fault. It was only because of those couriers. That's how he got the Crown.

The French couriers. What had they to do with this? He wondered where they were.

With a sigh, he slipped the Crown unsteadily back into its casket, closed the lid, and put it back within the wooden box. He packed the straw around it again but snatched his hand back with a sharp inhale. A bead of blood appeared on his finger. He'd pricked it. He looked in the straw and found a stray thorn. It must have fallen out of the Crown when he manhandled it. He drew it from the straw and dropped it in his pouch.

He concentrated his hate on Miles. Surely it was all Miles, not Lancaster. Jack was right, had to be. Lancaster was an innocent pawn in this.

There was much more to be learned. He needed answers not more questions. And if he was to learn anything he had to know more about why that Crown had not immediately been taken to court as it should have been.

He had to find those couriers.

14

THE KING'S HEAD WAS blazed golden by the late-afternoon light, but it belied a grimy interior, more so even that the Boar's Tusk. When Crispin entered, a haze of wood smoke hovered over the tables. Men hunched in a circle near the fire and lifted their heads from stooped shoulders long enough to look Crispin over before they gave him a dismissive flick of their lids and turned back to their coven.

A woman approached Crispin. Mislaid strands of her hair hung in lifeless strings before her eyes and she wiped her hands on her apron. She might be the innkeeper's wife, or just another wench who worked in the tavern's hall. It was hard to be certain. "Good day. What will you have?"

"I would speak with your Master."

She sighed. "Aye. He's in the back."

He followed her leisurely steps through a ragged curtain. The innkeeper was there filling jugs of ale from a keg. He was a tall man, bald, with a beaklike nose. He aimed a milky blue eye at Crispin. "Eh? What's your business?"

"The Frenchmen. Are they here?"

The man shot to his feet. "You're the one." His finger thrust toward Crispin's face like a dagger, and when he got close enough to make that finger uncomfortable, Crispin took half a step back and laid his hand on his own weapon. "You're the one that took my scullions. And I just hired them two. Where are they?"

"They needed to be kept safe."

"Safe!" He snorted. "After killing that man. Now I'll never be rid of those foreigners."

"They are here, then?"

His face squinted. He mashed his lips before spitting at the fire. He missed. "Aye, they're here."

"Where?"

"Top of the stairs." He leaned forward. "Oi. No trouble, mind."

Crispin showed his teeth. "No trouble."

He parted the curtain and trotted up the stairs to the gallery. He knocked politely. A rustle. A chair scraped. The door opened a sliver.

Crispin nodded his head in a slight bow. *"Mes seigneurs. Bonjour."*

"Ah!" said the man in French. "It is that smart Englishman."

"Will you allow me in?" continued Crispin in the same language.

The man closed the door in his face. Crispin heard him confer with his companion and then the door opened again. "Come in." He stepped aside and the other man scowled as Crispin entered.

Crispin assessed the two men, the table with its two beakers of wine, two bowls of half-eaten fare. "You had a fourth companion. Where is he?"

"He is not here," said the first. His dark hair, lustrous in the firelight, remained brushed away from his wide forehead.

"Any new insight as to why your friend was killed?"

"Gautier had an idea." Laurent turned to the other man with the dark hair and sour disposition. Crispin raised his face to him.

"Well?"

Gautier shrugged. "I thought I heard him say he saw someone he knew."

"Where?"

"I do not know. I was preoccupied."

"With the wench Livith?"

"I do not know her name."

Crispin looked at the first man. "What of you, *Maître* Laurent?"

"I was similarly occupied. I did not notice our companion was missing for quite some time."

"You were supposed to be guarding this most holy relic for your king. Now your negligence has cost you. And us."

Gautier hooked his thumbs in his belt. "What's another battle with England to us? This war goes on without ceasing."

"This relic was a goodwill gesture," said Crispin. "It could have meant lasting peace."

There was a pause, and then both Frenchmen erupted in laughter. Crispin's solemn face broke into a smile, and then he joined them. The Frenchmen pointed at him and Laurent clapped Crispin on the back.

"Sit," said Laurent. He pulled a jug from the shelf. "It is English wine, but it at least has spirits." He poured three cups and handed one each to Crispin and to Gautier. "To peace?" he said, raising his cup.

Crispin stood. "To the King of France."

The other two stood with cups raised. "To the King of *England*," said Laurent. They all chuckled and clanked cups.

They sat and Laurent refilled their cups. "A sensible Englishman. I never thought to find one."

"Oh, we do exist. Few are at court."

Gautier leaned forward. The hand clutching his cup had square, flat fingernails. "So. What is your interest in this? You are not the sheriff."

Crispin kept one eye on the door. It would not do well to have his back to it if their fourth companion returned. "No. It is my vocation to solve riddles. My name is Crispin Guest."

"You would solve the murderer of a Frenchmen? Why do you care?"

"I care about all crimes. Especially when they have to do with the assassination of my king."

"*Sang Deu!* Someone has tried to kill your king?"

"Have you not heard?"

The Frenchmen looked at one another a long moment before Laurent shrugged. "I suppose we have," he said in heavily accented English.

"So you do understand my language," said Crispin, also in English.

Gautier rubbed his smooth chin. "When it is convenient."

Crispin settled in. "I see. Well then. Let us speak plainly. Why did you come to the King's Head instead of going directly to court?"

"We told you," said Gautier with a frown. "We were to prepare for the English court."

"And that 'preparation' involved going off in separate directions to get your companion killed and the relic stolen?"

Laurent stared at Crispin. His dark eyes narrowed. "Are we being accused of this?"

"*Did* you kill Michel Girard?"

Laurent knocked back his chair as he jumped to his feet and drew his blade. "He's a spy for the crown of England!"

Gautier followed suit. Crispin didn't move and looked at them both. He leaned on his arm and sipped his wine. "If you only knew how humorous a suggestion that was . . ."

"Get up." Laurent waved the sword tip near Crispin's face. Crispin felt it itch his skin and longed to smack it out of the way. He sat nearly immobile instead and drank more.

"I think not. I'm not a spy. I want to get to the bottom of this plot."

Laurent tightened his grip on the sword. His knuckles whitened and shined with sweat.

Crispin set his cup down and swiveled on his stool to face them both. Two swords aimed at his chest. He kept his breathing steady.

Laurent's eyes made the barest of flickers toward Gautier. They breathed heavily for a moment more before they both withdrew their swords from Crispin's chest at the same time and smoothly sheathed them. "Then? Why are you here?"

"For information. Anything that will help me. I find it improbable that you met here to 'prepare' for the English court."

Gautier sucked in his lips while Laurent scowled at the floor.

"Just so. You will not say. Yet your companion is dead and you deny having to do with his murder. Is that correct?"

Without looking at Crispin, they both nodded.

"Mmm. Well, it is lucky for you that I already know the assassin. When did you discover *Maître* Girard was dead?"

"Not until the sheriff arrived," said Laurent. "We were as surprised as anyone else." And he looked it.

"Why did he kill your friend?" asked Crispin.

Gautier shook his head. "For the relic?"

It was Crispin's turn to lower his gaze. "Perhaps."

"Maybe," offered Laurent, "they knew one another. The killer and Michel. He said he saw someone he recognized."

Gautier dug his teeth into his bottom lip. "It seems strange, no? That Michel would be killed by someone he knew."

"On the contrary," said Crispin. "In my experience, I find that most murders are committed by acquaintances. Mostly in drunken tavern brawls. But this murderer also wanted to kill the king." He gauged their faces as he said it. There was a flicker in their eyes but he could not tell what it might reveal. "How would Michel have known such a man, an Englishman?"

"I don't know," said Gautier. "He has never been to England before."

"Then this killer has obviously been to France."

Laurent nodded. "So it would seem."

"Do you know a man named Miles Aleyn?"

The Frenchmen looked at one another. They slowly turned toward Crispin and answered, "No."

Crispin eyed them steadily and it was Gautier who dropped his eyes first.

"Indeed." Crispin glanced at his empty cup and left it where it sat. "What of this other companion of yours, the one searching for the relic. What is his name?"

After a lengthy pause, Crispin looked up again. The men stared at one another. Laurent stuck out his lower lip. "I do not think we are at liberty to say."

"No?" Crispin stared pointedly at Gautier who shuffled his feet. "We have our instructions, *Maître* Guest. We . . . may not say."

"I see." He rose. "I thank you, gentlemen, for your time and your . . . trust," he said with a sharpened expression.

"But you *will* do your utmost to expose Michel's murderer?"

Crispin turned to Laurent. "Oh I shall. But I do not need to tell you that the more information you can provide the easier it shall be for me to discover the culprit."

They were both as tight-lipped as before, though their gaze was steady on Crispin's.

"Very well," he said and bowed to both Frenchmen, put up his hood, and took his leave.

He stood outside their closed door and stared at it. What plot were they hatching that they would not divulge the reason for their stay at the King's Head or the identity of their fourth companion? Did it have to do with the attempt on Richard's life? Yet they seemed genuinely surprised by that news. Strange. And Miles Aleyn. The name had caused a spark of recognition in their eyes. They might not have killed their companion but they were hiding a great deal. Just what it might be, Crispin was yet uncertain.

The situation was getting more complicated than need be. It should be simpler. Miles did it. He had been in France. He told Crispin as much. He must have killed the Frenchman because the courier could identify him. Simple.

And the arrows? He stole them to deflect any identification from him.

But a bigger question remained. If it were a plot all along to kill the king, why the attack on Livith and Grayce? If they knew something, saw something that might incriminate the killer, then the scullions were in far more danger than he thought.

Where was that fourth courier?

He scrambled out of the inn and ran full tilt back toward Westminster Palace.

CRISPIN ENTERED THE PALACE kitchens easily and hurled down the steps. He scanned the room. It was even busier than before.

There, Livith was giving orders to Grayce while Grayce happily accepted them. They looked too busy to notice him. They were safe and none the wiser for their danger. Crispin bent over to grasp his thighs and breathed. He had imagined them both dead, arrows protruding from their necks. But now his thumping heart was tempered with annoyance. If only that damned Livith would let him force the information from Grayce's stubborn mind.

Blowing out a sigh, he straightened. Livith was probably right. Grayce was too dull-witted. She said she didn't remember, and in all likelihood she didn't.

The urge was strong to bundle them both and send them into the country, but where could he send them? He knew no one outside of London who would do him a favor.

He tapped his finger on his knife hilt. There was little choice in the matter. He had done what he could. Hidden in the largest kitchen in London was surely an adequate hiding place.

A scullion shoved Crispin none too gently out of the way. Crispin didn't take offense. He was the invader into their territory, after all. He was no longer a lord to be catered to.

The coming feast plunged the kitchen into raucous activity. Every hearth, every brazier vaunted roasting meats with a licking fire under bubbling pots. Servants scurried from one post to another, while women, wiping sweat from their foreheads with their bared forearms, stood over large cauldrons stirring two-handed with large wooden spoons, or sat on stools peeling onions and carrots.

Onslow Blunt spotted him. "Oi, Sir Crispin. Back again?"

"It's a fine feast you are preparing."

"To be sure. Mustn't let the world see the court is afraid." Onslow stared at Crispin and seemed to read his face. "Hungry?"

Crispin made a nervous chuckle and rubbed his belly. "As it turns out, yes, I am."

"Let's see how the capons are doing." Onslow wrapped the end of his apron around an iron rod that served as a spit, and with his wide hand, slid one of at least twenty capons off the rod and onto a long rectangular worktable in the center of the room. The plucked bird steamed and a pool of juices puddled beneath it.

"Geoff," said Onslow, stopping a boy hurrying to some task. "Bring us both a jug of wine. Get it from my larder, lad. Make haste, now."

Onslow turned back to the capon and in the middle of the busy kitchen chopped it in half with a handy butchering knife. He slid one half toward Crispin. "Here you go. It's been awhile since you've enjoyed my cooking, eh?"

"Too long." It was hot, but Crispin was famished. The small hocks that Jack managed to get hadn't quite been enough. He handled the capon's steaming flesh tenderly. The meat seemed to melt in his mouth. He licked the succulent juices from his fingers. "It's the pastries I miss the most," he said, mouth full.

"Oh, aye. I've got something special tonight, too. A miniature of

London, all done in spun sugar and cakes. I've been working on it for days."

"I can't wait to see."

"Are you staying?"

Crispin sucked the last of the meat from the bones and wiped his hands on a cloth just as the boy Geoff returned with drinking jugs. They both saluted each other. The wine tasted smooth and rich. Was it thicker? Was that possible? It was nothing like the fare at the Boar's Tusk. Most likely this wine was imported from Spain or France.

"I will be here, but unseen, if you get my meaning," said Crispin.

"In the kitchens?"

"In the kitchens, in the hall, in the corridors. You see—" He leaned in toward Onslow and Onslow matched his conspiratorial angle. Crispin's voice dropped to a taut whisper. "I think the assassin will try again."

Onslow's eyes rounded, revealing the whites all around his blue irises. "Christ bless me! You don't think that has anything to do with Master Peale?"

Crispin pulled the wine jug away from his lips. "What has this to do with Master Peale?"

Onslow dropped to a whisper. "Hadn't you heard? They found him dead not more than an hour ago."

15

CRISPIN SET HIS WINE down. Peale dead and his secrets with him. "By an arrow?"

"No," whispered Onslow. "Throat was cut. But not much is spoken of it. Most of the palace do not know, and the king wants it to stay that way."

His throat cut? "That's my fault," Crispin muttered. "I should have taken better care. I should have thought of this."

"How can it be your fault? No man can possibly blame you."

"I made too well known the point that I was identifying some arrows." And now there was no chance to prove identification. None at all. "My staying now is all the more imperative."

"Do you think the assassin will strike tonight?"

"I think it a ripe possibility. It is best I serve in the great hall."

"But Sir Crispin! They'll recognize you."

"Not if I keep my hood up and my head down."

"You're taking an awful risk."

"What would you have me do? I owe Peale that much."

Onslow ticked his head. "You serve the king, and he doesn't even know it."

Crispin said nothing, picked up the jug and knocked it back. He wiped his mouth with the back of his hand. "And the scullions. No trouble? No threats?"

Onslow shrugged. "Nought that I could see. They work hard. No complaints. Would you speak with them?"

"No. I would not vex them. I brought them here to be safe. I would have them believe that this is so. I will wander about, if you will allow it."

"Of course. My kitchen is your kitchen, Sir Crispin."

Crispin did his best to stay out of the way. He did not make himself known to Livith or Grayce. He reckoned they would be less likely to call attention to themselves if they didn't know he was watching them. Instead, he kept his hood up, and he walked along the perimeter of the kitchen, striding slowly, and nudging into the shadows when he could.

As the dinner hour approached, Crispin could feel the tension in the kitchens as the last-minute preparations were made. In the hall, the long trestle tables were probably already laid with their white linens, spoons, salt cellars, pipkins, and goblets. He detected music through the walls. That meant the diners had entered the hall and were assembling. Soon hands would be washed, a benediction prayed.

The king and his closest consorts would sit at the high table, but below that were tables for the noblemen of court. These were laid with tablecloths and less fine tableware than on the high table. They would be set with pewter chargers for the bread at each place, but the jugs for wine were of ceramic, not silver. Still, they sat closer to the king, and therefore it was a place of honor.

The low tables, farthest from the high table, would not sport the fine linen tablecloths, nor did they have their own salt cellars or even a bowl of their own. These men and women—lowest on the ladder of court hierarchy—shared their fare from the same trencher and their wine from the same cup. They might be pages. They might be minor nobles and rich merchants invited to eat with the king. They might be hangers on, ambitious men who sought the counsel and favors of some of the court's nobles.

In days past, Crispin's seat was at the middle tables, and sometimes at the high table itself, but only because Crispin was in the company of John of Gaunt. When Crispin was younger than Jack Tucker, he remembered serving the high table as a page. It was a privilege, after all, cutting the duke's meat for him and serving as ewerer.

He gave a thought to Peale, for he would not be part of this earthly feast tonight. Why had Miles killed him? To prevent Crispin from discovering the identity of the arrows' owner? But if they belonged to Lancaster, how did that incriminate Miles?

With a head beginning to ache with circular thoughts, Crispin found his way to the great hall's archway. Pottage was already being wheeled forward to the hall in big cast-iron pots. Platters of oysters were next, with servings of roasted eels.

Onslow looked like a marshal on the field of battle, directing his troops to form their lines. The roasters readied their meats and laid the entire animal on beds of greens. Some of the birds were dressed again in their feathers. All were laid on biers to be hoist by two servants.

Crispin decided to be a wine server. He could get close enough to conversations but not tarry too long for anyone to look directly at him.

He caught Onslow's eye amid the cook's wild gesticulations and nodded to him, but the look on Onslow's face seemed to say "be careful."

Crispin agreed wholeheartedly.

He drew the edge of his hood down low to his brows and grabbed a jug of wine. He followed a line of boys carrying long skewers of fist-sized quails all bunched together. He kept his head down and emerged into a hall already bursting with activity.

Crispin slowed and paused in the doorway. A wave of nostalgia rumbled in his chest. It had been a long time since he'd seen the hall in its full bloom. The coronas blazed with candles. Cressets burned. Golden light showered the hall's expanse. There were so many lights that the diners barely noticed that the sun had moved behind the clouds, making its long path toward the horizon.

But the noise. He'd forgotten the noise of diners talking and laughing. Musicians plucked and hammered and whistled merrily away, their notes dancing above the cacophony reverberating off the banner-draped walls. Jugglers and acrobats talked a patter as they tossed wooden balls and moved leisurely between the many tables.

Then there were the smells of smoke and roasted meats and sizzling butter and spices and fresh-baked manchets and sugar and honey and people and herbs.

It was almost more than he could bear.

"Oi! You. Move there."

Crispin scuttled out of the doorway so more servants could enter with their fare. He strode into the hall, keeping his head down but his eyes raised into the sheltering shadow of his hood.

He scanned the room. Where was Miles?

There. He sat on a bench at one of the low tables in the company of several men Crispin didn't recognize. The men were eating the food on their shared trencher with relish, reaching in with their fingers or jabbing a quail with the tip of their knives. In fact, all the men around Miles laughed, chatted, and ate—all except Miles. He leaned on his elbow and steadily drank from his clay goblet. And not once did he take his eyes off the king's dais.

Crispin turned toward the far end of the hall. At the middle of the high table on a fine wooden seat sat Richard himself.

Crispin drew closer even though his good judgment told him not to.

Absently, he poured wine for those who motioned him over, careful to keep his head down and say nothing. He moved between the benches and edged nearer to the high table.

Richard, now seventeen, was pale and round-faced, with those same heavily lidded eyes Crispin remembered. His fair hair fell in curls about his face, not quite long enough to reach his gold-embroidered collar, or his shoulders in their red velvet coat patterned in foliated circles. He wore a crown, a simple gold circlet with trefoiled points. He sported the beginnings of a goatee and faint mustache. He listened to the other diners as they talked, but his attention seemed to be diverted by his diminutive bride of over a year, Anne of Bohemia.

Sixteen years old and possessed of a simple face, Anne could have been the daughter of a merchant. There was nothing particularly regal about her. Perhaps that was what Richard found so appealing. Surrounded by the likes of his very regal mother Joan of Kent, his uncle John of Gaunt, his Chancellor Michael de la Pole, his chamberlain Robert de Vere, and his tutor Simon Burley, it was as imposing an entourage as one could endure.

Crispin tried not to stare at Gaunt. The duke's face was flush in a healthy if not slightly inebriated glow. His wife, Constance, sat several chairs away and kept a solicitous eye on him. Crispin couldn't help but suffer a strange feeling in his gut about Lancaster.

This was foolish. To be so close to the head table. Crispin knew he was asking for trouble. He should keep close to Miles and he turned to do just that when Joan, the queen mother, called out to him.

"Bring the wine, man."

Crispin would have clouted himself if he'd a free hand. He couldn't just run, could he?

He pivoted slowly. His heart hammered and he steadily approached the dais. He kept his head down and moved up the steps as if they were a gibbet.

Joan had kept her pert beauty, though now her face was etched with grooves, particularly at the eyes and mouth. She did not look at Crispin as she raised her goblet. Several of the others also indicated they needed wine and Crispin bowed his head so low he feared he might stumble.

He filled Queen Joan's goblet and then Richard raised his.

Crispin hesitated for a moment. Of all the places he could have been, of all the things he could be doing, he didn't imagine he'd be serving the king wine. Mildly he thought of poisons as the red liquor drawled into his Majesty's cup.

He breathed again when it appeared safe enough to leave. Wiping the jug's lip with his fingers, he turned on his heel when he noticed that his mentor the duke had raised his cup. Crispin paused. No. *Don't stay!* Crispin pretended he had not seen the duke's gesture and made to leave, but a page stopped him with a hand on his arm. "Knave," the boy hissed at him. "The duke of Lancaster needs wine."

Crispin stared wide-eyed at the boy, that *whelp* in his way, hindering his escape. The boy's audacious grip tightened on Crispin's arm. "Are you deaf?" Without warning, he spun Crispin around and pushed him toward Lancaster.

Crispin swayed for a moment. It wasn't fear exactly that froze him to the spot but an overwhelming sense of stupidity, that he could have avoided this. With a fatalistic sigh, he edged behind the throne and reached toward the duke as far as he could without getting closer. He tilted the jug and clapped its spout to Lancaster's raised cup. The pouring of it seemed to take the length of a small eternity. But once the cup was finally filled, he lifted the jug away and let out a long breath and even a chuckle. That wasn't so hard. At last. He was free to depart and no one had been the wiser. God be praised.

But then the duke looked up.

16

LANCASTER'S EYES ROUNDED AND his lips went white.

Crispin did nothing. He neither smiled nor implored with his eyes. If he were a dead man, then he'd rather get it over with.

Lancaster took the full goblet, put it to his lips, and drank deeply. He drank it down, but did not offer it up for a refill. He dismissed Crispin by curling his hand around the goblet and leaning on his arm.

Crispin wanted to ask him, wanted to cast the arrow pieces on his trencher and demand an explanation. Though he imagined Lancaster had his own questions for Crispin about now.

Instead, Crispin ducked his head and took the opportunity to slip down the steps to return to the main hall. He felt Lancaster's gaze on him but he couldn't worry over it. He had other things on his mind. He had to keep his eyes on Miles.

He turned toward the low tables and his heart lurched for the second time.

Where the hell *was* Miles?

Crispin hurried through the benches and people and stared at the place where Miles once sat, but it was empty like an open pit. He risked raising his head to look about the room, but he didn't see him.

"God's blood!" he hissed.

"Wine, here!" someone called over his shoulder.

Crispin cringed. Not him! Why did *he* have to be here? Crispin shook his head. Better and better. He lowered his face until the leather hood caressed his cheeks. He pivoted.

Simon Wynchecombe sat with his cronies at a low table and lifted his clay cup toward Crispin. Deep in conversation with the man beside him, the sheriff never raised his eyes. Crispin poured quickly and hustled away before anyone else at the table could ask him to serve them.

He looked for Miles in earnest. The man had simply vanished. How had he done it? Should he ask? No, that would be dangerous and someone was sure to recognize him. He slid as quickly as he could through the crowd, looking over heads, searching faces.

Suddenly everyone stood.

The duke had risen from his seat and was making some sort of pronouncement with his wine cup raised. Crispin was at the other end of the hall by then and Lancaster's voice did not carry. But he surmised that Lancaster had called for a toast to the king. Everyone raised their cups.

Crispin put down the wine jug on a table. He didn't want to be bothered with any more requests. He *had* to find Miles and quickly.

A juggler blocked the aisle but Crispin shoved him aside, and one ball fell and rolled under a table. The man swore an oath and Crispin pressed forward, moving toward the edge of the room.

Lancaster talked on.

Miles had to be here somewhere! Crispin shoved courtiers out of his way. It didn't matter anymore if they saw him. What did it matter if he couldn't stop Miles, for he knew with the blood singing in his bones that Miles would make another attempt sometime this night.

Had he seen it? There was an abundance of jewelry on both men and women alike; men with their swords in decorated scabbards and women with jeweled baselards secured at their girdles. With all the glittering finery, he couldn't be certain he saw a flash of something.

He wasn't even sure in what direction he saw it. Whatever it was it didn't belong, but he couldn't make his mind locate it a second time.

Frantically he searched, saw it again, and froze for the span of a heartbeat.

The tapestries. They fluttered throughout the hall from the movement of the diners and the servants, from the heat of the fires and candles. But this one, hanging on the south wall halfway between the king's dais and the exit, did not flutter. It bulged.

And an arrow was slowly edging its way farther and farther from behind it.

All sound—diners clinking goblets, trilling laughter and hoarse guffaws, music piping merrily—were all suddenly swallowed up by the quick inhale of the universe. The racing thump of Crispin's heartbeat replaced them; a hollow thud growing steadily faster.

He sprinted forward.

With an unapologetic heave, Crispin shoved a servant. His tray of cooked peacock dressed in its indigo plumage tumbled to the floor. The peacock's head snapped off and rolled between the legs of a merchant who stumbled to get out of its way, and in turn, tripped a woman behind him. She screamed and teetered backward and fell into the arms of the juggler. The four balls scattered. One bounced into a large kettle of pottage. Two others rolled under the feet of two men carrying in the confection, Onslow's prized creation of the city of London in spun sugar and cakes.

The man carrying the front of the bier stumbled but recovered. But the man behind him was not as lucky. He tried to right himself but couldn't without dropping his end of the bier. He let one handle go as he flung a hand outward to steady himself. The shifted weight dislodged the first bearer and he slid backward. The bier tipped and, in slow degrees, the whole confectionery slid off the bier and crashed in upon itself onto the floor in splatters of frosting and crackling sugar. The horrified forward bearer stared at it helplessly. The other slipped on a wayward cake and fell face first into the rest of it.

Crispin dived through the crowd; his only thought was to stop the arrow from launching. But there were too many damned people in his way! *Move!*

In the back of his mind, he could hear that Lancaster had stopped speaking. A buzz of conversation amid high-pitched yelps of surprise followed in his wake. None of it mattered. All his concentration was centered on that tapestry.

The bow advanced. He could see it now peeking from the tapestry. If he couldn't make it in time— No! He wouldn't think of it. Couldn't. He doubled his efforts and threaded quickly between the courtiers.

Finally shoving his way past the last stragglers at the crowd's hem, Crispin leapt for the tapestry, grabbed the exposed weapon, and slammed it to the wall.

The arrow shot forward, drastically off target from its intended mark. It flew and stuck in the wall just above the king's chair.

Richard leapt to his feet and snatched his wife's hand, pulling her behind him. Someone screamed. The men on the dais threw themselves before the king, drew their swords, and whipped their heads around, searching.

By then, the archer had released his grip on the shortbow and rumbled behind the banners and tapestries to make his escape. The tapestry flew up, furling like a sail. Footsteps ran.

Crispin tried to get to him, but now there was a crushing throng pushing against him. He stumbled. He reared up. His hood fell back, but it was too late. The crowd closed up again. Confused heads turned every which way. Women were wailing and everyone seemed to be shouting.

And then someone gasped. Before Crispin knew what was happening, the crowd parted and left a wide circle around him. He suddenly and unaccountably found himself alone.

Not so unaccountable. With a sinking feeling in his gut he knew exactly why.

Crispin stared back at the anxious and horror-struck faces. A trickle of sweat dribbled down his temple to his cheek.

"It's Crispin Guest!" said a voice, shock spinning it to a whisper. The hall fell silent.

Crispin didn't need to look down at the guilty bow still clenched in his left hand.

"Holy Christ," he muttered.

17

AS CRISPIN SAW IT, there were only two choices: he could stay as he was and get captured and executed for a crime he didn't commit— or he could run.

He chose the latter.

He threw himself forward into a knot of women. Screams filled his ears, but at least the women had no weapons. He felt the cascade of silk and satin on his hands, smelled their perfumes and sweat, and pushed ahead, crisscrossing amid the tight throng. All at once, he burst free of the crowd. Men with swords approached from one side, guards with guisarmes from another. The crowd of people shrank back.

He looked at the shortbow still in his hand and cast it away. At his back, a tapestry and a solid wall.

This was not good.

His eyes searched, mind churning. Escape. There had to be a way. There was always a way.

He looked behind him at the tapestry, up to its stern iron rod, to the windows above.

The men were coming, murder in their eyes. He was done for. No trial. No gaol. Just a bloody death right here in the great hall.

Crispin spun. He grabbed the edge of the tapestry with both fists and pulled himself up, hand over hand. A spear whistled past his ear, moving his hair. He stopped only long enough to stare wide-eyed at the quivering shaft imbedded in the plaster before he threw his strength into reaching higher.

The iron rod. He felt his hand curl around it and then the other hand. Now he dared look up and saw the window. It was farther than he thought.

Another spear clanged against the wall just below his right thigh. He swung his leg up and his boot managed to just grab the rod. He'd have to stand on it to reach the window.

He felt a tug on the tapestry and looked down. Two guards climbed up below him.

No time to think. He pulled his other leg up and crouched on the rod like a frog, both sweaty hands clutching the rod between his feet. He walked his hands up the wall until he stood.

He lurched. Why was the rod suddenly leaning? At his left, the rod hung precariously from its hanger imbedded in the plaster-covered stone. The damned thing was pulling away from the wall! Too much weight.

A bit of plaster fell from the hanger. The rod lurched again as it slipped farther.

"Better and better," he muttered, shaking his head.

He looked up at the window. There was a sill but it wasn't very wide, only enough for his feet. He reached up to grab it.

Too far.

He heard a grunt and told himself not to look down, but in the tense state his mind was in, he didn't listen very well to himself. One of the guards climbing the tapestry had almost reached him. He thought of kicking him in the face but a better idea occurred to him.

The man stretched his hand forward and gripped the rod. The whole tapestry shifted again. The man raised his head and looked over at the unstable hanger. His expression opened into fear. It was a good fifteen feet to the floor. He looked up at Crispin and whitened his knuckles on the rod.

Crispin smiled and slid along the rod toward him. The man's features changed to one of horror as he saw what Crispin was about to do, though he misunderstood the reason.

Crispin raised his foot, but instead of kicking the man's face, he stepped up onto his head. Crispin's boot slid on the man's hair and the human stepping-stone heaped a set of fine old curses upon Crispin, questioning his paternity as well as his sexual practices.

Crispin ignored it. Now tall enough, he reached up and grabbed the sill. He pushed away from the man's head to get a good grip. That was also enough to dislodge the guard. The man lost his hold, tried to regain it, and tumbled down. He knocked the other guard free and landed on a knot of men gathered below. Then the entire rod let loose from the wall. The men below scrambled out of the way before the rod and tapestry clanged heavily to the floor.

Crispin dangled like a plucked goose from the windowsill. Halberd heads clanked against the wall in an attempt to reach his feet. If he couldn't swing up to the window, he was as good as a dead goose.

He grit his teeth and swung his foot, missed, swung again.

Got it! He pulled his body up on the narrow ledge. For once grateful at his meager diet, he stood, facing the window. Unable to resist, he turned his head and got his first look at the hall.

Chaos. All its inhabitants glared up at him, curses on their lips. Spears shook, swords flashed. They wanted his blood, that much was certain.

With his chest pressed to the glass he felt the window with his fingers, the edges of glass, the lead dividers, looking for a latch or hinge.

Then his heart burst with a shot of warmth. The window didn't open. He *was* a dead man.

He looked back down and wondered who he should land on for the best effect. It would be the last choice he ever made so he wanted it to be a good one.

He saw it like a story woven into a tapestry. The man below cocked back his arm and took aim at Crispin. The spear released in a long and graceful arc, straight at him. If he didn't move it would surely pierce him, and he wondered in the few heartbeats it took for the spear to leave the guard's hand, if he shouldn't let it do its work. The aim was good and would, no doubt, do great damage to his chest. All he had to do was stand as he was and make no attempt to move. A simple thing. Better than the death Richard would choose this time. Crispin ruminated on the possibilities—on who would mourn him, where his miserable body might be buried if allowed such an ennobling thing as burial. But then his instincts took over, made the decision, and forced him to lean to the side just as the lethal missile slid past him. The spear crashed through the window in a barrage of broken glass and twisted lead.

Crispin windmilled his arms, trying to keep his balance. He stared at the window's suddenly gaping hole. That would do.

He closed his eyes, gave in to faith, and hurled himself through.

18

CRISPIN FELL A LONG time, or so it seemed. A belly-churning ride toward the unknown. He did not know whether a grassy square awaited or a stone courtyard. Either way it was a long drop and likely to hurt.

He struck the thorny bushes right away like many sharp knives pricking his skin through the coat. It broke his initial fall, but then he continued his momentum through the cracking branches and pointed twigs. The sounds of snapping wood were only slightly louder than his own grunts.

He hit the ground on his shoulder, heard a crack, and exhaled with a wave of pain. He had a feeling the bone had just dislocated. As much as he wanted to lie on the ground and moan out his suffering, he knew he didn't have time for it.

Rolling to his feet, he assessed his surroundings. Still within the walls of the palace, he knew he had to get out at once. Oh for a sword! A glance at the walls made his sore shoulder twinge. Never mind the sword. Wings would be better appreciated about now.

Holding his sore arm, he pushed forward and trotted along the wall's perimeter. With a groan, he knew he'd have to climb.

The palace grounds meandered. It wouldn't be an easy thing to simply scale the wall and be out into London. Whose courtyard was this beyond the wall? What did it matter? He just needed to rest for a while. He was getting dizzy and slightly dazed. He needed to find someplace safe and quickly. Crispin took a breath and found that the pain in his shoulder made it difficult to draw a deep one. Maybe staying in the palace was the best course. They certainly wouldn't suspect he'd be fool enough to remain.

A tree near the wall offered a good place to climb, but it wasn't a nice gnarled oak to give plenty of easy footholds. It was a tall, thin larch with a gangly arm thrown over the wall, a branch barely thick enough for a man's weight.

No time to debate it.

Crispin hugged the tree and clenched his teeth. His shoulder was definitely misaligned. Nothing he could do about it. It was climb or die. He raised his knees and shimmied carefully up the rough bark. He felt as if he were traveling up an inch at a time. There was no telling when his pursuers would appear and he wanted the chance to get over the wall before they made it to the courtyard. If they didn't know what direction he'd gone he'd have a better chance to get away clean.

At last. He reached the limb hanging over the wall. He maneuvered toward it and tried to swing his leg over. His shoulder screamed its reluctance. He dug into the bark with his fingernails, tightened his arms around the limb and dragged his body forward, inch by inch, until he could open his eyes through the pain and look down. He would chuckle if he had the strength. "Out on a limb as usual," he muttered. Below was the gravel, mud, and grass of another courtyard, but it was a long way down. The wall was covered in thick ivy. Their bright green leaves shone silver in the dying light. If he could get to the wall itself, he might be able to slide down the ivy, alleviating a lot of pain. It was worth a try.

He'd have to fall just right. *And what are the chances of that?* Not much had gone right this evening, except he did stop the assassination. But what of tomorrow? He'd never be able to get into the palace again. In fact, after tonight, it might not be possible to stay in London at all.

He stuffed that thought away for another time. If he dwelled on it, he might give up altogether and he certainly wasn't prepared to do that now.

Crispin drew a long breath and assessed the wall. He wiggled to the edge of the limb, looked down, and let his body peel over the side. His feet hit the wall first and then his knees collapsed under him. He rolled in the wrong direction, tearing off large swaths of ivy, and then managed to right himself and slid down through the foliage, bouncing off the last bit near the ground. He tumbled into the quiet courtyard and saw that it ran along Saint Stephen's chapel and the palace. He lay propped against the wall. With a shudder, he realized he was in the same pose as the French courier shot with a deadly arrow two days ago, but there was little he could do. He had to get his breath back before he could rise.

He listened. No sound. No shouts or running feet. He was safe for the moment but knew it wouldn't last.

Crispin pushed himself up the wall and stood, panting. His shoulder was bad. Something would have to be done soon, but first things first. He ran along the long courtyard and finally slowed when he reached another wall. He didn't think he had the strength to climb another wall. He looked up at the apartments instead, saw a gentle light through the tall windows, and staggered toward them.

IT WAS POSSIBLE CRISPIN slept only a few minutes. It was also possible he slept for a few hours. He wasn't certain when he opened his eyes. Huddled in a dark corner beneath the shadow of a chessboard, Crispin stared at the darkened window. Shards of moonlight slid across the panes, and these were only visible riding on the brief slant of rain pelting the obsidian-dark glass. The room seemed familiar but his hazy mind would not supply an answer.

The rolling ache in his shoulder told him not to move. His mouth felt dry. He spied a flagon sitting on a tray, its belly lit by a single candle and the glow of embers in the hearth that did little to warm him. His cloak had been left behind in Onslow's kitchens. He supposed many a day would pass before he could fetch it, if ever he could. He'd have to make due with the short shoulder cape and hood.

A step. He cringed into the darkness. The door opened and a figure entered. Crispin couldn't tell who it was in the gloom and he waited until the figure approached the fire, picked up a poker, and jammed it into the wood, stirring the coals to flames.

Without a sound Crispin rose and stood behind him. He hated like hell to do it, but he drew his dagger and pressed the tip to the small of the man's back.

"Don't turn around."

The figure tensed. Crispin could tell the man wanted to swing out with his arm. He saw the arm curve, the fingers curl into a fist.

"You're a dead man," whispered the man.

"Yes. I've lived under a sentence of death for seven years now."

The man almost turned.

"Don't!"

And then Crispin noticed too late that familiar profile.

With a gasp, Crispin dropped the hand with the dagger and sheathed the weapon. He stepped back and bowed. "Your grace."

Lancaster turned and glowered. Crispin slumped or tried to, but his shoulder caused him to yelp and he staggered back.

Lancaster's glower turned to something else. "You're hurt."

"My shoulder. Dislocated it." He fetched up against the wall.

"I can fix it."

Crispin's eyes met his and stayed there. Neither man moved. It was a common enough battle wound for a knight. Tumbled from one's horse, a knight was lucky to have only dislocated a shoulder joint.

Lancaster's bearded jaw slid. His teeth gleamed in a grimace below the mustache. No doubt, he liked this situation as much as Crispin.

The pain and dizziness made it difficult for Crispin to go on, and if run he must, he had to fix his shoulder. He nodded to Lancaster and the duke moved forward and took his arm.

"This one?"

Crispin nodded again.

"It's going to hurt. And might I say, you deserve what you are going to get for putting a knife to my back."

"Forgive me, my lord."

Lancaster sneered. "Brace yourself."

Crispin straightened, forced his back against the wall. Lancaster propped his foot to the plaster wall, took hold of Crispin's arm with one hand and his wrist with the other. "Ready?"

"Do it."

Lancaster yanked. Farther . . . farther . . . until they both heard a pop. It hurt like hell, but the relief was instant, except for a radiating ache across his back and chest. Crispin resisted the urge to roll his shoulder.

"Much thanks," he grunted. He leaned against the wall.

Lancaster released him and stepped back. "What the hell are you doing here at court?"

Crispin almost chuckled. The breath he blew out nearly rumbled itself into an ironic snigger, but too much sourness wore it away. "On my honor—that is, whatever you may value of what my honor once was—I did not try to murder his Majesty. In point of fact, I stopped it. The assassin is still at large."

Lancaster's shoulders relaxed, but his pacing and posture showed anxiety still stiffening his body. "Much evidence to the contrary."

"Evidence?"

Lancaster bore down on him. "God's wounds, Crispin! You had no business being at court, and you had the cursed bow in your hand! Did you think that little detail could be overlooked?"

Crispin ran his dirty fingers through his sweat-damp hair. "I know it looks bad—"

"*Bad?* Catastrophic!"

"There's little to be done now. My objective is to leave the palace. Alive."

"You will have to take your chances with the king's men."

"I have no intention of being turned over to the guards. Unless that is *your* intention."

"I haven't decided. I haven't yet reckoned why you are here in my chamber. Am I required to rescue you? How many times must I do so?"

Crispin tried to smile. "Seventy times seven."

"Don't be flippant."

"Your grace, if you surrender me, I will most certainly be tortured."

Lancaster heaved a sigh and turned toward the fire. He scowled into it. "I know that."

Crispin followed him to the fire and stood behind his back. "Then you also know I will have nothing to confess."

"Yes. I know that, too."

"And then I will die."

"Yes."

Crispin spat an ungrateful chuckle. "Forgive me, your grace, but so far, your logic escapes me."

"I cannot be seen with you. Especially today of all days. In case you haven't noticed, you are accused of high treason and murder. I stood up for you once when you were guilty, but not again."

Crispin walked to the other end of the hearth and stared into the flames. His voice was flat. "I see. Of course, this time I am *not* guilty." He bared his teeth. "Miles Aleyn is the assassin. Are you surprised to hear it?"

Lancaster made no sound, so Crispin turned to look at him. The duke's face maintained its glower. His dark beard and mustache framed his tightened lips. His bushy brows arched over his eyes with all the menace of a demon's claws. "Strangely," he said, voice quietly controlled, "I am not."

Indeed. "I have more to say," said Crispin. He reached into his pouch and tossed the arrow pieces to the floor.

Lancaster stared at them. The once smooth feathers were now crushed and twisted. "What's this?"

"Portions of arrows that have been involved in several misdeeds. One was found in a dead French courier. Another tried to kill me, and another an innocent scullion. I've no doubt that if the arrow that tried to kill the king were pulled from the throne it would match these others."

"So. What do these events have in common?"

"Nothing. Except these arrows. They belong to you."

Lancaster looked up at Crispin. He didn't growl or bellow as Crispin expected. In fact, he didn't act in any way Crispin remembered from long ago. He merely blinked, dropped his gaze from Crispin's, and stared into the hearth. The glow trembled yellow light across his craggy features and velvet cotehardie. "What is on your mind, Crispin?"

Crispin suddenly felt exhausted. The fire in his blood that had propelled him up the tapestry and out the window was ebbing. He felt no strength left in his limbs. "What is on my mind?" He wiped the sweat from his face and let his hand drop to his side. *Sweet Jesu. Every horror is on my mind.* "I wonder if I may ask a question."

"You should take care, you know. Tonight alone you have been caught with a weapon of assassination and put a knife to my back. What next?"

"My lord, I know that time can change a man. Change him in ways no one would ever expect."

"Yes," said Lancaster slowly. "I expect it could. Circumstances, too, can change a man."

"Make him different. Send him in different directions."

"Yes."

Crispin heaved a sigh. "And so I ask you, your grace, why were your arrows used so heinously in the last few days?"

"What proof have you that those arrows are mine?"

What indeed? The maker was now dead. And who would need to silence him? Who but a man hiding something from the light of day? "The proof is dead along with Master Peale. But he did identify them to me. Much good that is."

Lancaster turned. His dark eyes revealed nothing. No spark. Not a twinkle. His lips twisted slightly and then parted. His voice was dangerous. "Do you dare accuse me, Guest? *Do* you?"

The sickening feeling in the center of Crispin's gut throbbed. "I only know what I know, your grace. That those arrows are yours. That Miles Aleyn was hired by an unknown person seven years ago to plot against the king and probably hired by the same man today. That these arrows killed and tried to kill. And that Edward Peale is dead."

"If that is all you know, then it is wiser to keep silent on the subject."

"Your grace—"

"*Do you have a death wish!*" Lancaster fisted the hilt of his dagger but kept it sheathed. "Is it your desire to be slain here and now in my chamber? Who would accuse me then? An assassin killed? A man witnessed by all the court holding the foul murder weapon? I will be a hero. What's to stop me, Master Guest?"

Crispin straightened. "Nothing. You may do what you wish, my lord. I am at your mercy. I only want to know if we are opposing forces. I do not desire it. You know how I feel."

"And you know me not! Get out, before I take a sword to you."

"I made an oath to you once. I swore to be your man until my death. I have never foresworn that. But know this: I will not turn myself in. I will unmask the assassin—*and* his associates—and clear myself. To do that, I've got to escape this palace. I know you will not help me, but will you at least let me leave without raising the alarm?"

"I will give you a quarter hour lead."

Crispin stood as he was, back to the wall, and stared in disbelief at the man. He wanted to remind Lancaster how he'd served him as a household page all the young years of his childhood, his adolescent years as a squire, and when he was eighteen how the duke had made him a knight, dubbing him with his own sword.

But he couldn't. It wasn't because his throat was too warm and thick. He just wouldn't say the words. He glanced at the floor instead and clenched his jaw.

Lancaster closed his eyes and raised his fist to his mouth, sliding the back of his hand over his lips. After a long silence he said, "You'll never make it over the wall. It's a fifteen-foot drop. There is a way out that few know of. A secret way."

Crispin raised his eyes.

"It is still used on occasion. It might be guarded."

"Where?"

Lancaster explained how to get to it, how to avoid the guards. Crispin understood.

"Can you make it from here?"

"Yes."

"Then go."

Crispin turned to leave.

Lancaster took a step, hesitated, stopped. "I hope you can prove your innocence. It's going to take a great deal."

"I will throw the assassin at the king's feet myself."

Lancaster raised a brow. "Indeed. It will take that. Are you up to it?"

Crispin nodded but didn't look at Lancaster. He couldn't afford to. "Whatever it takes."

Crispin stared out the window he had pried open, out to the rain-wet courtyard. He squeezed himself through over the sill and dropped with a splatter onto the muddy grass and stayed in a crouched position, which did nothing for the state of his shoulder. When all seemed clear, he dashed for the bushes along the palace walls and made his way to the west corner. Lancaster said there was a secret door in the garden wall that led to a long passage that let out to the wharves.

Crispin hoped it was true.

The rain steadied, drumming his head until his hair hung like moss to his scalp. He dared not obscure his view by raising his hood. After slogging through the muddy yard and sodden foliage, he neared the place Lancaster said he should explore and he thrust his hands forward searching for the wall. The darkness had fallen suddenly, like a cord cut in the heavens. He swore an oath when his fingers smashed against the hard stone. His hands searched, muddy, slimy from the walls and God-knows-what. Then he felt the edges, found the secret latch, and sent up a quick prayer of thanks when it soundlessly opened.

He slipped through and trotted a long way down an extended passageway. The smell of the wharves gave away his location and he stepped out into a back alley. The odor of rotting fish and sewage assailed him, but he thought it never smelled as sweet.

Crispin ducked into the street and jogged down the slick cobblestones. He saw the Thames ripple through flashes of torchlight and slanted rain, and he hurried along the river back to London. He only hoped he could make it there before the king's men.

19

"JACK!" CRISPIN THREW OPEN the door. The room was dark except for the faint glow of the peat embers in the hearth. "Jack." He heard a yawn and fell on the sleepy boy in the hay. "Jack. You're still here."

"Aye, Master. 'Course I am. What's amiss?"

"You've got to get up now. We're going to the Boar's Tusk."

"I ain't thirsty, Master. I'm just weary." He tried to lay back down but Crispin yanked him to his feet.

"I said get up! There's no time to waste. It's not safe here."

"Not safe? 'Slud. What you got yourself into, Master?"

Crispin started to light a candle but then thought better of it. "I went to Westminster Palace to try to stop an attempt on the king's life."

"And did you?" Jack was fully awake now and pulled on his cloak.

"Well . . . in a manner of speaking. I mean, I did stop it, but—"

Jack grabbed the sore arm and Crispin winced. "You're hurt. What's happened?"

"I got myself accused of the assassination attempt. And now I'm on the run. So if you don't mind, make haste!"

Jack threw his arm across the doorway to block Crispin. "Wait. You mean to tell me you got yourself blamed for trying to kill the king? Did anyone see you?"

Crispin tried not to look at Jack. "Did anyone see me? Only all of court." Crispin made a halfhearted attempt at a laugh. "It doesn't look good, Jack. We must leave."

Jack raised his hands and made a plaintive plea to the heavens. "I leave you alone for a few hours—"

"We must go!"

"Wait! What about the Crown o' Thorns?"

Crispin's glance darted toward the corner. "God's blood!" He stomped to the hay pile and freed the wooden box. He cast open the lid, pulled out the gold box and opened it. His fingers touched the Crown and he yanked it out and looked at it. "Where was your invincibility tonight?" he accused. He stood with it a moment, clutching it in his hands. What was the purpose of holding on to this any longer? Well, it would certainly do Crispin no good anymore, but there was always Jack. If Jack took this to court, perhaps he would get a reward. No, no. Better he take it to the sheriff when he could. The sheriff would surely realize that Jack was no marksman with a bow. Wynchecombe *might* have the bollocks to defend the boy, but then again . . . Crispin ran a hand up his face. He couldn't think. His shoulder still pained him, still muddled his mind. Only one thing was clear. He had to keep the Crown safe until he could let someone know where it was.

He glanced at the hearth and strode to it. He leaned down and, braced against the heat, he reached up inside the chimney as high as he could and tucked it on the smoke shelf.

Done, he made for the door.

"What of the boxes?" Jack pointed to the courier boxes in the hay.

"Cover them up again and hope for the best. Then come on."

He didn't wait for Jack. He knew the boy would catch up. Crispin rambled down the steps and onto the street. It was past curfew but it didn't matter. His long strides took him quickly to Gutter Lane and even as he turned the corner Jack drew up beside him. He expected a smile on the boy's normally cheerful face, but those ginger brows were instead wrinkled over worried eyes.

Crispin knocked on the tavern's door and a sleepy Ned answered. "Master Crispin, it's far past curfew."

"I know it, Ned, but we need to come in. I must talk with Gilbert."

Ned had already shuffled out of the way, his hair more disarrayed than usual. Crispin didn't know if the boy was heading for Gilbert's room or not, so he pushed him out of the way and began shouting. "Gilbert Langton! Awake!"

Crispin turned at a sound and saw Gilbert, wearing only his knee-length chemise, leaning in a doorway. Gilbert was rubbing his tosseled head. "What's the matter? Crispin? For the love of the Virgin, what are you doing here at this hour?"

Now that sanctuary seemed close at hand Crispin was ready to crumble. He needed rest. Food could wait. "Gilbert." It felt good to drape his hand on his friend's shoulder. He really wanted to drop into his arms. "There's a lot to explain, but simply put, the king's men are after me. I need a place to hide out for a few days until I can get out of London."

"Out of London?" Gilbert was now fully awake. He dragged Crispin by the arm and hurried him down the stairs into the wine mews. Ned followed with a candle. It barely lit the big bellies of sweating casks, a stone floor, a table, two chairs, and a cot the scullion sisters recently shared. "Crispin! What have you done?"

"I've done nothing but try to save the king, and it's got me only trials and evils!" He slammed his fist to the wall. "I saved him! And now I am blamed for trying to kill him myself!"

Gilbert looked at Jack, whose pale face had nothing to offer. "We need wine." Gilbert found a jug and put it under a spigot. "No need for straws, lads. Jack, fetch the bowls. One for each of us."

Crispin sank to the chair and put his head in his hands. Ned stood warily next to the other chair as Gilbert sat. Jack offered the bowls and Gilbert filled them, Crispin's first. They all drank silently until Crispin shook his head and grasped the bowl with both hands. "I've gotten myself into a right fix this time. I truly do not know how I am to come out of it alive."

"The trick is," said Gilbert, "to find the real assassin."

"I can't do that if I'm not at court." Crispin gulped the wine and set the bowl down again. Gilbert refilled it and he watched the alluring flicker of ruby red and yellow candlelight play against the sides of the clay bowl.

Gilbert drank his wine. "The king has it in for you. Always has. Probably jealous of you and Lancaster. After all, a man can tell the difference between fawning and true affection."

Crispin rubbed his chin, feeling the stubble. He looked up into the shadowy faces of Jack, Ned, and Gilbert. "I can't think anymore tonight. Let me rest. But Gilbert, you must keep watch. The sheriff may come here looking for me."

ONCE NED AND GILBERT left them alone, Jack settled Crispin on the cot, and as soon as he hit the straw he lost track of Jack and everything else.

Until the sound of men shouting awoke him.

He scrambled out of bed. His knife was in his hand and he looked up the stairs where Jack pressed his ear to the door. He motioned down to Crispin to be quiet and hide.

Crispin cast about for a reasonable hiding place. Behind the large tun cask. A tight fit with his nose pressed against the damp wood. His nostrils filled with the smell of must and old wine.

Wynchecombe's voice trembled the rafters. "I know he's here!" He crashed through the door sending Jack tumbling down several steps. Crispin squeezed his dagger hilt. If anything happened to the boy because of him . . .

"Bring a candle," bellowed the sheriff.

One of the sheriff's men thrust a candle at him. He took it and held it aloft. "Ah, Jack Tucker. Where the lapdog is, the master is close at hand."

"No, my good lord. I don't know where Master Crispin is. What is all this about?"

"Get out of my way."

Crispin heard a slap. He held his breath, ready to pounce.

The sheriff's heavy footfalls thundered down the steps. He paused at the bottom and then silence.

It had been folly coming to the Boar's Tusk. Now Crispin endangered all those he loved. He should have taken his chances on the Shambles or simply gotten out of London completely. Of course it was all too late. What was the use in hiding? There was no way out of the cellar and Wynchecombe was going to catch him. It was over.

The sheriff blew a long breath through his nose. "Go out to the tavern and wait for me." He called this up the stairs, Crispin assumed to his men.

"My Lord Sheriff? And leave you alone with a desperate criminal?"

"He can't get out except up the stairs. Leave me, I say."

Crispin listened to the sound of the men's retreating footsteps until they finally disappeared.

"Jack," said the sheriff, his voice low and slick. "Close the door."

"My Lord Sheriff, I'm telling you—"

"Close the damn door!"

Jack's miserable steps trudged slowly upward and then the door clicked closed. "He's not here, my lord," repeated Jack in a desperate voice.

Wynchecombe didn't reply. His echoing steps made a slow meander. The flat of his boots crunched damply on the stone floor. "Crispin." His voice echoed hollowly. Each cask tossed the sound back to Crispin.

"Oh Crispin. I know you're here. Best come out and talk to me. It's your only and last chance."

Crispin didn't think he could stomach being thrown into prison again. And he did not relish the idea of more torture. This time, they would devise something better, something more lingering. And then his execution was bound to be long and agonizing. Perhaps he could use the sheriff as a hostage. It was worth a try.

Crispin squeezed out of his hiding place and stepped before the sheriff. The candle in Wynchecombe's hand lit his face with enough malevolent light to sharpen his features to demonic proportions.

"Well, well. Here he stands." The sheriff laid his hand on his sword pommel, seemed to consider, and let his hand fall back. "A merry chase, but now it is done."

"You have something to say to me, Wynchecombe?"

He shook his head and chuckled. "Must I constantly remind you, Crispin, that you must address me as 'my Lord Sheriff'? Why is that so difficult to remember?"

"I have no time for games. If you've come to arrest me I warn you. I won't go quietly."

"I didn't expect that you would. I will be happy to see you in gaol again where you belong and to collect the reward for your capture." He smiled. The candlelight caught it. His teeth glowed like bones. "Give me a good reason why I shouldn't."

Crispin glanced down at his hand, and turned the dagger in the candlelight.

Wynchecombe looked at it, too. "Are you going to use that?"

Crispin tightened his hold. "I haven't decided yet."

Wynchecombe's smile flattened. "I'm still waiting for a reason."

Crispin tried, as he had tried many times before, to discern the man behind those dark eyes. Wynchecombe was greedy, self-important, vicious, cruel, and ambitious. But his dealings with Crispin had been fair, tempered, of course, by Wynchecombe's threats and imperious style.

The sheriff seemed to be offering him a chance—whatever that chance was. His other options didn't look so good.

Crispin took a breath. "I can't bribe you. You know that."

"Intimately."

"All I have is our history. We've known each other for a full year. I've helped you more often than not, surely you recall that. Little compensation have I had for it. You usually garnered the credit for work I did—"

Wynchecombe canted forward. "There's no need to go into that, is there?"

"You know I didn't do this, Lord Sheriff."

"I know no such thing. I was there, after all. The bow was in your hand. So many witnesses."

"And none of them saw what truly happened."

"Now you weave tales. How can you possibly dispute the testimony of so many eyes? Even if *you* do not, *I* see the writing on the walls."

"I didn't do it."

"So says the condemned man. I've heard it so many times before."

Crispin shook his head. "After all this time, you haven't a sense of me?"

Wynchecombe opened his mouth to speak but held it in check. He looked around the dark room as if for the first time.

Crispin moved his fingers over the knife's handle. "Simon . . . you can't be that much of a bastard."

"What kind of bastard I am depends on you. No, you're as enigmatic as they come, Guest. You wallow in it. Maybe you tried to kill the king and maybe you didn't. It would still be a prize for me to bring you in, guilty or not."

Crispin glanced at Jack. His face was pasted with an expression of terror, marking it white and longer than usual.

"You know I would never have a chance to prove my innocence. I'm a dead man the moment I walk back into court."

"You didn't let me finish." Wynchecombe sauntered toward the tun and kept a careful eye on Crispin's movements. Crispin followed the sheriff's progress and kept his knife drawn but lowered.

The sheriff sneered and sniffed the spilled wine dripping from the spigot.

"I was going to say," said Wynchecombe, turning toward Crispin, "that though you are a great prize, so is the Crown of Thorns. I think I am in a good bargaining position now. I do not think it will cost me the usual to get it from you. Will it?"

"Are you that certain I have it?"

Wynchecombe laughed. "Now I *am* certain. Come, Crispin. Is this relic worth your life?"

"Will you help me bring the true culprit to justice?"

"Bring me the Crown and I'll consider it."

"I don't have time for you to consider it. Yes or no?"

Wynchecombe chuckled and nodded. "Very well. Have it your way. Get me the Crown and I will forget I saw you. *And* look for the culprit."

"I know the criminal. It is Miles Aleyn, the king's Captain of the Archers."

Wynchecombe raised a brow. "Indeed. Can you prove it?"

Crispin made a sound very like a growl. "No."

The sheriff looked up the stairs. Jack had pulled his knife and was breathing hard. He glared at the sheriff murderously. "Then it won't be easy. How about that Crown, then. Get it."

"You'll let me go?"

"I'll have to, won't I? Take your mastiff with you before he hurts himself."

"What about your own dogs? I don't want to be let free only to be cornered by one of those heroes up there."

Wynchecombe was still smiling. "You there. Tucker. Tell my man I want to see him."

Jack hesitated and looked to Crispin. Crispin nodded for him to obey and Jack opened the door and went through it.

"You'd better hide again, Master Guest," said the sheriff.

Crispin saw the sparse light from the open door illuminate the first bit of stairs. Wynchecombe's smile galled but he had little choice. Reluctantly, he slid in behind the tun cask again—*hiding like a rat*, he thought—just as the sheriff's man appeared at the top of the stairs.

"My lord?" he said.

"There's nothing here. You men go along back to Newgate. I want to talk to the innkeeper a bit longer."

"He'll await you here, my lord."

The man left and Crispin peered out of his hole. Jack stood in the doorway, one half of him lit by the firelight in the tavern, and half in the darkness of the cellar. He watched until every man left before he nodded to Crispin that it had been done.

Crispin crept back out from the shadows, stared at Wynchecombe, and reluctantly sheathed his knife. "I thank you, Lord Sheriff. Trust can be an uneasy thing."

"I never said I trusted you. I still have the upper hand. If you don't return with that Crown, your precious innkeeper and his wife will be hauled to prison on the charge of treason." Wynchecombe opened his full-toothed smile again. "No risk. You see, I *do* have a sense of you." His smiled fell away. "Make haste. I weary of this."

Loathsome bastard. Crispin edged past the sheriff, expecting like some unruly schoolboy to receive a blow, and climbed the stairs. "Come along, Jack."

Crispin stared at the silent Gilbert and Eleanor sitting in the near darkness of the tavern hall, at Ned who sat on a stool by the door and looked back at Crispin as if he were the Savior himself. *Nothing like it.* If anything, he was the portent of doom to them all.

He cast his feelings of dread aside, concentrating instead on his mission. Crispin stood beside the tavern door and nodded for Jack to open it. He saw Jack step into the moonlit street and look carefully down one way and then the other. When his pale face turned back to Crispin, he gave a solemn nod.

Crispin slid carefully out the door and shivered in the cold. He regretted for the thousandth time his lost cloak, but there was nothing to be done about it. He was grateful, however, for the dark, for there would be fewer prying eyes when shutters were closed and shadows hid him.

He took the lead of Jack and trotted ahead, with Jack trying to keep up beside him. Neither said a word. Nothing needed to be said. They both knew the situation well. Handing over the Crown now was a small price to pay for the lives of his friends. He hoped it might spare his as well.

The moonlight lit the way, shining the muddy street like a ribboning beacon. They turned at Cheapside and followed it to where it became the Shambles. Passing the quiet shops on the dark street, Crispin suddenly felt more alone than he had for a long time. The poulterer who shouldered Martin's tinker shop was shut up and silent. Not even the soft sound of clucking could be heard from its depths as they passed. Martin's window, too, was shuttered and barred, though a splinter of light lined the sill where a candle no doubt rested.

Crispin nabbed the key from his pouch. He crept as silently up the stairs as he could, cautious about the creaking step. Jack was silent behind him. If there was anything the boy excelled at, it was stealth.

He brought the key forward, but it slipped from his fingers and fell with a tinkling clunk. He turned to Jack with a wince and they both froze, waiting for the shadows to pounce upon them. When nothing happened, he dropped to the floor with a whispered oath, and felt with his hands along the darkened wooden landing until he touched metal. Rising and rubbing his aching shoulder, he thrust the key in the lock at last and pulled open his door.

One glance at the corner and the pile of straw told him the reliquary lay undisturbed. He went directly to the hearth. The fire had burned down to ash but was still warm. He dropped to one knee and reached up into the fire box. His fingers ran along the shelf, and then he leaned into the hearth, twisting, reaching, the peat embers cooking his back and choking him with a puff of smoke and a swirl of ash. His fingers scrabbled as the panic slowly rose in his gut.

No use. The Crown was gone.

20

"COULD IT HAVE BURNT up?" Jack pushed Crispin aside and searched for himself. He didn't notice when his cloak caught fire.

Crispin hauled Jack from the hearth and stamped out the flames. "It won't do anyone any good to set yourself afire." He sat back on the floor and rested his chin on his fist. "Someone has taken it. Who knew that the Crown of Thorns was hidden here?"

"You. Me. Them wenches. The sheriff. Who else?"

"Who else? No one. Who could have guessed?"

Jack jumped to his feet. "Abbot Nicholas! He guessed."

"Yes, but he would not have stolen it, nor sent anyone. Who else? Help me, Jack."

"I can't—no one else knew of it. Neither Master Gilbert nor Mistress Eleanor would guess its hiding place."

"True. It was hidden. It would have to take a desperate man— Desperate *men*. God's blood."

Crispin rose and made for the door, then stopped. If he delayed by investigating his hunch, Gilbert and Eleanor would be in danger. "Jack, I need you to go to the King's Head."

"What for?"

"The Frenchmen are staying there. I need you to follow them. It may already be too late."

"Right, Master. Did they take the Crown?"

"It is a wild hunch. But their mysterious fourth companion may very well have told them about me. They would have come here at least to talk to me and discovered the Crown for themselves. At least it is a possibility I cannot afford to leave alone. Keep a close eye on them, Jack. Don't let them out of your sight."

"Where will you be?"

Crispin looked around his small room. He wondered if he would ever see it again. "With any luck, I won't be in Newgate. And I shan't stay at the Boar's Tusk. That's already caused too much trouble." He ran his thumb over his knife pommel, polishing it smooth. "Find me at the Thistle." Jack made to leave but Crispin grabbed his shoulder. "Jack, if I am arrested, don't stay here. Go. Leave London."

Jack's face was as sorrowful a mask as Crispin had ever seen. He bit the inside of his cheek to keep his own emotions in check.

"Leave London? Where would I go?"

"I don't know. You're a smart lad. You'd get by."

"But Master, I'd never leave you."

"Jack, if I'm arrested there will be very little left to leave. You'd need to fend for yourself."

"But I'd stand by you. I'd not have you die alone." Jack's eyes welled. Two large tears rolled down his dirty cheeks.

Crispin closed his eyes and cursed. "Don't, Jack. We haven't got time. Just promise me you'll leave London. That's a command!"

"I won't make that promise!" He shook himself free of Crispin's hand and threw himself down the steps at a run.

Crispin swiped at his eyes once with the back of his hand before he turned to the room with a trembling breath. He gathered the courier bag with its two boxes and hauled the strap over his shoulder. He rushed down the steps, hoping to see Jack one last time, but the boy was too swift. There was no one and nothing on the blue-gray street but the silver shimmer of moonlight on puddles.

Crispin wondered if a life of sin had led to this moment. He wasn't much of a praying man. In fact, his prayers more often than not became blaspheming tirades to the Almighty. But as he glanced skyward, thinking about what had been in the box slung over his shoulder, he again asked, as he had asked so many times before, "Why me?"

Why had he stepped into trouble time and time again? Always, he thought he was doing right when it was always so wrong. Hadn't he tried to help Richard this time? Was his intent not good enough, his heart not pure enough?

He stopped when he turned the corner and spied the Boar's Tusk. The building sat quietly in the gloom, its bright windows dark except for the faint glow of candle and hearth behind the shutters. He swallowed a lump in his throat. "Well, I've had a good run. I can't say I won the race, but neither did I lose it."

He adjusted the courier bag and headed straight for the door. It wasn't barred and so he opened it. Four white faces turned to him. The only one who stood was Wynchecombe.

"Ah!" said the sheriff. He gestured to the table and Crispin brought the bag over and put it down where Wynchecombe pointed.

"My Lord Sheriff, there is something I need to tell you."

"Oh?" Wynchecombe was distracted by the boxes, especially the gold one. He set it on the table and put his hand on the lid.

Crispin rested his hand over Wynchecombe's. The sheriff looked up with a quizzical expression. "My Lord, this is the courier box—intact as you see it. But the Crown, alas, is gone."

"What?" He flung the lid open and looked inside. He drew his dagger and grabbed Crispin's shoulder cape. "What game do you play, Guest?"

"No game. It is gone. Stolen."

"You're hiding it."

"No, my lord. On my honor."

"Honor?" He threw Crispin back. "You have none! I'm a fool to have trusted you."

"I would never sacrifice my friends. Take me, if you must, but for the love of the Holy Rood, do not hurt these innocent people."

The sheriff glared at Crispin, turned to the white-faced Gilbert, to Eleanor who clutched Gilbert's arm, to Ned who sucked on his fingers.

"Where's the cutpurse?"

"He hasn't got it. I swear by our Lady."

"Where is he?"

"I sent him away. If I couldn't save myself—"

"You're the fine nobleman, aren't you?"

"I came back, didn't I?" Crispin thrust his chin defiantly, perhaps his last act of defiance.

Wynchecombe cocked his head and pursed his lips. He swiveled toward the others. "I knew you'd be back."

"Then you also know I'm not lying. I am at your mercy. You know that, too. To come back meant I'd be walking to the gallows myself."

"Crispin." He nearly purred it. He shook his head.

Damn the man! The sheriff wanted to arrest him. Truly wanted to see him hang . . . Or *did* he?

The sheriff continued shaking his head until his smile turned to a frustrated sneer. "You are the damnedest man I ever met!" He paced, stood before the fire, paced again, then stopped before Crispin and aimed his finger at him. "You *will* find that Crown of Thorns for me. You will return it only to me. Understand?" He looked once at Gilbert and Eleanor. "I will do what I can on this other matter, but I make no guarantees."

Crispin's heart beat a step faster. "You will not pursue me?"

"No. But remember"—he gestured with his head toward the others—"I know where these live."

21

THE THISTLE WAS DARK. Crispin hovered under the eaves, considered bedding down in the stable, but decided against it.

Then he heard it. A step. He saw a figure moving among the shadows and he pressed against the wall. The short figure moved along the edges much like a rat would do and Crispin lowered his hand from his dagger. He crouched and slid along the wall right behind the shadow and when they both reached the darkest corner, Crispin said, "Greetings, Lenny."

Lenny jumped. His arms flailed and his cloak blew out. He looked like a waterlogged bat falling from a belfry.

"Master Crispin!" His hushed whisper cut across the space between them in a spitting cloud of fog. He pressed his hand to his heart. "I nearly shat m'self. What by blessed Christ are you doing?"

"Trying to stay alive." He leaned against the wall and looked up into the drizzling sky. The moon had disappeared behind a ragged sea of clouds.

"Oh, aye. I heard. You ain't a safe man to be hard by, beggin' your pardon." Lenny turned to go, but Crispin touched his arm.

"Don't discount me yet. I haven't quite given up."

"Your trouble is you don't know when to surrender."

Crispin smiled for the first time that night. "No."

"Now take me, for instance. When you told me to stop me thieving ways, I give it up, now didn't I?"

"Was this before or after I had you arrested? Three times."

Lenny chuckled and rubbed the spot where an ear had been. "Well, I take a bit o' convincing."

"And your being out well after curfew. That couldn't mean anything sinister, could it?"

"'Course not, 'course not." He waved his hand in dismissal but an object fell out of his sleeve to the ground and both he and Crispin bent to get it. Crispin was faster.

"What's this?" Crispin raised the small metal goblet into what remained of scattered moonlight.

"Oh that?" Lenny ran a hand over his rain-slick bald dome. The long, stringy hair around it hung down in straight lines like a steady drizzle. His brows wriggled, dripping rain on his cheeks. "That's a . . . that's a . . ."

"A gift?" Crispin's lopsided grin nudged his brow upward and he dropped the goblet back into Lenny's open palm. The man closed his long fingers over it and stashed it quickly within the pouch at his rope belt.

"Thank you, Master Crispin."

"Lenny, I've a favor to ask."

"Oh anything, Master Crispin. Anything at all. Old Lenny is helpful if nought else."

"Where do you live?"

"Oh, here and there."

"I know it is mostly here, near the Thistle. But where? Exactly."

Lenny pulled at his ragged cloak. "Why would you be wanting to know that, Master Crispin?"

Crispin dropped his voice even softer. "Because I need a place to stay. Somewhere the authorities will never find me."

"Oh no, Master! No, no, no." Lenny shook his head vigorously. His wet hair spun out around his head and slapped his face, sticking there. "Not nigh me. With all the world after your hide? No, no." He turned and jerked free of Crispin's grip and scurried along the wall.

"Lenny, I haven't got many more options."

The voice of the Watch suddenly sprung from the darkness. In the next alley, he called for all to be in their beds. It wouldn't be long before his lamp's light would cast its weary glow along the street and catch them. There were fines for being out past curfew, but in this part of town, the Watch was likely to arrest them, call out the hue and cry.

Crispin followed Lenny's brisk pace. "Lenny, look at the advantage you have of me. Look at the favors you can garner."

"What good are favors from a dead man?" Lenny stopped, turned to Crispin, and made an apologetic sneer. "Beggin' your pardon." He turned again and hurried.

Crispin looked back. The echoing voice of the Watch drew closer. Crispin thought he could see the beginning of the halo of light from his lamp.

"Lenny, for the love of Christ!"

"What do you hope to gain?"

"My innocence."

Lenny stopped and swiveled his head on his hunched shoulders. "Are you sayin' you *didn't* try to kill the king?"

"Yes, I am."

Lenny's look of disbelief almost made Crispin lash out at him. He grit his teeth instead and pressed against the wall. He snatched a glance back. The lamp's glow brightened the alley's entrance. The Watch approached.

"If I help you, what's to be gained?"

Crispin had only a few pence in his money pouch. Pence. All he had left in the world. "The next time I see you stealing . . . I shall look the other way." He scowled at himself. The words left a bad taste in his mouth.

"*Every* time?"

The Watch's step crunched the uneven cobblestones on the road. The lamp glowed the edge of Crispin's hair. "Yes, yes," he hissed. "Every time, then, you scoundrel."

"Well then." Lenny threw his hood up over his head. "Come along."

He ducked down and disappeared into the dark and drizzle. Crispin shot a glance back at the Watch and cursed Lenny, until the thief tugged on his wrist.

"Down here!" whispered Lenny, and Crispin saw the arch of stone set in the wall at street level.

Lenny disappeared into the blackness and Crispin dove for it. He couldn't see, but he followed the sound of Lenny's steps and descended. The air smelled damp and close, as if they were somehow under the Thames. Ridiculous. Too far away. Yet the feeling of cramped closeness remained. He raised his hand and felt the roof, slick with mold. It was some kind of tunnel. Some Roman construct. No wonder Lenny looked so much like a rat when he lived little better than one.

At last Lenny let out an exhale. Crispin stopped, straining his eyes to see. Flint and steel threw a bright spark into the darkness. Another, and a fluff of rags took a small flame. Lenny lit a candle to it and threw the flaming rag into the hearth. The room jumped into view, the light startling the shadows, which remained wary but black.

The room was disgusting. Dank, dark, and wet; an undercroft long abandoned because of the encroachment of the Thames seeping through its walls. Perfect for Lenny.

"Home and hearth," said Lenny, rubbing his hands briskly before the small peat fire.

Crispin considered for a moment whether it would be better spending time in one of Newgate's cells than here, and then dismissed it. This might be the lowest he might stoop, but the alternative meant a nasty death.

Crispin stood in the center of the room and stared at his surroundings, loath to touch anything.

"I've never had guests before," said Lenny. He laughed. "Guests. *Guest.* That's you, ain't it?" Laughing, he choked on his jest, leaned over, and coughed.

"Lenny, I need to sleep. Is there a place?" He looked around trying not to show his distaste.

"There's a pile of fine straw in that corner. Not too damp. You don't mind if I leave you, do you? Nighttime's the best time for me to, well, you know."

Crispin trudged toward the pile and sank into it. He waved Lenny off. He was too tired and achy to debate it. He nestled down into the straw and fell asleep with the smell of moldering grass in his nose.

"HOW ABOUT A NICE cup o' broth?"

It wasn't Jack's voice. Crispin bolted upright, his dagger in hand.

Lenny flung back. Hot broth flew into the air. The wooden bowl landed on the floor, face down. "Master Crispin! You're tight as a bowstring." He picked himself up and merely brushed the broth into his already dirty clothes. "Should have expected as much." He picked up the bowl from the floor and shuffled toward the crock on the fire. He scooped the bowl in and drew out more broth. Liquid dripped from the bowl's dirty edge.

Crispin sheathed his knife and ran his hand over his hair. "Apologies, Lenny. I forgot."

"Understandable." He handed Crispin the bowl.

Crispin took the bowl and tried not to sniff it or look at it before pressing the rim to his lips. He gulped without tasting and wiped the excess from his mouth with the back of his free hand. "Much thanks, Lenny. What is the hour?"

"Early morn. The sun ain't up yet."

Crispin pushed up from his bedding and stood, brushing bits of straw from his coat.

"The king's men are wasting no time searching for you, Master Crispin. There's a reward offered."

"Indeed." He stretched his back, careful of his tender shoulder, and walked the length of the tiny room, shaking out his stiff legs. He found a bucket of fresh water in a corner and splashed the icy liquid on his face and rubbed a finger into his mouth to brush his teeth. "A reward big enough for a man to do well, no doubt."

"Aye. A goodly sum." Lenny smiled. He rubbed his hands together, like a rodent cleaning himself.

Crispin spat on the floor and cocked an eye at the thief. "You plan to turn me in, Lenny?"

Lenny looked skyward and scratched his stubbled chin. What remained of his long greasy hair rested on his shoulders. "Now let me think. A tidy sum of gold or your festering hide? Which would you choose?"

Crispin sat on a rickety stool and balanced himself by placing his hands on his knees. "Well by God, Lenny. I think I would choose the money. Did you?"

Lenny's smile opened wider and then he guffawed. "Aw, Master Crispin! You ain't got no faith at all. You forget. I know you." He squinted over the finger he pointed at Crispin. "I've slipped through many a grasping fist, but not yours. No, sir. A man thrown down to the gutter like you. But did you stay there? Indeed not. Either God or the Devil is defending your hide." Lenny vigorously poked the fire to little avail. "If I turn you in for thirty pieces of silver I'm the one who'll hang. No, sir. You've got more lives than Lazarus. You're the cock that'll win this fight, mark me. Don't know how, mind, but I know you'll fare well. You always do, curse you."

"Why, Lenny, I'm touched."

"Don't go weepy on me. I know you. I'll not have you come back and smite me. And you would, too."

Lenny's words would be humorous if the situation weren't so dire.

Crispin stared at the floor. For the first time in a long time, he didn't know how to proceed. He wished it was Jack Tucker sitting across from him and not the bald-pated thief Lenny.

"What will you do now, Master Crispin?"

Crispin rubbed his chin. He needed a shave but it might be many a day before he got one. "I was thinking that very thing, Lenny. Right now the most important thing is to recover a certain lost item before my friends suffer further."

"Ain't the most important thing to unmask the real assassin?"

Crispin looked up. "You don't believe I did it."

"'Course not. You ain't that addlepated."

"Unfortunately, I was caught with the weapon in my hand."

Lenny tried unsuccessfully to hide his chuckle behind his hand. "Oh my. That don't go down well."

"Indeed."

Lenny sidled up to him and sat on the floor. "What is this lost item you'd be looking for? I'm good at finding things. Almost as good as you are."

Crispin dropped his face in his hands and rubbed his brow, his eyes, his nose. "Does it matter? Gilbert and Eleanor will be in danger from the sheriff if I do not recover it soon."

"Master and Mistress Langton? Oh that's a shame, that is. Getting your friends into trouble. You shouldn't aught to do that, Master Crispin. You should be more careful."

Lenny's oozing tone reminded Crispin with whom he spoke. Lenny could only be trusted so far. If at all.

Crispin stood. "I can't do anything about it lying low in this rat hole—" Crispin showed his teeth in a mordant smile. "Begging your pardon, Lenny."

Lenny smiled back. His uneven teeth were long and slightly protruding. "Aye. You'd have to go disguised, now wouldn't you. Can't walk about in that cotehardie. Don't everyone know it by now?"

Crispin ran his hand over the coat's breast, feeling where the weave had worn away. The material was very thin now, patched and repaired numerous times, its buttons chipped and cracked. "Disguised?"

Lenny fussed over the fire, prodding the peat, which only offered a meager flame and smaller heat. "'Course if you're caught, it's over for sure. King Richard has no love for you. There might be no trial. After all, you ain't no lord no more—beggin' your pardon."

Crispin paced the small room again. "A disguise is a good idea, Lenny. I might even be able to get into court."

"Oh Master Crispin. You *are* mad. You'd never make it past the guards. My, my. You've got bollocks, to be sure. Who's the guilty bastard, anyway? Some lord?"

"This isn't the toughest task I've ever had." But Crispin knew that wasn't quite the truth. His life had been in danger before, but never like this. "If I can prove this once and for all, I might be able to clear my name completely. Maybe the king will not distrust me anymore."

"You fancy you'll go back to court?"

"I've got no other choice, Lenny. It's this or leave London for good."

"What's so good about London?" Lenny grumbled. "I'd leave in a tick if I could."

"And how would you make your living?"

Lenny's scowl widened into a grin. "Aye, you got me there, Master Crispin. A wily one, you are. Where would old Lenny go, eh? Straight to the Devil!"

"Lenny, I need another favor from you."

"Another favor from old Lenny?" Lenny turned to the fire and crouched before it. His rags hung about him like a great fur cloak. "Giving you shelter, feeding you. That's more than I done for anyone, Master Crispin, and that's a fact. And only because I know you well. Even if most of our association comes from your arresting me."

"Of course I've no right asking anything more of you."

"That's the truth. I done more than a Christian should. Charity, it is."

Crispin nodded and reached into his pouch for a coin. A sharp pinprick. He yanked his hand out. A bead of blood formed on his finger. Gingerly, he reached inside again and pulled out the thorn.

"What's that, Master Crispin?"

Crispin stared at its black, sleek surface, turned it over in his hand. "Madness. Foolery." He reached into his pouch with the other hand and grasped a coin. He held it out for Lenny. "For your kindness, Lenny. And for the favor."

"Well now. Ain't that generous of you." Lenny snatched it. The coin disappeared somewhere on his person. "What favor?"

"I'd like you to find Jack Tucker. I need his help. I know the fool didn't leave London as I told him to do. But he should be nearby. Tell him to meet me at Westminster Abbey."

Crispin rubbed his fingers over the thorn. He didn't want to believe it, but his hand tingled where the thorn stuck him and he felt the growing sensation of confidence in his chest.

Crispin squinted at the man. "And Lenny. I also need to borrow your coat."

22

THE SUN SENT A puss-yellow glow into a wash of clouds, dissipating the morning shadows and leaving London to awaken into another dismal and overcast morning. Crispin trotted along the edges of the houses and shops, not looking up, but keeping his gaze concentrated on the street or on the feet of horses and passersby. Lenny's coat of rags, now resting on Crispin's shoulders, stank of sweat, mold, and decay, as if something had died within its folds.

Crispin suspected that this was entirely possible.

The last he saw of his own rust-colored cotehardie was over Lenny's hunched body. *This better be worth the sacrifice.* He didn't mind holding his breath all the way to Westminster as long as he could get there undetected.

The king's men were everywhere. They trotted down the lanes two by two. The closer Crispin got to Westminster, the more numerous they became. He forced himself to move slowly, even limp, and always, he kept his head shaded by his leather hood.

He hobbled to the alms door at Westminster Abbey and pulled the bell rope. After a few minutes, a monk appeared at the barred window. "There are no alms today, friend. Come back tomorrow."

Crispin raised his head and winked when Brother Eric's eyes widened in recognition. "The only charity I need, Brother, is to talk with the abbot."

Brother Eric took a moment to compose himself. He stretched his neck looking past the barred window before he put his key to the lock and opened the door. "Master Crispin," he said in a husky whisper. "What by blessed *Jesu* are you doing here? Do you seek sanctuary?"

"Not yet, Brother. I merely need to speak with the abbot."

"He is at Prime with the others."

"May I wait for him in his quarters?"

Crispin's aromatic coat must have finally reached Eric's senses. The monk wrinkled his nose and ran his gaze over the offending garment.

"I promise to leave the coat outside."

Eric hesitated a heartbeat longer and finally nodded. He opened the door and Crispin stepped through. He stood in the cold porch while the monk closed the door and turned the key in the lock. Crispin shrugged out of Lenny's coat, let it fall to the stone floor, and kicked it aside. A cold draught slithered along the colonnade and whirled around Crispin. He shivered and rubbed his hands up his arms. He was cold, but much relieved to be rid of that putrid coat.

He followed the silent monk through the cloister and up the steps to the abbot's lodgings. Eric opened the door for Crispin but stood aside for him to enter alone. "My Lord Abbot will be in anon, as soon as Prime is over. I must return to my duties."

"Brother." Crispin reached out and touched his dark sleeve. Eric raised his pale face to Crispin. The monk's eyes were rimmed with red from lack of sleep and his pale hair was cut in wisps on his high forehead. "I must ask you to tell an untruth should anyone inquire if you have seen me."

Eric's expressionless face brightened momentarily. "Seen who?" he said, and turned to retreat down the colonnade.

Crispin smiled and stepped over the threshold. He was grateful the room was warm as he was clad only in his chaperon hood and shirt. He stood by the fire, its soft crackle the only sound. Or did he hear the distant song of the monks chanting their devotion in the church's choir?

The peace and quiet should have pacified, but it only set his teeth on edge. He paced before the fire, glancing once at the chessboard frozen in the midst of their play, and once at the large crucifix on the opposite wall. The figure of Christ lay in shadow even as the morning light rose through the stained-glass window. Crispin ignored the crucifix at first and strolled to the chessboard. He examined the pieces, his mind jumping five moves ahead. His fingers closed over a pawn and he edged the piece toward the white king. "Your king is still in jeopardy," he whispered to the empty room. He saw the game play itself out, saw the white king fall, Crispin's black pieces surrounding it. But his gaze snagged on the black knight, superbly carved in ebony. A knight in full harness, his lance lowered, the charger reared. Compelled by its intricacies, he closed his fingers over it and raised it up for a closer look. Each detail of mail and surcote, all amazingly reproduced in miniature. He looked at the board again; at his pieces closing in on the white king. "After all the careful strategy, it is the pawn who brings down the king despite everything the knight does."

He turned the piece in his hand and noticed the pinprick on his finger. He placed the knight back on its square and raised his hand to examine the fading mark, rubbing his fingers together. He turned again to the crucifix.

The carving of the crucifix was a realistic study of agonizing death, that promise of redemption for sacrifice. The figure's arms were outstretched almost beyond endurance, the feet cruelly nailed. On his head, a carved wooden crown of thorns.

Crispin reached into his pouch and carefully felt for the large thorn. His fingers examined, smoothed, grasped the object and then let it go. "Invincible?" he murmured. "I've never felt more vulnerable."

If he couldn't find that Crown and give it to the sheriff, he dreaded to think what would happen to Gilbert and Eleanor. Lenny's mocking tone rang in his head. No, he hadn't been careful. It was the height of idiocy ever setting foot again at the Boar's Tusk. What had he been thinking?

He glared at the crucifix again. "I *need* your help," he whispered. "If those bastard Frenchmen have the Crown, then I'll never get it back, and Wynchecombe might suppose I tricked him. I will *not* have harm come to my friends!"

"Are you giving orders to God?"

Crispin whirled. The abbot stood in the entryway. Under the dark cowl his face wore a frown.

"My Lord Abbot," said Crispin with a bow.

"Crispin." The abbot tossed back his cowl and strode to the fire. He stretched his hands over the flames, turning them. "Forgive me if I do not say I am happy to see you."

"Understandable. But I had little choice in coming."

"Are you seeking sanctuary?" The abbot's voice was gentle but his expression seemed to infer he'd rather not agree to it.

Crispin stood several paces from the abbot and the fire, but he never moved closer to the hearth. He shivered. "No. I can't do what I need to do if I request sanctuary."

Nicholas aimed a reddened eye at him. "And what is it you 'need' to do?"

"Find the true assassin." The abbot's expression of doubt drew a ball of heat from Crispin's chest and up his body. He clenched his fists. "I am *not* a killer!"

"This is not what I heard."

"Forget what you heard. What do you *believe*?"

Nicholas sighed and sunk into his chair. He dragged the fur wrap over his legs. "I'm not quite certain what to think. But—" His eyes, a glossy gray, studied Crispin, his lack of cloak or coat, and finally rested their gaze on Crispin's face. "I do not believe you are a murderer."

Crispin snorted. "I'm relieved to hear it," he muttered.

"So why are you here?"

Crispin sat in the chair opposite the abbot and closed his head in his hands a moment. Had it only been yesterday that all hell had broken loose in the palace? "I think I had better tell you everything."

Nicholas settled back and clasped his hands over his chest. He lowered his lids. "I'm listening."

Crispin smiled. The abbot looked as if he were prepared to hear Crispin's confession. "Four days ago, a simpleton, a scullion, came to me confessing that she killed a man. When I reached the scene of the murder I realized she could not possibly have killed him."

Nicholas raised his head.

"The man was shot with an arrow," Crispin explained.

Nicholas nodded and eased back, though his eyes weren't as lidded.

"It happens this man was the French courier transporting a certain relic from the court of France."

Nicholas snapped opened his eyes. "The Crown of Thorns!"

"Yes. It was there. I took it."

"*You* took it? Why?"

Crispin smacked his fist in his palm. "I wanted a bargaining chit. I wanted a way back to court. I would appear clever and devoted if I could deliver the Crown into Richard's hands."

Nicholas said nothing, but his expression was a changing mask between tolerance and reproach. "Where is it now?"

"That's just it. The sheriff knows I have it. He's agreed to let me go, but in return I must give the Crown to him. But now it's been stolen from me."

Nicholas had been steadily leaning forward and now he almost rocked out of his chair. "Dear me. Do you have any suspicions as to who might have it?"

"I think the remaining French couriers stole it—or, I suppose, regained it. But now my friends are in danger—those held under house arrest by the sheriff—and the true assassin is still afoot."

"Do you know who the assassin is?"

"Yes. It is the cursed Captain of the Archers, Miles Aleyn." Crispin scowled deeply and stared at the flames. "But the most troubling aspect of it all is the arrows. Those used to kill the courier, to try to kill me, and to try to kill the king. They belonged to my Lord of Gaunt."

Nicholas popped up from his chair and paced before the fire. "This is all very troubling."

"There is something more."

"More?" The abbot swiveled toward Crispin. His brows couldn't go any higher.

"The Crown. As a jest . . . in a moment of indulgence . . . I put it on my head."

Nicholas's glance took in the crucifix behind Crispin. Crispin could not help turning as well and he strode to the object to stand below it. "Yes!" said Crispin, shaking a fist at the corpus. "I put it on my own cursed head and I've been in no end of trouble since."

Nicholas's voice washed over Crispin like a cool hand to a fevered forehead. "And what happened?"

At first he was going to tell the abbot that nothing happened. But with his eyes transfixed to the wooden carving, his lips parted, and he said instead, "I don't know. An odd sensation of confidence." He rubbed his fingers together, feeling the tips tingle. "That I could do anything, be anything."

"I see. I did hear tell of that magnificent escape of yours up the tapestry."

Crispin never shifted his gaze from the corpus's crown. "It wasn't the Crown. The effect had worn off by then."

"Are you certain?"

"Yes, dammit! I had to do it myself. No great power of God interceded to save me. I climbed the damned tapestry myself and fell out the damned window, all on my own."

"Crispin, Crispin. Why do you doubt so much? God watches over all we do. He cares for us as His children. Can you not put your faith in God, your fate in His hands?"

He shook his head. "I find it impossible to do so."

"But why? You strive to do good. Look at this holy relic that came into your hands. God is using you through the Crown."

"I know no such thing."

"Your deeds will be rewarded. Mark me."

"No good deed goes unpunished, eh, Father Abbot?" He tried to chuckle, but it came out more like a bark. Crispin thought it was due to his dry throat and he walked to the flagon for a remedy.

Crispin felt the abbot's eyes on him as he poured himself a goblet of wine. He gestured to the other goblet and Nicholas nodded. Crispin poured another, drank a dose of his own, and handed Nicholas a full cup.

The abbot took a sip and stood thoughtfully with it. "It is no accident that the Crown fell into *your* hands, Crispin. You experience its power but you are loath to believe it."

Crispin tipped up his goblet. "'It is the mark of an educated mind to be able to entertain a thought without accepting it.'"

"You quote the pagan philosophers well," said the abbot. Crispin smiled, a genuine one, and saluted with his cup. "But I find it telling, Master Guest, that you would rather quote a pagan than a holy saint."

"Very well." Crispin held up his goblet. "'O Lord, help me to be pure . . . but not yet.'"

The abbot's narrowed eyes held no humor in them. "So you know your Augustine. But did the venerable saint not also say: 'Miracles are not contrary to nature, but only contrary to what we know about nature'?"

Crispin's smile faded. He looked into the bottom of his goblet and regretfully set it aside. "I am not here to debate theology with you. I must get into the palace again."

"Crispin, no! That would be foolish, dangerous, and unwise. I must beg you to put it out of your mind."

"The Crown may be there. The murderer most assuredly is."

"Then why come to me?"

"This is the best place I knew of to come for a cassock."

"A disguise?"

"I know of no other way."

This set the monk's head wagging again. "Dangerous," he muttered. "You have no friends there. If Lancaster is implicated as you say by these arrows, then he cannot help you either. Though I cannot believe he is involved."

"It does concern me."

"You pledged yourself to him. What if it comes to a matter of him or you?"

Crispin sneered a glance at the discarded goblet. "I made an honorable oath. But not to fall into treason again. If it comes to it, I prefer to side with myself."

"Distressing," Nicholas muttered. He eased back to his chair and cupped the goblet's bowl with both hands. He stared into it thoughtfully. "The Crown of Thorns. These French couriers. It all reminds me of something."

"Oh?" Crispin wasn't listening. He pulled out his dagger and toyed with the point of the blade. He was thinking how satisfying it would be to thrust it into Miles's chest.

"It was a few years back," said the abbot, "in the early days of King Charles in the French court. I recall two French nobles were killed. Two who supported a treaty with England. Strangely, they were both killed by arrows."

"Eh? What's that?"

"Yes. By arrows. I'm afraid it was during the worst part of your difficulties a few years back."

"You mean when I was losing my knighthood."

The abbot missed the sarcasm in Crispin's tone. "An assassin slipped in to the French court, blended in, killed his targets, and slipped away just as easily."

Crispin leaned forward. "The assassin was never found?"

"No. This would seem to follow the same pattern."

"Except this one missed. He missed me and the king. Twice."

"Thanks to you."

"And he also missed the scullion."

"The one who thought she killed the Frenchman? The witless one?"

"No. The other. Her sister."

"Why would an assassin trying to kill the king waste time on a scullion?"

"Because she knows something. Saw something."

"Yes, I suppose. Poor creatures. We do sometimes think of our servants as expendable. As less important."

"But if I were killing a mere scullion . . ." Crispin lifted his eyes to look at the abbot. The hearth flames warmed the side of his face. "I wouldn't waste an arrow. I would slit her throat, something quiet and discreet. I could get as close to her as I wanted. A servant, after all, is only a menial. I can approach them at will. An arrow is a distant weapon. I should have used my dagger or a garrote."

Nicholas rubbed his neck. "You do travel in odd circles."

"So why an arrow?"

A knock sounded on the door. Crispin and Nicholas snapped to their feet, looking at one another. It could be Brother Eric, but if it were not, Crispin wanted as few people as possible to know he was there.

With a gesture, he silently told the abbot he would hide behind the window's drapery. The abbot watched him, poised over his chair. Crispin retreated once again into temporary hiding, pulling the heavy material in front of him. It smelled of incense and smoke. He watched the abbot through a sliver of space where the drapes met. Nicholas sauntered toward Crispin's goblet and tossed its excess wine into the fire. He set the cup on the sideboard, straightened his cassock, and calmly called, "Come."

A monk bowed as he entered. His face was hidden beneath his cowl. "There is a boy at the gate, my Lord Abbot. He insists on seeing you."

"A boy? Who?"

"He gives his name as Jack Tucker. But he is garbed as a beggar, my lord. He claims he is in service to a knight."

Nicholas cast a shrewd glance toward the drapery. "Send him to me, Brother Walter. I will see him."

"But my lord—"

"It is all well, Brother."

The monk bowed and left for the gate. Nicholas turned as Crispin emerged from behind the tapestry. "How did your servant know you were here?"

"I sent a message. Will you loan me that cassock, Father Abbot?"

Nicholas took a deep breath and shook his head. "Crispin, I truly fear for you this time. This is not some scoundrel on the street. This is the King of England. Already he likes you not. He needs little excuse to do you ill."

"I know. But if this is not done, I will lose everything. And I've already lost so much. I can't afford to lose more."

"Your life?"

"The least of my worries."

Nicholas trudged to his chair and wearily sat. "Of course I will give you the cassock. And I pray that all ends well for you."

Crispin scowled into the fire. "It can't get much worse."

They both turned at the knock. Crispin needed no prompting to steal behind the drapes again, but when he heard the apologetic murmurs of Jack Tucker he slipped back out.

"Jack! I'm glad to see you."

"Oh, Master Crispin! I am pleased to see you alive! I didn't believe Lenny at first. What are you doing here? You're not going to become a monk, are you, sir? It ain't as bad as all that, is it?"

The abbot straightened his shoulders. "Young man—"

"Oh! Beggin' your pardon, my lord." He bowed to the abbot and crossed himself, and then quickly turned back to Crispin. "Master Crispin, I'm here at your service, sir. What would you have me do?"

"You are going to get me into the palace."

Jack cut his gaze toward the abbot. "He's mad. How many times have I said it? He's barking mad."

"Jack, I may be foolhardy, but I am not mad. Tell me about the Frenchmen. Where are they?"

Jack ran his hand up into his floppy mane of ginger hair. "I followed them to court."

"Do you know if they have the Crown?"

"I don't know. But they was carrying an important bundle. At least they took great care with it."

Crispin sat heavily on the chair, his hands hanging over his thighs.

"I know, sir. Master Gilbert and Mistress Eleanor. Won't the sheriff be reasonable? Can't he see you had no choice in the matter?"

Crispin hung his head. "I don't know, Jack. I was greedy about the Crown myself. How can I blame the sheriff for the same sin?"

"Then if you would go to court again, I'm your man. Let's do it as quick as possible. Before I change me mind."

DRESSED IN A BLACK cassock and cowl, Crispin hurried across the lane to Westminster. Jack, too, was dressed like a monk—much to his protestations.

"I don't like it," Jack muttered for the thousandth time. "It's blasphemy, that's what it is."

"Be still. This is only to get us into the palace. Do you want to be arrested?"

"No, but what are we to do once inside?"

"You locate Miles and I'll find the French couriers."

"Oh, as simple as that. And just how am I supposed to find the Captain of the Archers?"

"You could ask."

"And get caught?"

"No one knows you, remember? It's me they're after."

Jack tugged on his cincture and straightened. "That's right. The tables are turned, eh? They ain't after me for a change."

"Yes. It must be a unique experience for you."

They reached the gate and both fell silent. The guards had been doubled since the last time Crispin was here—less than twenty-four hours ago.

Crispin approached the gate with head down. He raised a benediction to the guard who approached. "My brother," drawled Crispin. "My Lord Abbot of Westminster bid us come to the palace and offer what succor we may."

The guard looked them over and, without further question, allowed them through.

That was a little too easy. Crispin looked back, but the guard did not follow. The palace seemed eerily quiet, none of the usual sounds of merrymaking or chatter; no raucous laughter and drunken challenges. It was as if everyone had crawled into their shells to await the coming tempest.

"It's quiet here," said Jack.

"Yes, I was thinking that very thing. You'd better be on your way, Jack."

"Where shall we meet again?"

In Heaven? "When all is finished, the abbey seems the safest place. Off to it."

Jack nodded unsteadily and Crispin stopped him by touching his arm.

"Good luck, Jack."

"God's blessings on you, sir."

Crispin watched the becassocked Jack amble down the corridor and finally disappear around a corner.

"Now, if I were a French courier who had recovered my lost package, where would I go?" Crispin smiled. The French ambassador, of course.

He cast a glance down the corridor. The rooms along the Thames were generally where they put foreign dignitaries. At least that was so in Crispin's day. He pulled his cowl down to shadow his face, and headed down the passage.

He looked behind to make certain no one followed, turned a corner, and nearly slammed into an entourage. They chattered in French, calling him an oaf with one side of their mouths and asking for forgiveness with the other. Crispin looked up and saw the two French couriers Laurent and Gautier beside another man, older, wearing a long gown and a long gray beard. The French ambassador. He fussed with a bag slung over Laurent's shoulder.

Two guards were also with them, their bland expressions hidden beneath mail coifs and helms.

The man whom Crispin took as the French ambassador turned to Crispin and said in French, "Our apologies, Brother. But it seems this encounter is the wheel of fortune turning in our favor. We must have you bless this happy event."

"Of course," replied Crispin, disguising his voice.

But instead of allowing Crispin to gesture a benediction over them and mumble some Latin, the ambassador said, "Come. We go to see the king."

The entourage moved forward, but Crispin hung back.

One of the guards turned. "Well? Let us go, Brother."

He watched the backs of the couriers, the ambassador, the guards, and raised his eyes to Heaven.

Crispin recognized the way. They were heading toward the great hall. *Richard will be there and doubtless, I will be out of the pan and into the fire. I hope I don't bleed too much on Abbot Nicholas's cassock.*

When they reached the archway, Crispin could tell by the rumbling conversation that there were more present than Richard. Many courtiers were there, including Richard's cadre, the queen, and Lancaster. Among the milling knights and courtiers stood the sheriff, the reliquary at his feet. The scowl on his face told Crispin that he was none too happy. In any case, the proceedings should prove to Wynchecombe that Crispin had nothing to do with any trickery. At least, not yet.

He scanned the room, looking for Miles. No surprise he was nowhere to be found.

The ambassador and his entourage placed themselves before King Richard, who was standing on the dais. The crowd hushed.

"Your most gracious Majesty," said the ambassador with a flourishing bow. "At last, we have recovered the sacred relic. I am charged by my sovereign, the gracious King Charles of all France, with presenting this sacred Crown into your safekeeping."

He turned and reached into the bag over Laurent's shoulder. Slowly, and Crispin thought with a great deal of theatricality, he drew forth the Crown of Thorns and held it up as if he were the archbishop on coronation day.

Then he looked at Crispin.

My cue. Crispin walked in a slow, careful amble—the kind of walk he expected a monk to make—and stood between the ambassador and the king. He eyed Richard out of the corner of his cowl while keeping his head low. He raised his hand and made the sign of the cross over the Crown. Everyone followed suit. Under his breath, Crispin intoned, "*Putresco in inferni, o taeter rex.*"

Richard hadn't heard him but the ambassador glanced at him sideways, an uncertain glint in his eye.

Crispin ducked his head and made the sign of the cross again. "*In nomine Patri, et Filio, et Spiritu Sancte.* Amen."

Richard's face showed little emotion, though Crispin and all of London knew his devotions were sincere. Oddly, he looked as if he would rather be anywhere but there. Crispin supposed that two attempts on his life were getting the better of him. No wonder this ceremony was conducted in haste and inside palace walls.

Richard dutifully stretched out his hands to receive the Crown, bowed to the French ambassador who bowed back to Richard, then handed the Crown to a page, who raised a velvet pillow to receive it.

It was done. The Crown was now safely in Richard's hands for the moment. But until the Crown was returned again to France, no one in England would breathe any sighs of relief.

The men and women of the court moved forward, hailing Richard. Servants arrived from all directions to offer celebratory wine. Crispin took this moment to fade into the crowd, backing away, especially from Wynchecombe. He aimed for the kitchens, hopeful he might retrieve his cloak. He walked backward, bowing to any who happened to look his way, though most did not. He was forgotten, just as he wanted to be.

The kitchens lay at the opposite end from the king's dais, making a large expanse of floor to traverse. But he made his backward progress with little interference from milling servants and reached the kitchen archway without once being stopped.

When he looked up from under his hood one last time, something caught his eye.

Across the hall, almost exactly opposite the destroyed tapestry on which Crispin made his escape, he saw Miles, teasing the shadowy edge of a pillar.

Across from Miles, the French couriers stood apart from the English throng. But Crispin saw the moment they spotted Miles and recognition flowered on their faces.

Miles did not notice them, however, and took a step back, shielded from the king by the column. Something was in his hand.

Without thinking, Crispin reached for his dagger, but he was hindered by the cassock, and he wrestled with the unresponsive garment, trying to free it.

Before he could draw his blade, his shoulder—the same dislocated only the night before—slammed against the wall as if punched, ablaze in fiery pain. He staggered forward with a choked gasp, suddenly woozy. He took a step back—one, two—until his foot found no step at all. Darkness was closing in as he lost his balance and tumbled down the kitchen stairway. When his head hit the bottom step, he was already unconscious.

23

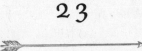

CRISPIN OPENED HIS EYES a crack, but as soon as he did, it seemed the whole world burst upon him in a roiling sea of hot pain. His head—no, his shoulder hurt more, the same one he had dislocated, and felt as if a demon jabbed it with a hot poker.

He tried to roll toward the shoulder, but strong hands pushed him back. His eyes looked up, tried to focus, gave up.

"Don't try to move." A woman's voice. Familiar. Her hands were tearing open the cassock. "I'm going to fix you up."

His dry lips parted as his mind caught up. "Livith?"

"Don't move, I say. I found you at the bottom of the stairs."

"Where am I now?"

"You're in my room. It's only a storeroom, but we call it home. For now." She smiled at Crispin, a pleasant sensation out of so many discordant ones. "You went and got yourself shot with an arrow, didn't you."

Crispin turned his head and looked at the shaft protruding from the space between his shoulder and collarbone. Hawk fletching.

"Damn Miles to Hell." Crispin jolted upright, or at least tried to. The searing pain flattened him again. "The king! Is he well?"

"He is. No harm came to him. You must keep your strength. I've got to get that arrow out."

Crispin was about to protest, but realized Livith couldn't very well get a physician or even a barber. He wasn't supposed to be in the palace in the first place, and if caught, an arrow in the shoulder would be the least of his troubles.

"Very well," he grunted. He felt the sweat burst out all over his body and a queasy feeling rumbled in his belly.

She nodded and looked behind her. Crispin was on the floor and she grabbed his arm and yanked. "It'll be easier if you were on the table."

He rose to his feet and stood on his two legs, though they did not feel as if they belonged to him. She maneuvered him toward the table and he sat on the edge and slid the rest of the way. "You'll have to slide your shoulder to the edge. I'm going to drive the arrow through."

"Christ's blood."

"It ain't Christ's blood I'm worrying about."

She helped him to maneuver his bad shoulder off the table's edge. He felt her at his belt.

"What are you doing?"

She smiled a sly grin full of immodesty. "Now then, Master Crispin. You think I'll take advantage of you?" She kept her smile even as she crawled up on the table and straddled him. Her thighs tightened around him. "I like my men fully aware and conscious. And they like it that way, too."

He managed a smile. "I've no doubt of that."

She unbuckled the belt, stretched the leather between her hands, and held it toward his face. "I want you to bite down on this."

He nodded and dutifully opened his mouth to receive it like a horse receiving his bit. The leather tasted of dirt, oil, and the dull tang of tanning. He bit down hard, especially when Livith brought up her wooden shoe and Crispin's knife. She put the shoe on his chest and grabbed the arrow's shaft. She cut the shirt away from the arrow wound and began running the blade around the shaft, sawing an even line around its circumference. "I'm going to break off the arrow as much as I can," she said, hair falling in her face. It was the first time she hadn't worn her scruffy linen kerchief and he could see the thick tendrils of the ash blond hair falling about her cheeks. He reached up and touched a curled end of one lock, and Livith slowed. She watched his fingers entwine, the hair curling around his hand. She looked into his eyes and he smiled again and spat out the belt.

"I thank you for this."

"You can't go about with an arrow in you, eh?" She smiled and replaced the leather between his lips.

His gaze fell away from her's as the pain of the arrow overwhelmed. He stared at the shoe on his chest, ran his glance over its contours, the mud on its sole. Something about the shoe disturbed him, and he tried to unwind the hidden thoughts about it, but another wave of pain forced a groan from his lips through the belt, and he forgot all else.

Livith grabbed the arrow shaft at the base at Crispin's shoulder, grasped the other fletched end, and suddenly snapped it.

Crispin arched and grunted through his teeth.

Livith steadied herself on Crispin and took up the shoe. "When I count to three, I'll drive it through with this. Then I'll have to pull it out from below. I've no way to tie you down and there's no time to get help from anyone. Do you understand?"

He nodded and clenched the leather. *Just get it over with.*

She put her one hand firmly on his good shoulder to keep him still, and raised up the wooden shoe in the other hand. "One . . . two . . . three!"

Crispin screamed through his teeth. The leather belt took the brunt of it. He wanted to thrash out, to arch his back, but he held himself firm and stretched his neck sinews as far as they would go.

When he felt her yank the bloody arrow through his back, blackness encompassed him. The last conscious sensation was a wave of relief and his head smacking against the table.

* * *

CRISPIN AWOKE AGAIN, THIS time on a straw-covered pallet. His shoulder was packed solid with cloth and a sling was tied around his arm and neck. The cassock had been removed completely and lay in a heap beside the bed. He thought about sitting up for the grand span of a heartbeat and gave up the idea when the pain told him to stay where he was. He stared up at the dusty cobwebs and beams, inhaled the musty air, and licked his dry lips, praying for wine.

A door opened. He lifted his head enough to see Livith shutting it carefully, and she had something in her hand and over her arm. "I brought you wine," she said, raising the bowl. "Master Onslow gave it to me when I told him what it was for. I also brought your cloak."

She handed him the bowl and spread the cloak over his nakedness like a blanket. She slipped her arm under his shoulders, cradled him, and lifted him enough to drink. He thirstily drank the bowl dry. "There. That will be good for the blood." She helped him back down and sat beside him on the straw.

"Livith, thank you again. Did you see what happened?"

"I saw you tumble down the stairs at me feet with an arrow stuck in you. That's all I saw."

"Damn Miles. The audacity of him. I must stop him before he harms the king." Crispin tried to rise and made no argument when Livith pushed him back.

"You'll not get up today. You didn't lose a lot of blood but it's still a shock to the body."

"I've been wounded before."

"Aye." She slid the cloak down revealing his naked chest and torso. Her finger traced the many sword and knife scars. "There's probably the whole map of France here."

He inhaled, careful not to jar his shoulder. "You may be right."

"But this—" She pulled the cloak down farther and ran her finger over the old burns just below his rib cage. "This is not from war. Who did this to you?"

Crispin gazed at Livith's clouded eyes. They narrowed with scorn but it was not directed toward him. "That was the king's men trying to extract a confession."

Her face hardened but she did not take her hand away. "I'd'a thought you'd want King Richard dead."

"Not by the hand of an assassin. He is still my king."

She raised a brow. "And did you think so when you was committing treason?"

"That was then. This is now."

She made that low laugh deep in her throat. Crispin felt it somewhat lower.

He tried to survey the room, but all was too dark. He got the vague impression of shelves and barrels, but that was all. "You shouldn't be alone with me here," he said. "I feel you are safer back with the kitchen staff."

"No one will trouble us here."

"But the killer was after you, too."

"I tell you no one has troubled us."

She hadn't replaced the cloak. Instead, her fingers slowly ran up his breast, combing through his dark chest hair. She talked softly as she stroked, though at this point her words sounded more like the sighing of wind in the trees, or the soft sibilance of a waterfall. Maybe it was the wooziness in his head or the stabbing pain in his shoulder and arm, but he found himself intrigued with her mouth; that tart moue spouting all sorts of blasphemies and brash statements. He thought of her thighs tightening about his hips when she ministered to him earlier and it was suddenly impossible to concentrate at all on what she was saying. He reached up and clasped his fingers to the back of her neck and brought her face down. He covered those taut lips, thinking to silence her, but she moaned her pleasure into his mouth, opened her lips, and mashed her nose against his.

She slithered atop him and straddled him again, yanking his cloak completely away and tossing it aside.

"Are you extracting another arrow from me?" he gasped when she pulled her lips from his.

She smiled. Her eyes became slits, those faery eyes. "I *am* looking for a shaft," she said, then grasped his braies and tugged them down.

"I should protest," he said mildly, lifting his hips to accommodate.

She looked down. "I don't see any objections." She chuckled and raised herself.

Crispin closed his eyes and allowed her to do her will on him. A small portion of his mind warned him, but he ignored it, much as he ignored the pain of the hole in his shoulder.

She rocked over him, a soft moan escaping her lips. And then she leaned forward, mouth taunting his, teasing with feather touches. "*Mon péché,*" she breathed before she licked his open lips.

He heard a cry, but it wasn't the one he expected. He snapped open his eyes and turned. Grayce stood in the doorway, her apron hem brought up to her mouth to stifle another scream. She shook her head, wild eyes glaring at Livith, and then she sprinted back into the shadows, feet slapping the stone floor.

"Mary's dugs!" cried Livith, and rolled off him. Crispin caught the sight of white buttocks before her skirt fell back into place. She stared at the archway and then glanced back at Crispin with an apologetic smile. She hoisted his braies back into place. "Sorry, love. I must discover where she's got to. Explain it to her." She leaned over and kissed Crispin once, shook her head and made what he could only describe as a half-growl, half-purr, and lit off after Grayce.

Crispin threw his head back. *Damn!* But the creeping cold of the room did much to sober him. Livith had replaced his braies but not the cloak. He rolled to his good side and slowly edged into a sitting position. He found his cast-away cloak, and slid off the pallet to retrieve it. He decided to get his shirt on, even as bloodied and torn as it was. Better than nothing. She had conveniently torn away the left sleeve, so he shrugged into the right sleeve, eased it up his shoulder, and let the rags drape over the sling. He slung the cloak over his shoulders, and then slipped the shoulder cape and hood over his head. This proved more difficult, for the leather chaperon hood was fashioned to fit the body, and his sling got in the way of the cape sitting properly on his shoulders.

He swayed from weakness and pain. "I wish she'd brought more wine." He needed warmth. He needed to get out of the palace. He needed Jack Tucker.

He stared at the door and made his way to it, then rested against the wood. Opening it a crack, he peered up the dark stairway and trudged up the stairs.

When he reached the top landing, he looked about. He could hear the sounds of the kitchen staff nearby. He opened a door and found the kitchen. Leaning heavily in the doorway, he watched the servants scurry, no doubt under Onslow's direction. They carried platters, pots, and baskets, crossing and recrossing the wide expanse of the cavernous kitchen. But the perfected madrigal of servants dodging between each other was suddenly interrupted. Several servants near the great hall's archway fell forward, colliding with others until the whole arrangement fell into disarray. Crispin soon saw why. Spear points danced above the crowd. Guards. And they were heading toward him. Someone had called the alarm. *Grayce!*

Crispin darted forward, forgetting for a split second the pain of his shoulder. He tumbled, remembering it, and fetched up against a table.

The guards tromped forward and Crispin peeled back. There had to be another way out. A door! He staggered toward it, hauled it open, and found himself out in a courtyard. Bloodied tree stumps served as butchering blocks. Empty barrels, feathers, and other refuse littered the yard. He looked for weapons. At least his knife was still in its scabbard on his hip, but it wouldn't be enough to fend off a garrison. He passed through a door in the wall and hopped another low wall, ran a few yards, and felt a disturbing sense of familiarity when he looked up and found the window he'd crawled into before. Lancaster's. Dare he try the duke's patience a second time?

He looked back and heard the scramble of men and the clack of spears. They found the door and would soon be upon him. No choice, then.

Crispin climbed to the window and looked inside. The duke was there before a bright and appetizing fire. A short monk was talking to him.

No. Not a monk. Crispin froze in disbelief. It was Jack Tucker still in his borrowed cassock, but his slight frame drowned within the large, black gown. The boy shivered, head low between his shoulders in a half-bow of obeisance and fear, and he spoke in hurried sentences.

"Who are you?" cried the duke. "How did you get in here?"

"I am Master Crispin's servant, m'lord." He peeled back the cowl. "Jack Tucker."

"*Crispin's* servant?" Lancaster took a step back. He looked toward the doorway but no one was there. "Who allowed you in here?"

"That doesn't matter now, m'lord. What matters is Master Crispin."

"Did he send you?"

"Oh no, m'lord! He'd flog me good if he knew I was troubling you."

Lancaster frowned. "Away with you. I haven't time for this."

"M'lord, please. I beg of you. You must help him. He's in powerful trouble. He's trying to help so many people and all he gets is vexation in return. You must know he didn't try to kill the king. You must know it!"

"I said get out. Must I use my sword on you?"

Jack dropped to his knees and tore open the cassock, baring his chest. "Do with me what you will. But I won't stop begging for help."

Lancaster drew back his hand and struck Jack across the face.

Crispin gasped when Jack tumbled backward. But the boy recovered and brought his hand to his reddened cheek. "I won't take 'no' for an answer, m'lord. Master Crispin is in danger of his life. He was trying to *save* the king, not kill him."

Lancaster stepped forward and struck him again.

Crispin grabbed the sill. What was he to do? What could he do?

Jack rose to his knees again, only more unsteadily. "You can beat me within an inch of me life, but I won't stop beggin'. My master's missing. He might be dead."

Lancaster glared down his nose at Jack and eased his palm back and forth over the pommel of his sword. "Does he still think the culprit is Miles Aleyn?"

"Aye, m'lord."

"Does he say why?"

Jack licked his bruised lips. "He does."

"Why, then?"

"He bid me say nought and nought I will say."

Lancaster drew back his hand and delivered another blow that echoed throughout the chamber. Jack's whimpers reached Crispin, and he curled his hands into fists.

"I will not say. My master bid me be silent and I will not say!"

Crispin pushed so hard the window shattered and he rolled into the room. He snapped to his feet and faced Lancaster. Somehow Crispin's dagger was in his hand. "Strike him again and liege lord or no I swear I will drive this knife into you."

Lancaster's face whitened with shock. He lowered his hand and postured. "You're a fool."

"Am I?" He looked at Jack staggering to his feet and gathered him against his good side. "Then I *am* a fool. But I'm a fool with the most steadfast servant in all England. Shall I tell you what Jack in his faithfulness would not? Miles Aleyn was the last conspirator in the plot to overthrow Richard. It was he who lied and tangled England's youthful knights into that deadly conspiracy. Only he and I walked away from it. He by the honor of those he cajoled, and me by your good grace."

Crispin and Lancaster engaged eye contact and held fast to it like two wrestlers loath to release the other. A long moment passed. Finally, Crispin lowered his eyes to look at Jack. "Are you well, Jack?"

Jack snuffled, wiping the blood from his nose with his sleeve. "Well enough, Master."

"Go get yourself some wine." He pushed Jack toward the flagon. Jack hesitated and looked toward Lancaster. "I said get yourself some wine. My Lord of Gaunt will not object."

Lancaster directed a sneer at Jack. "No. Why should I? I have lost all control of my own household. What's a little wine for a servant boy?"

They watched as Jack poured wine into a goblet, took it in both trembling hands, and tipped it to his bruised mouth. The wine dribbled down his chin.

Crispin staggered and took a breath. Tumbling through the window and facing off with Lancaster was taking its toll. He cradled his arm.

"What's happened to you now?" asked Gaunt, gesturing to the sling.

"I was shot with an arrow."

"Oh Master!"

"I am well, Jack. For the moment. I would merely like to know why someone is trying to kill me. I would like to know why they are using your arrows."

Lancaster studied Crispin's arm a long time. The packing at his shoulder began to stain with red. Lancaster clutched his sword pommel, fingers whitening. "Seven years ago, Miles Aleyn stole my arrows before he went into exile to France."

Crispin never expected Lancaster to speak, especially in that sighing, resigned tone. "I did not know he was exiled," said Crispin. "It was never spoken of at court, or rumored outside it."

"Very few knew. Even the king did not know. Which was why he appointed Miles as his Captain of the Archers." He snorted contemptuously. "If I had known that his Majesty had chosen Miles, then I certainly would have said something. Alas, it was too late by the time I heard the news." He stared at Jack still sucking down wine from his bowl. "I believe Miles told those willing to listen that he was going to France to join the king's army, which was partially true."

"Why was Miles exiled to France and why steal your arrows?"

"His exile included every comfort. But, of course, it was to get him out of the way."

"Why?"

Lancaster strode to the sideboard. He gave a sideways glance to Jack and poured wine into another goblet. He knocked the cup back and drank the wine in long, rolling swallows. When he lowered the cup, he ran his hand under his dark mustache to wipe it free of wine droplets. "Because seven years ago *I* hired Miles to begin the conspiracy against the king."

24

CRISPIN STAGGERED BACKWARD. AN iron fist grabbed hold of his heart and squeezed. He couldn't breathe, couldn't think.

Lancaster hired Miles? Then that would mean all his life was a lie. Everything he'd known and believed—all lies.

"I never meant for you to become involved," said Lancaster hastily.

Jack was at Crispin's side. "You're pale, Master. Sit down. Let me help you."

Hands led Crispin to a chair. Crispin sat while his lord stood, a breach he never would have engaged in were he in his right mind. But he knew he'd never be in his right mind again.

Lancaster continued. He pressed his hands to his back and straightened. He was tall, taller than Crispin. He looked regal, majestic; far more so than Richard ever looked. "I needed to root out my enemies. In those early days, there were far too many. Conspiracies abounded. Many of them plotted my death, but there were also those who sought to discredit me against Richard. Those especially I could not afford. And so I devised my own plot. It was to flush out those rascals who would make trouble in the years ahead. And yet . . . I never knew how many young bloods were willing to put their prince away in favor of me." He took a drink and lowered the goblet to his breast. He looked at Crispin and his eyes softened. "And I never suspected you would be foolhardy enough to join with them."

Crispin's eyes were hot. He blinked hard. "How could I not? I would have followed you into Hell if you'd asked."

"Yes, I know."

Crispin panted. His mind couldn't catch up. Light-headed, he prayed he would swoon to spare him from this moment. He heard the fire spit and crackle over the logs, smelled the toasty oak burn. But he felt the warmth of the room as something distant, something just beyond his reach. He languished in a cold bubble while the rest of the world gloried in golden light. Was he asleep? If so, he lived in a nightmare.

It took a few moments for the sensations to dissipate and his mind to clear before he could absorb all the facts. Lancaster said his plot flushed out his enemies as well as his friends. "The plot worked too well," Crispin said, voice hoarse. "You almost decided to go ahead with it."

"Not enough of the right men supported it. I had to let it collapse."

"And me with it."

"When I found out you were involved, it was too late."

Crispin took in a long breath. "Why didn't you let me die?"

Lancaster's stern glare softened and finally looked away. "I . . . couldn't. I couldn't."

Crispin mustered his strength and rose. He stood unsteadily and straightened his shoulders. His entire body ached; the hole in his shoulder, his sore limbs. But mostly his heart. A blackened tear rent it ragged and wide. "You bastard," he whispered, feeling on the one hand he had uttered blasphemy, and on the other righteous indignation. "I thought it was Miles. All these years I hated him. All these years when I thought it was him . . . it was you."

"And now you hate me."

Crispin's lips peeled back. "What do *you* think?"

"I suppose I can't blame you."

Crispin stared at the broken window and beyond it to the rain-glittered garden. Spears marched by, some milled near the broken glass, and heads appeared at the sill. Lancaster took swift strides to stand before the casement, blocking the rest of the room. He leaned out the window and pointed. "I heard a noise that way. Go investigate."

None of the men dared question the duke of Lancaster, and they withdrew. Lancaster pulled the drapes across the window, casting the room into velvet shadows. He turned back to Crispin.

Crispin stared at the floor. Was it only a few short moments ago he was immersed in an intimate encounter with Livith? To be back there now, to forget this horrifying truth and drown himself in the pleasures of a sensuous woman! There didn't seem to be any point in pressing on, in capturing Miles. Who cared about the murder of a Frenchman? Or the king, for that matter, if Richard's staunchest supporter was equally guilty? What a fool he'd been! It should have been obvious. If Crispin had only opened his eyes he would have known. Lancaster was a ruthless statesman. He conquered. He devoured. He took. Crispin should have known it. But in all his naïveté, all his trust, he hadn't.

"Tell me the truth," rasped Crispin, not looking at Lancaster. "Are you trying to kill the king? Are you behind this new plot?"

Lancaster never moved. He stood in that regal manner of his, the manner that brought men to his service, made them pledge oaths to him, ride to war with him, die for him. There was a solemn set of his mouth. "No" was all he said.

Crispin edged his glance up and looked at the face of his mentor. Lancaster didn't flinch, didn't blink. He stated his position simply. He denied his involvement. Crispin wanted to believe him, but *was* it the truth? Crispin was beyond being able to distinguish truth from lies.

As if Lancaster could read these thoughts, he stepped closer and said more quietly, "Crispin, I had nothing whatsoever to do with this new evil. And I have been involved in many plots. I am not afraid to admit to you my complicity in those. But in this, I am innocent."

"Innocent," Crispin echoed.

Lancaster nodded. They both sensed the poor use of the word, considering the context.

"Master," urged Jack. He glanced back at Lancaster, who stood in silhouette against the large hearth. Jack's face was purple with bruises. "Master Crispin, we must go. You were right. There's no place left for us here. We must leave London." His voice was dull and full of weary maturity.

"What difference does it make?" Crispin whispered. "When Miles kills the king, I will still be blamed. Nowhere will be safe."

"We can go to France, maybe. You're always talking about France. Maybe we'd be welcome there."

"The English king's assassin? Oh yes. They'll welcome me with open arms."

Jack looked to the duke. "M'lord. Tell him. Tell him he must go. Tell him to forget Miles and the Frenchman. Leave it to the sheriff."

"I should have confessed seven years ago," said Crispin dully. "I would have been dead by now. Unconsecrated, and my soul wandering in Purgatory, but surely it would be a better Purgatory than this."

Lancaster snorted. "Surrendering, are you?"

Crispin raised his face. He didn't know what he looked like, but his expression startled Lancaster enough to take a step back. "Don't I have every right to?"

"Of course. You have earned the right. But I expected that after so long, you would know how to survive, how to circumvent your enemies."

Crispin struggled to push himself from the chair. Jack tried to help, but Crispin swung his good arm and Jack got out of its way. Crispin rose and squared with Lancaster. "Until this moment I thought I knew who my enemies were."

"I am not your enemy."

"Oh no? That's right. You were my savior. Of course, I would not have needed a savior if your henchman had not deceived me into committing this most unforgivable act of treason!"

"You do not realize your situation."

"Oh, but I do."

"No, you don't." Lancaster raised his royal head. It was only by an accident of birth that he was not king now. Richard. The resemblance was slight between the faces of uncle and nephew, but there was no mistaking what color of blood pulsed through Lancaster's veins.

"No one has ever committed high treason in this realm and lived," he told Crispin. "You were spared for a purpose."

"Who do you think you are? Do you play at prophet now?"

"I am the one who pleaded for you. Richard had no cause to accede to my pleas. It was his choice and he knew it. His counselors advised him otherwise, to take your life. But he chose not to. I don't know why."

"I do not care. I know well the life I have lived since. And I tell you, I would rather be dead!"

"Well then, why not let the guards take you? Walk out into that corridor now and shout it to the heavens. You'll be dead soon enough."

"M'lord!" Jack lunged forward, his fingers outstretched as if trying to capture the duke's last words. "Please don't tell him that. Tell him you will champion him."

"Crispin, tell your servant to be still or he will find a sword in his gut."

"The both of you! Be silent!" Crispin raised his hands to his ears. The wounded shoulder, however, would not allow him to raise that arm so high. He grabbed the hurt shoulder instead and trudged across the room to a shadowed corner where the chessboard sat. He remembered playing many a game with the duke on that very board. He wiped the sweat from his upper lip. "Can't you both be silent," he whispered, "and let me think?"

Lancaster's confession had been demoralizing and terrifying. He stared at the chessboard and felt his sore shoulder heave with each heavy breath he took.

The chess pieces gleamed in the sallow light, their proud knights mocking. He swept his arm over it and cast the pieces to the floor. One of the knights broke in half, forever separated from his stallion.

A decision needed to be made. And yet it seemed already made for him. "Jack." Crispin said it so quietly, even he wasn't certain he uttered it. He stared down at the broken knight.

The boy edged forward. Crispin heard his shoes scrape against the wooden floor behind him. "Master."

"If I stay to do what I feel is my duty—to stop this assassin from killing the king—then I will be captured. It will be the end of me. My Lord of Gaunt here will no longer have a voice in the matter."

Jack frowned. Crispin noticed the beginning of a ginger whisker. No, he was far too young. Perhaps it was only another freckle on the burl of his chin. The boy's voice was unsteady, but his words were strong and did not falter. "I would just as soon see you free, sir, but I know it is not your way. And if you die this time, then it is for a noble cause. Not one of treason, though all the world may still think it. *I* will know. And all your *friends* will know. *Anyone* who knows you well will know." He said the last looking directly at Gaunt. The duke's mouth did not move. His lips formed a thin, tight line. But Crispin thought he detected the merest trembling of his chin.

Crispin smiled briefly. "Then, for your sake and the sake of my friends, I must do my best." He straightened and cradled his bad arm. He pulled his cloak about him and lifted his head, though he did not look at Gaunt. "I will take my leave of you now, your grace. I will trouble you no more. Indeed, I think there is very little either of us has left to say to the other."

"Crispin—"

Crispin bowed deeply. "I take my leave. With or without your permission." He headed toward the door and leaned heavily against

Jack when the boy offered his arm. It wasn't until they stood outside Lancaster's apartments that Crispin breathed again. He looked both ways down the empty corridor.

He looked at Jack, and the boy offered a sincere and sorrowful expression. Crispin squeezed Jack's shoulder. "Thank you, Jack. For everything."

Jack nodded. His face was on the verge of tears.

"Did you find Miles Aleyn?" Crispin asked.

"No, Master," he replied in an unsteady voice. "I'm not even certain he's in the palace."

"He is. I saw him. In fact—" Crispin remembered Miles's face masked in shadows by the column in the great hall. "The French couriers. They saw him, too. And they recognized him. They knew him."

"But they told you they didn't."

"They said they didn't know him by that name." This was better. Immerse in the problem and then all the other hurts could be forgotten for a time. The puzzle was the place to hide. The puzzle was a safe haven.

"He'd been to France," said Jack.

"Yes." Crispin minced through the puzzle in his mind. "Yes. France."

Crispin stood that way for a long time, his face blank. Jack finally nudged him. "Something else troubling you?"

"Yes, but it has to wait. I'm not leaving here until I find Miles." Crispin set off down the corridor, cradling his arm.

Jack trotted after him. "What happened, Master Crispin? To your arm."

"Miles. There was an arrow. Livith found me and ministered to me." Pain radiated throughout his left side, especially where the wadded cloth blotted the hole. He looked down and saw blood soaking the linen. He needed to be sewn up like his old coat, but he didn't have the time.

He took a deep breath and started running. He grunted out the pain but he couldn't stop, wouldn't. If he had killed Miles the day he saw him in Islington he'd be in better stead now.

He didn't know where to look, but his feet took him near the great hall. He slammed himself against the wall just within the shadowed archway and breathed. *Jesu, this shoulder hurts!* "Jack. Go look. I can't risk being seen."

Jack straightened his cassock and pulled the cowl up over his head before he leaned toward the archway and peered around the corner. "Only a handful of courtiers," whispered Jack, "but Miles is not among them . . . Hold there. Someone running."

Crispin heard the scramble of feet, shouting, and then more feet, marching feet pursuing.

"The poor bastard is down!" hissed Jack. "A cluster of guards wrestled him to the ground. He's in for it now. Been there m'self." Jack edged farther into the hall, extending his body. In his black cassock, he looked more shadow than boy.

"They're picking him up," Jack continued. "It looks like . . . it looks like . . ."

Jack's spine snapped to attention and he rubbed his eyes and looked first at Crispin and then back to the hall.

Crispin stared at Jack and whispered, "What is it, for God's sake?"

Jack shook his head. "It looks like they've captured . . . *you!*"

25

CRISPIN'S FACE DID NOT change for a heartbeat and then he threw back his head and gave a hearty laugh. "Captured *me*, did they? How do you know?"

"Well . . ." Jack hugged the edge of the pilaster. "I see a man wearing that cotehardie of yours—"

Crispin continued laughing though it hurt his shoulder and he ceased abruptly. "My decoy has arrived. What are they doing now?"

"They're ushering him away. Out the other door. Everyone's going. The hall's empty."

Crispin stepped tentatively toward the archway. "Good. We'll go this way, then. It will save me time."

"Who was that poor bastard?"

"That was Lenny."

Jack smiled. "And he agreed to be your decoy?"

"Not exactly. I hinted to him that he might earn a reward at court. Looks like he just got it."

"Why is he wearing your coat?"

"I needed a way to get across London without being detected. We traded coats."

"Now, Master Crispin, that wasn't a very nice thing you done to old Lenny. He won't appreciate it."

"I imagine he's spilling his guts about me now. That will keep everyone busy enough. I hope."

Crispin checked again to see if anyone remained in the hall and then slipped out onto the stone floor. Heading across the hall was the best shortcut to the courtyard. Miles might be there and Crispin needed to conserve every step.

The tapestry that Crispin climbed in his escape had been removed, leaving an obviously blank space on the wall between more tapestries and banners. The broken rod still hung there by one hanger. Gouges in the plaster pocked the stone wall, reminders where spears had penetrated. The window was covered with boards hastily nailed into place to keep the weather out.

"What happened there?" asked Jack. "Looks like a whirlwind swept through."

Crispin looked up. "No, only one desperate man."

Jack turned to stare at Crispin. His jaw slackened and his widening eyes inquired, but he said nothing.

They'd made it halfway across the floor when Crispin stopped. He saw movements in the shadows by the kitchen entrance, the figure of a man and the gleam of a sword pulled from its scabbard.

The figure strode into the light and took a few paces forward. He wagged the sword at Crispin from across the expanse of floor, his gloved hand wound taut around the sword hilt. "Why, Crispin Guest!" Miles said tightly. His voice conveyed a smile even though his face did not. "It's a miracle. Did I not just see you taken away by the palace guards?"

Crispin stiffened. "No miracle. A trick of the eye, perhaps."

"So now the king must add sorcery to the charges against you. One wonders how many times and in how many ways you can be executed."

Crispin raised one edge of his mouth not quite into a grin. "I'll wager none. It is not my execution that is close at hand, but yours."

Miles stepped closer. The sword bobbed toward Crispin. "Mine? I think not. For I am not guilty of anything."

"Do not make the angels weep, Miles."

Miles's smile was that of a reptile. "You credit me with far more than my due."

Crispin backed away from Miles's advancing blade, running his gaze over the three feet of steel. He raised his voice. "Miles Aleyn, you are under arrest in the name of the king."

Miles laughed. "And what authority gives you the right—or the gall—to utter such nonsense? Are we talking of the faery kingdom?"

"The sheriff gives me the authority."

"The sheriff. I wipe my arse with London's sheriff."

"We've all had enough of your bow work, Miles." He gestured to his own arm. "Especially me."

Miles stepped closer, only ten feet from Crispin now. "I wish I can take the credit. But alas, I did not. Besides, I would have rather put an arrow in your heart than your shoulder."

"Lying to the last."

Miles chuckled and raised the blade. He stood only a few feet from Crispin.

Crispin eyed the blade again, feeling himself at a distinct disadvantage with no sword and the use of only one arm. "What is your intention, Miles?"

Miles whipped the blade through the space between them. The steel sang in the cold air. "Cut you down to size, perhaps. And pray, what is yours?"

This time, Crispin's smile was wide. "To beat the shit out of you."

Miles flicked a dismissive eyelash at Jack and directed his gaze again to Crispin's bandaged arm and sling. He laughed. "With what?"

"With this." Before Miles could react, Crispin kicked Miles's sword hand with all his might. The sword flew across the room.

A surge of hot blood pumped through Crispin's chest. That had gone better than he hoped.

Miles shook out his gloved hand and looked back at the now distant sword. "Damn you, Guest!"

But Crispin wasn't done. He slammed his foot to Miles's kneecap, and the archer went down. Without hesitating, Crispin threw a kick into Miles's chest. A whoosh of air expelled from the archer's lungs and he folded, legs splayed.

Crispin panted and stood over him. "Well now. Maybe you will tell me—"

Miles's fist arced upward and caught Crispin in the gut. Crispin stumbled back a few steps, his good arm pressed to his belly. Miles tried to rise but his buckled knee would not allow him. Instead, he half-limped, half-slid across the floor like a beached whale. He pulled his dagger free.

Crispin gasped, looked up, and saw the knife. He yanked out his own and slashed at Miles. Miles jerked back.

Crispin's mouth set grimly and he jumped away from Miles's blade and instead caught the side of the archer's head with his boot. Miles fell forward and the dagger skidded free across the floor. Jack scrambled to retrieve it and held it aloft, aiming it toward Miles.

Miles leaned on his arms and heaved his shoulders, sucking in air. Blood rimmed his lips and plastered the hair on the side of his head where Crispin kicked him.

Crispin looked down at him, satisfied he'd done sufficient damage. He turned to Jack. "Go get the duke's men."

"Right, sir!" Jack saluted with Miles's dagger, turned on his heel, and ran, feet slapping hard on the floor.

Crispin faced Miles. "Now, you turd. I have a few questions for you."

"Go to Hell, Guest."

"I've already been there. And I will soon see you there. Save your breath and keep your lying to a minimum. I know all about your association with Lancaster."

Miles snapped up his head, eyes wide. He slid his jaw but said nothing. A trickle of blood painted a crimson line down his chin.

"Yes, I know. Tell me why you stole those arrows. Trying to make it look as if Lancaster were guilty?"

"Enough, then! I stole the goddamned arrows. But that was seven years ago. You didn't think I was going to go to France without some proof of Lancaster's involvement, did you?"

"He could have killed you. He should have."

"No, instead he exiled me."

"With money enough to set you up well, I imagine."

"That was all very well—for a while. But a man gets a hunger for his homeland. So I joined the king's army."

"As an archer."

"Yes, as an archer."

"And you used that skill for treason, trying to kill the king."

"No, damn you! How many times must I say?"

"Why do you lie now? You are a dead man already. Lancaster's men will be here soon. Torture will extract the rest."

Miles's brows winged outward. Sweat dotted his face and trickled down. "I tell you I did not try to kill the king. It is impossible."

"Not for the likes of you. You are a deceiver, an extortionist, a murderer. There is no honor in you. There is nothing but evil and death, and that is what you shall receive."

Miles tried to rise but Crispin used his foot to kick him back down. "Stay on the ground where you belong, dog!"

"I tell you it is impossible! I did not try to shoot the king!"

"And why is that so impossible?"

Miles grimaced. He glanced back toward the archway where Lancaster's men would soon emerge. His face shone with sweat, his tunic equally dark with perspiration. Breath trembling, he looked up at

Crispin and locked eyes with him. "This is why." He raised his gloved hand to his face and grasped the leather fingers with his teeth and yanked off one gauntlet and then the other. He tossed the gauntlets at Crispin's feet.

Crispin looked.

Miles had only a thumb and two small fingers on each hand. The forefingers and middle fingers had been hewn off.

26

"THEY CAPTURED ME," RASPED Miles. "The damned French. And they did what they do to all captured English archers: They made certain I could never use a bow again. And I can't. Satisfied?"

Crispin stared at the gloves. Yes, he saw it now. Some of the gloves' fingers were artfully stuffed so that no one would be the wiser. And if Miles kept his gloves on at all times, as he had, no one would know. No one did.

Crispin kicked the gloves toward Miles, but Miles ignored them. "So, you did not use the bow yourself. You hired someone."

"No."

"Then how do those French couriers know you? Don't deny it. I already know they do."

Trapped. Miles knew it. Crispin saw it on his face. And it was only a matter of time before Lancaster's men arrived. Miles glanced again at the empty archway.

"The more you tell me now, the less torture you will endure."

Miles rubbed his hand over his lips, those misshapen fingers. "After . . . after my capture, I used my wiles to work my way into the French court. That's where Lancaster's funds made their mark. I could live well on English coins and also be in the French king's employ."

"You are the fourth man."

His lips snarled and he shook his head. "You are very cunning, Guest. How did you know?"

"Their companion never reappeared. When they saw you they were surprised, perhaps not expecting to see you here. I simply put two and two together. But a question remains. Why did you force the couriers to meet you at the King's Head? If you are so innocent, why were you plotting? Who told you to bring them there?"

"I was to warn them." He looked uneasy, scraping his bottom lip with his teeth. "They were to delay going to court."

"To give the assassin time to work his will."

He continued to chew on his lip. His eyes darted to the archway. Without raising his head to Crispin, he nodded.

"Who, Miles? Who told you to do this?"

"I . . . I cannot say."

"Cannot or will not?"

He looked up then, fragile defiance in his eyes. "Will not, then."

Crispin narrowed his eyes. He nearly drew back his fist, but decided he wasn't worth the split knuckles.

"When it was clear Lancaster was through with me," said Miles, looking again over his shoulder toward the archway, "I had to make other plans. They believed a lot of things about me at the French court. Like you, they gave me more credit than was my due. But I didn't disabuse them. It was to my advantage to appear craftier. I became a double agent, so to speak, working in both courts and spying for France."

"You are a true whoreson, Miles. I have never met a more foul man than you. You regard your honor very low."

"I don't regard it at all. What has honor ever gotten me?"

Crispin heard Gilbert's words suddenly in his head uttering the same sentiment. What had honor ever gotten Crispin? But Crispin had no need to question it as others seemed to do. He couldn't understand a man like Miles. Noblemen were trained from birth in the philosophy of uncompromising honor. It was as natural as breathing. Or at least Crispin always thought this was so. "What about self-respect?" said Crispin, face warm. "What about dignity, pride, nobility? Our honor is ourselves. It is who we are."

Miles laughed nervously. "Listen to you. You, who has not a scrap of honor left."

"I have far more honor than you have ever had, Master Aleyn. You don't even understand the concept."

"I understand gold. That's what I understand. And I understand compromise. I stole Lancaster's arrows in order to be in a better position to negotiate. But then some bastard stole them from me. Then where do you suppose I next saw them? Hmm? Not at the English court. Not what you think."

Crispin squeezed his hurt shoulder. It didn't help. He felt woozy again. He knew it was from loss of blood and exertion. He glanced at the archway. Lancaster's men were certainly taking their sweet time about it.

"Where then? If you are so keen to tell me."

"Seven years ago. In the necks of two French noblemen. It seems these courtiers supported a treaty with England and that made the king too uncomfortable."

"Which king?"

"The French king, of course. They supported the English treaty against the good wishes of their sovereign. An assassin took them out. Imagine my chagrin when I realized they were my good English arrows. That's why they were stolen, of course. At least that is why I thought so. Because they were English arrows the blame would be put on England, if anyone cared to look that closely at the arrows. Only someone like you would care."

"The assassin was never found?"

"No. And it was not me."

"I have no reason to believe you."

"No, you don't. But when that boy comes back with Lancaster's men, I will keep nothing secret. I have no taste for torture, especially my own." He scooted closer to Crispin. "Listen, Crispin. There's truly no need for this. I've told you what I know. You've discerned the truth about Lancaster and about me. That should be enough to satisfy you. Help me to get away, and I will make it worth your while."

"Are you insane?"

"Look at you? You look like a beggar. I have gold aplenty. You'll never hunger again."

"Have you not listened to one word I've said?"

Miles jerked his head. He, too, heard the approaching footsteps. He turned desperate eyes to Crispin. "Crispin, I've got the gold. You can have it. All of it. Just help me get away. I'll never trouble you again. You're a fair man, I can see that. Let me do this for you, if you will do this for me. Guest! I'm begging you."

Crispin took a step back and raised his chin. "I have a word of advice, Miles."

Breathing hard, Miles glanced at the archway and back to Crispin. "Crispin, for the love of Christ—"

"When they use the hot pincers on you, relax your muscles as much as possible. There's slightly less sensation when you do. Only slightly, mind. Probably not enough to make a difference."

Miles implored with trembling hands. "Crispin! Help me!"

The heavy footfalls increased and there were suddenly many figures filling the archway. They headed straight for Miles and lifted him struggling in their midst. Miles's face degenerated into grimaces and tears. His pleas and wails echoed in the hall and receded with him once they dragged him away.

Crispin smiled.

But the smile faded. Lancaster made the man into a criminal, whether Miles tended toward that demeanor or not. That was disturbing enough. But Miles had also confessed that he had nothing to do with the assassination attempts, and for some reason, Crispin believed him.

The notion of English arrows being used for the very fact they were English struck a chord. It reminded him of shoes.

27

JACK EDGED NEXT TO Crispin and they both watched Lancaster's men disappear with Miles. "He's a coward," said Jack. He said it simply, a pronouncement, like "my soup is too hot." He raised his chin to look at Crispin, and his bright eyes shone with the flush of pride.

Crispin supposed the pride was for him.

He leaned against Jack and the boy gave a cry. "Oh Master! We must attend to that arm."

"There isn't time, Jack. There is still an assassin to stop. Verily, there are at least two."

"Two? Isn't Miles one of them?"

"No. He had his own secrets, and they distracted me from seeing what I should have all along."

Jack slapped his forehead. "Them French couriers!"

Crispin lifted his shoulders in an effort to breathe. "Jack, do what you can to get Lenny out of shackles. Here." He reached into his pouch and gave a little hiss when he jabbed his finger on the thorn. He pulled it out again along with some coins, and dropped the coins in Jack's outstretched hand.

"Oi! Master Crispin," he said pointing to the object in Crispin's palm. "That looks like one of them thorns."

Crispin looked at the thorn, and then at his finger. He had so many holes in him now he wondered how he had any blood left. "It *is* one of those thorns. It fell out of the Crown."

Jack backed up, hands fanning the air and head shaking. "Christ's toes! You must return it. Take it away."

"If only I could. I will give it to the proper authorities when all this is over."

"Oh!" Jack covered his mouth and then pointed a trembling finger at Crispin. "It's that power. It's the thorn protecting you. Jesus mercy." He hastily crossed himself multiple times.

"Don't be a little fool. Go now. Rescue Lenny. You still look like a monk. It will put you in good stead. That silver will go even further."

"Where should I go?"

"The captain of the guard. Or the sheriff, if you must."

Jack nodded but eyed Crispin warily. He fisted the coins and took off at a trot, looking back at Crispin once before disappearing through an arch.

Crispin took another deep breath. He hoped he had enough strength to go on. But almost the same moment he thought it, a feeling of comforting warmth began in his chest and spread outward like a sunburst. It radiated into his sore shoulder, not exactly dulling the pain, but making it that much more bearable. He felt taller, straighter. He should be feeling exhausted. He should be in too much pain to lift his foot one more step. He should be fainting.

He looked down at the thorn in his hand and slowly shook his head in his refusal to believe. "You can't be doing this. I don't believe you can do this."

The thorn lay in his palm. It looked like any other thorn: black, unimpressive yet somewhat dangerous.

He looked at his finger. Already the pinprick was disappearing.

He swiveled his head to look back at the direction he'd come, to the archway that led back to Lancaster. But thinking of the duke left him cold and desolate. Since his degradation, he and Gaunt had spoken little. The few times they had, Lancaster had used distant tones to protect his good name from association with Crispin's. *His good name.* And Crispin had taken it like the properly chastised servant he was, feeling all along he deserved it. *Like a fool!* Where was the honor in all this? Even Lancaster proved that in order to protect his own interests, he was willing to sacrifice his fiercest supporters. The young knights in the conspiracy had given their lives. And Crispin had given his life, too, in a sense. Was there anything or anyone worth dying for?

He clutched his hands into fists and just as quickly snapped them open again. The sharp thorn still lay in his palm. The words whispered over his lips. "*'Greater love hath no man than this, that a man lay down his life for his friends.'*"

The sheriff had seen the Crown being presented to the king. He hoped Eleanor and Gilbert were safe now. The sheriff would have nothing left to surrender to the king—except Crispin himself, of course.

He sighed and dropped the thorn back in his pouch. Wearily he raised his head and scanned the large and ominously empty hall. How much had these old timbers seen? How much honor? How much degradation? How much death? Crispin shivered and pulled his cloak about him.

Behind him lay Lancaster and the French ambassador, the couriers. But he made no move in that direction. Instead, he headed for the kitchens.

He strode beneath the shadow of the arch and opened the door. He trod down the stairs and was struck by the warmth blasting up the stairwell, the aromas, the sounds of iron pans and brass kettles clanking. But it did not comfort today. At the bottom of the stairs he simply stood, watching the many lives move about him, going about their tasks with their own cares tucked neatly behind their caps and wimples. What did people like these think about? Probably much as he thought about these days: Was there going to be enough money to last the winter? Was there enough to tuck away for the eldest daughter's dowry? What would happen to their families if sickness came to them? Mundane thoughts. Mundane cares.

But he knew from experience that some harbored other thoughts, not so mundane. Greedy thoughts. Illicit. Dangerous. And these thoughts came from every level of society, whether king or beggar. But only a king could make such men act on their evil thoughts, because only a king had the power and money to use at his will. And the others, the lowly ones, fell easily to the temptation. Was it their fault, to be enticed by the Devil as they were? *Adam and Eve were so enticed. Free will can be a dangerous thing. On one hand is Heaven, but on the other sin and damnation.*

Crispin glanced at the faces; hard faces, lined, dark from smoke. But he did not see the faces he sought. He saw the other door, the one to the small storeroom that lay in shadow, went to it, opened it.

No one was there. He pulled a stool from its place at the table, sat, and waited.

IT MIGHT HAVE BEEN an hour until Livith stepped through the door and shut it. She flinched when she noticed Crispin sitting in the dark.

"Well!" she cried, her hand on her heart. "God bless me! You startled me, you did. I wondered where you'd gone. That arm can't be doing too well."

"Well enough." He painted a design on the table with his finger and slowly lifted his gaze.

She smiled and flew to him. She threw her arms about his neck and settled in his lap. "Now," she said, lips caressing his. "Where were we?"

He grasped her arm and pushed her back. She stood back unsteadily and stared at him. Her face and eyes registered their puzzlement.

"There's no time for this now," said Crispin. "It's time for answers."

She stared at him. Her head was cocked to one side. Her angular features were shadowed by the uncertain flicker of a single candle. But those faery eyes studied him like a fox hiding in the brake. "What nonsense is this?" Her hand went to her hip and her whole body swayed into it; all the curves and undulations of Woman. "Don't you want to finish what we started?" she said softly. Her tongue peeked from between her lips and traveled over them in one slow, gliding meander, leaving a path of moisture glistening on that small but succulent mouth.

"The time for games is over, Livith. Where's the bow?"

Her eyes widened slightly but her lashes swept down and covered anything that might have been revealed by her eyes. "What are you talking about?"

"The bow. I'm certain you each possess one. One is lost, of course, but there must be another."

The luscious s of her body straightened and she crossed her arms over her chest. She shook her head and a smile sprouted on that tart mouth. "I knew you was too clever. I told myself not to trust you."

"So where is it?"

"How the hell did you discover us?"

He blinked for a moment then flicked his gaze down to her feet. "Your shoes."

"My what? My sarding shoes?"

"Those wooden clogs. They are a French design. They are not made quite the same way in London. That is how I knew you had been to France. And you spoke French to me. Did you realize?" He could see she didn't, but it made little difference. "There was no possible reason for your being in France except as clever executioners. After all, what is more invisible than a couple of scullions?"

"A couple of *women* scullions, that's what."

"Just so. So where is it?"

Livith gave a chuckle, a low rumble in her throat. "Oh Crispin, why are we arguing? We had the makings of a splendid time together."

"Why hire me if you only intended to kill me?"

She threw back her head and sighed. "*I* didn't hire you, remember? I had no choice. Not with the famed 'Tracker' sniffing about."

"So Grayce *did* kill the courier."

Livith slid her foot forward and sauntered toward the table, her hips rocking. "Aye. He must have recognized her from the French court. It was the only thing she could think to do." She meandered all the way around the table and back toward Crispin. She dropped her fingers lightly to the back of Crispin's hand, trailing up his skin to his wrist. He jerked it away. Frowning, she stood back, looking down her nose at him. "After she'd done it, she didn't know what else to do and I wasn't there to tell her. She got confused as she is wont to do. So the idiot went to you. She never thought it out. She can't."

"If you had been there instead of Grayce no one would have ever known."

"Aye. And the king would be dead by now and I'd be fifty pounds richer. And, of course," she smiled, "*you* wouldn't be dead."

"But I'm not dead."

She smiled, revealing one chipped tooth. "Not yet. But you will be. That's twice I struck your shoulder with an arrow. And that's twice I hadn't wanted to kill you. If I had, you'd've been dead long ago."

"Why didn't you?"

She smiled. "I didn't want to. But your messing about at court made me a might anxious. I shot you here to lay you low. And to play." She licked her lips. "A man who's a little helpless . . . well, it's a bit of merriment, ain't it? And you were enjoying it right well as I recall."

Crispin turned away from her leering grin. "And the attempt on the king in the garden? Missed on purpose, did you?"

Her smile faded. "Sarding servant. He saw me. Gave the king the warning. I shot him instead to teach him a lesson. It wasn't easy reaching over that wall."

"How did you escape detection?"

"I told you. No one looks twice at a woman servant. My bow is small enough to easily hide under me cloak."

"I find it incredible that a woman knows how to shoot at all. Though you did say your father was an archer. . . ."

"And a damn good one, too. But without sons, there was no one to teach but us girls. And we learned right well."

He eyed her pointedly. "Your Southwark speech sounds authentic. You *are* English, then?" She nodded. "And this is how you earn your keep? Only pretending to be scullions so that you may kill for money? If I were not so disgusted I might very well admire your audacity. But as it is, I find the waste of talent pathetic."

"I don't need your judgment. I get me gold. And that's good enough. I make more wages than you do, to be sure." She laughed. "I'd even consider paying you in full. But I don't see what good it will do you now."

"Then that performance at the Boar's Tusk. The clothes strewn about the storeroom. The arrow strike you took. Staged?"

"Didn't want you getting too suspicious. Grayce shot me. I told her to. I'm afraid it truly rattled what she's got left of a brain. But we had to get out of there. It was just good luck you got us into exactly the place we needed to be: court."

"What about Miles Aleyn?"

"That peacock? He's more talk than show. He had but one task, and could he accomplish even that? No! Nearly fouled it all with his carelessness with them couriers. It ain't Grayce's fault she didn't know what to do. She can only stick to the plan when I'm there to tell her." She shook her head as if it were merely a bit of burnt toast she was worrying over. "Found Miles Aleyn at first strutting about the French court. My employer knew him well. Thought it a merry idea to use foreign arrows for a job I done several years ago."

"The French noblemen, you mean?"

She shone her teeth in a guffaw, and slapped her thighs. "You are a one, ain't you? How'd you know about that?"

"And you happened to have a few good English arrows left to take to England?"

"Aye. My employer seemed to know a thing or two about them arrows. Thought it amusing to use them. Do you happen to know why? You know everything else."

"Yes. Because Miles stole them from the duke of Lancaster and they can be identified as his."

She put her hand over her mouth and laughed into it. "That's a pretty notion, that. Someone's trying to be especially naughty."

"Indeed. About that 'someone.' Just who *is* your employer?"

She put up one finger to her pursed lips. "Oh no. Mustn't tell. Especially to the likes of you."

"You know I am being blamed for this."

"Aye. That's the funniest part of all."

Crispin made a grimace. "Strange. I don't find it amusing whatsoever."

Her taut shoulders drooped. She edged closer to him, leading with her hips. "Come, Crispin. Let us put our differences aside. Let us recapture the moment. Who would know? I'll leave off killing the wretched king and disappear, if that's what you want, and you can go about your business none the wiser and no one else hurt."

"I would never soil my hands with you again."

She stopped. Livith's face soured. Her eyes narrowed "Very well," she rasped. "Have it your way."

Crispin was waiting for a move, but he didn't expect her fist. She punched hard into his shoulder just at the point of injury; rapid punches, three, four times. It took his breath away, the pain so intense, so penetrating. He gurgled a protest, went rigid, and fell backward to the floor.

Livith cast the table into the air, upending it. She snatched the short-bow from its hiding place on the underside of the table and slammed an arrow to it. She straddled him, aimed the point of the arrow right between his eyes, and pulled back the string.

Supine, Crispin looked up at Livith's eye taking aim down the arrow shaft. No time to think. He swung his legs up behind her and clasped them around her waist. The arrow shot forward, skimming the top of his bare head. He yanked his legs down, pulling Livith backward.

The same moment he released her, he rolled to the side. He managed to get to his knees just in time to feel the crack of the bow against his head. Stars, flashing light and dark. Pain bursting in his head. He sunk down, but knew if he succumbed he'd be a dead man.

She swung the bow from the other direction, and Crispin raised his good arm to block it. At least it *used* to be his good arm. He spun his leg outward and tripped her. She fell hard to the floor on her backside and swore.

Crispin was down on his knees again, trying to breathe, trying to get a fix on what was up and what down. His head was light. Loss of blood, a blow to the head—all of it was taking its toll. *Wish I'd told Jack where I was going to be.* Funny how that seemed to matter more and more these days. What Jack thought. Where Jack was. Maybe Eleanor was right. Jack was more to him than a servant, but it was too late to do anything about it now. For the first time in a long time, he didn't think he was going to make it. Defeated by a woman! That was especially galling.

Crispin groped for his dagger and yanked it out. He fisted it tightly. That was all he had left. He hadn't the strength for any more punches, no more kicks. Just the weapon. If she knocked it out of his hand, then he'd only have time for about half an Ave Maria, then all would be over.

Crispin heard a noise and realized that it was Livith, sobbing. "That hurt, you bastard! Me bum. You broke it." Out of the corner of his eye he watched helplessly as she struggled to her feet. She rubbed her backside and drew her hand over a sloppy, wet nose. "I am going to take an arrow and burrow it deep in that hole in your shoulder. That should feel right good, eh Crispin? That'll be like the fires of Hell, I should think." She kicked his hand, and the dagger flew. Sorrowfully, he watched it go. She limped to where it lay against the wall and picked it up. She turned it in her hand. "Nice. A fair piece, this. I think I'll cut off your ear first. Then the other. Then a few cuts to the neck—not the artery, mind. I want you to linger. I want you to see your blood flowing away."

"After all we've been to one another," he said.

She chuckled, deep and smooth.

Crispin watched her approach and forgot to pray. His mind was full of blasphemies instead, and he licked his lips to utter a few choice ones aloud.

Just then the door flung open. Livith turned. That's all Crispin needed. He projected all his strength, all his weight forward and head-butted Livith in the belly. She flew backward into the arms of Grayce.

Crispin fell to the side, trying to roll to a sitting or crouching position. Livith lay on her back. Her knees jerked up like a dying crab. Crispin saw the knife across the room on the floor. So did Grayce. She was a slow thinker most of the time, but she had no trouble reckoning this situation. She dove for it the same time Crispin did.

Her fingers reached it first, but Crispin closed his hand over hers, trying to wrench it from her. He was weaker than he thought. He wasn't getting anywhere. They rolled along the floor, Crispin doing his best to get the knife. He slammed her hands against the stone floor, once, twice. She leaned forward and dug her teeth into his wrist.

He cried out, but knew he couldn't let her go. He gritted his teeth, sucked in a breath of icy air, and rolled again, this time slamming her head to the floor. That loosened her, and he did it again. She released the knife and he had no trouble rearing up and punching his fist into her face. Now there was blood on his hands, and it wasn't his for a change. For good measure he took her head in both hands and slammed it hard into the floor. Twice. He heard a crack and then a blossom of blood oozed under her head. Her wild hair partially covered her cheek, and strands lodged in her slightly opened mouth and glaring eyes. If she were alive she'd move that hair off of her tongue and teeth. He had a feeling she wouldn't be moving it.

A scream behind him. Livith had risen and stared at the specter of her dead sister. She raised her hands to her head and shrieked again. Then she focused her eyes on Crispin. The pain in her eyes turned to fury and she opened her mouth to emit an animal scream. She picked up the heaviest object within reach—the stool—and raised it over her head, ready to cudgel him.

He wasn't entirely certain what happened next, but the stool seemed to be frozen in midflight, and many hands closed over Livith and dragged her backward. The stool hit the floor and cracked.

Crispin swayed for a moment. Not much left for him to do. Might as well fall to the floor and lose consciousness—which he did.

28

THEY HAD CRISPIN SITTING up in no time. He was grateful to be back in his own lodgings, though he had no memory of the actual journey. Visitors had come and gone, and he had little recollection of them, though he remembered vaguely Gilbert's hand patting his, and Eleanor weeping into her apron.

A man had come, too, a man he didn't know. An older man in a long, black robe, who removed Crispin's shirt and stuck a needle into the hole in his shoulder. Crispin seemed to remember black thread, a ragged sort of pain, and then the sense that he was drunk, or something like drunkenness without the taste of wine. The man, of course, had been a physician, and he sewed up Crispin's shoulder like a tailor. A tailor would have been cheaper, but since someone else had paid for the physician's visit, Crispin didn't worry. The only thing that made him worry later was discovering that Lancaster had sent the man.

A clean bandage covered the packing on his shoulder, and a sling wound about that. A blanket covered what was left of Crispin's modesty, and his coat—the old one recovered from a much relieved Lenny—sat draped over his shoulders. Jack sat on the end of the bed and tried to fill in the gaps in Crispin's knowledge of events.

"Miles Aleyn told all, as you suspected he would," said Jack excitedly. "It was him what killed Edward Peale. Didn't want the arrows to be known as Lancaster's. But ain't that why he stole them in the first place, Master?"

"Yes, Jack. But I can see why he would not want the implication now. It would only turn unwanted attention to him. Did he know about the assassination plot?"

"Aye," said Jack. "Though he didn't know it was Livith and Grayce. It was his job to detain the couriers so that the assassins could meet with them and that was how they were going to get into court. He never noticed them scullions either, neither in France nor here." He shook his head before he looked up, beaming. "Oh! And the best of all, he confessed that *you* had nought to do with it. And that was the last thing they got out of him."

Crispin sipped red wine from a wooden bowl. He knew this flavor. The Langtons had sent it from the Boar's Tusk. "Why so?"

Jack smoothed out the blanket in front of him. He didn't look sorrowful when he said, "The torture killed him, is why. He's deader than a post, and mourned as much."

Crispin lay back and rested the wine bowl on his chest. He couldn't muster a smile, but closed his eyes in satisfaction. Yes. This felt good. Miles had finally gotten his due. Crispin only wished he had been allowed to witness it.

He took a deep breath and opened his eyes. He looked at Jack and found a smile after all. "What of Gilbert and Eleanor? Are they well? Is the sheriff still after them?"

"No. The Lord Sheriff left off after Miles's confession and that of Livith, that whoring bitch. She survived her torture but it won't do her no good. They're set to execute her tomorrow. It should be good and bloody. Want to go?"

Crispin lifted the wine bowl, looked at the blood red wine, and lowered it without drinking. "No. But you may go, if you wish. What of Grayce?"

"Dead. It is rumored that the king of France hired them two. But now I suppose we'll never know."

"No," muttered Crispin. "We'll never know."

"That was a close one this time, Master Crispin. I'm beginning to think that a more quiet life would suit me better."

"Oh? Are you looking for another situation?"

"Ah, I didn't mean that, Master. It's just that . . . you ain't as young as you used to be."

Crispin narrowed his eyes. "Thank you very much."

"I worry over you. Like a mother hen."

"Eleanor does enough of that."

"I can't help m'self. I like looking after you. It makes a man feel . . . important."

"Well, Jack," said Crispin, settling lower on his pillow. "I know I am in good hands."

They both turned toward the door at the sound of many feet climbing the stairs. "More visitors?" sighed Crispin. "Please, Jack. Tell them I'm asleep. Tell them I will not see anyone today."

"Right, Master." Jack jumped up and skipped to the entry. Before the visitors had a chance to knock, he cast open the door. Nothing happened. He stood in the doorway and said nothing, not moving.

Crispin eased up and tried to look over Jack's shoulder. "Who is it, for God's sake?"

Jack turned with a horrified expression. He stepped aside and two men entered, pushing him out of the way. Shiny helms. Arms encased in mail and armor plate. Swords jutting up from scabbards. But worst of all, their surcotes were quartered with red fields of yellow leopards, and blue fields with yellow fleur-de-lis: the ensign of the King of England.

"Crispin Guest," said one. "You are to come with us." A camail of linked steel rings ran up either side of his head from his helm and formed a metal mesh like a wimple over his chin. The edges of his mustache flattened under the steel.

Crispin remembered to breathe. "On what charge?"

The other shook his head. "You are to come with us," he said.

"Where?"

"To court."

A long pause. Crispin's gaze rose toward Jack. The boy froze by the door. *So, this is it.* Crispin cast the blanket aside and eased his naked legs over the edge of the bed. "Jack, help me with my shirt and cotehardie."

Once Jack helped him dress and shave, Crispin stood and allowed the boy to drape his cloak over his shoulders. He turned to the men who had been watching dispassionately. "Gentlemen, I am now ready."

The one who originally spoke grunted, and they both waited for Crispin to open the door before they followed him. Jack threw on his mantle and started after, but one of the guards turned. "You stay."

Jack looked up with frightened eyes at both steely faces. "But I'm Master Crispin's servant. He needs me!"

"He has no need for you. Get back, boy." The man drew back his arm as if to strike. Crispin caught it and held it with his one good hand.

"There's no need for that." He turned back to the boy whose face shone white with panic. "It's all well, Jack. I want you out of this, anyway. You'll be safer here."

"But I thought this was done with! What do they want with you now, Master Crispin?"

"I don't know. But you must stay here. If I do not return . . . then go to the Boar's Tusk. They'll care for you there."

Jack grimaced. He wiped his hand across his face spewing sloppy tears.

"Now Jack. I expect better." He wanted to tell the lad not to worry, to have heart. But he couldn't quite bring himself to utter the lies. Somehow it had all gone too well, too pat. He had been waiting for the other shoe to drop. Well, now it had. "Farewell, Jack. Be good. And . . . thank you for all you've done."

"Master Crispin!" Jack's cry was the last he heard before the guards slammed the door in the boy's face. Crispin sneered at them for their loutishness, and then threw one end of his cloak over his shoulder and proceeded down the stairs.

He had plenty of time to think as they made the long walk to Westminster, they on horseback, he on foot. He spent the time looking at London, at her wharves, her inns, her wretched streets and hovels. When he was a rich lord, Crispin had always taken London for granted. The city was there to supply his needs, both physical and spiritual. Many of his household servants had come from London. He himself was born in London, though he spent his early childhood on his family estates in Sheen. But he knew, as indeed every Englishman knew, that there was nothing to compare throughout the rest of the country with London's markets and shops. No country village possessed the same visceral stench of London, her streets teeming with workers, beggars, thieves, whores, and brigands; but also with nobility and kings, queens and ladies. London was England in miniature, as certainly as Onslow Blunt's spun sugar creation had been.

They reached Charing Cross. The spires of Westminster Abbey and the palace were finally visible. Crispin's heart began a drumbeat. Not that he wasn't ready for the inevitable. He had been ready for a long time. He supposed it had been overdue. But he had set his sights elsewhere, on other things. There was Jack Tucker, for one. The boy had blown into Crispin's life like a whirlwind. He had been just another thief on the streets, with a life sure to end on the gallows. But after only a few short months, he had become smooth like a river stone, doing his best to fit into a world Crispin barely felt comfortable in. He had much he wanted to teach Jack. Now there would be no time.

Gilbert and Eleanor had been good to him, too. There had been no advantage in it. He was no lordling to grant favors. He was even incapable of paying them on time, and he still owed a great deal to them for food—but mostly drink. It seemed they made a friend of him simply because they had wanted to, and this, to Crispin, was a novelty. Was this the advantage in a lack of pedigree? Had he learned this secret only at the end of his life?

He fully expected to enter the palace by the stables or the prisoner's gate, and was slightly surprised to be entering by the grand entrance of the great hall.

Crispin's heart pounded in his ears, so much so, that he could hear very little else.

The hall brimmed with light and people. The rustle of gowns, the buzz of low voices. His recently laundered coat clung to him with sweat.

The crowd parted for him and the hum of conversation died away in whispering echoes. His gaze darted uncertainly from face to face, very few he recognized.

The guards directed him to the dais with Richard's throne, and Crispin inhaled sharply. Richard was there, leaning on his throne, flanked on one side by Michael de la Pole and Robert de Vere, and on the other by John of Gaunt.

Crispin finally stopped before the dais and bowed low to Richard. The king raised his languid lids and studied Crispin. He wore an ermine-trimmed gown covered in gold netting. His hair was neatly trimmed and curled just above his shoulders. His sparse goatee and mustache looked enhanced by a brush of darker powder. He inclined his head—not so much to acknowledge Crispin's obeisance, but to hear the proceedings. The gold crown—a substantial ornament with gems and points—gleamed.

Crispin waited. What was supposed to take place now? Was he to throw himself on the floor and beg for mercy? *Richard can wait till Doomsday.*

The king glared at him. He leaned his chin on a bejeweled hand. "You saved our life," he said.

Crispin almost fell to the floor anyway. With a steady voice and another bow, he said, "Your Majesty."

Richard edged forward. His small eyes studied Crispin. "When was the last time we spoke, Guest? Eh? I was quite young then. Just a boy."

Steady, Crispin. "Seven years, your grace."

Richard sat back. "That's right," he purred. A smile curled the edges of his lips, as careful a couture as his hair. "Seven years. We were newly crowned. Fresh from Westminster Abbey. They brought you before me, remember? In chains. We wanted to look at you; to see the man who would have deposed us for our uncle." He turned his face toward Gaunt who didn't so much as quiver a lash. Richard snorted at his uncle, and turned back to Crispin. "We knew who you were, of course," Richard went on. "You were always polite but . . . unfriendly. We never liked you before, and we certainly did not like you that day. No, indeed." He leaned forward, hands on his knees. "Ever wonder why we never executed you?"

The hall seemed to hold its collective breath. Crispin made certain he kept his gaze riveted to the king. In his head drummed the litany: *Don't look at Gaunt, don't look at Gaunt . . .*

"Many a time, sire," he said aloud.

Richard smiled. It was practiced this time. He clearly enjoyed hearing Crispin's words. "'Many a time,'" he echoed. "It was something you said once. I was quite young, but I remembered it. You said, 'It would be worse for a nobleman to lose all than to lose his life, for all *was* his life.' Do you recall saying such a thing?"

"Not in so many words."

"But certainly your philosophy, eh?"

"It . . . sounds like me, your grace."

The king smiled again. He toyed with a gold chain around his neck. Crispin noted the width and design of the chain and considered that the proceeds from the sale of one link of this decoration could feed Crispin for an entire year. "Today, Guest, you stand before us a different man. Though, by God's wounds, I think you were wearing the same clothes!" The courtiers laughed politely at that, and just as quickly quieted.

"No matter. Today, we are here to recognize the fact that you saved the life of your monarch. Certainly this calls for a reward. What sort of a reward would suit you, Guest? You saved the life of a king. You have saved England. What would be suitable?" He put his finger to his lips in mock speculation.

Crispin dared a glance at Lancaster. Gaunt's face was tight, his lips pressed so firmly they paled.

"I know!" Richard stood. He took a step forward and looked down on Crispin. "Shall we restore your knighthood? Is that your desire?"

The room fell to silence.

Crispin's eyes widened. He swallowed and licked his lips. *What goes on here?* His gaze cut to the other courtiers, but they were just as perplexed as he was. With a suddenly hoarse voice, he softly replied, "As it pleases your Majesty."

"Not as it pleases us, surely," Richard said a little too loudly. "As it pleases *you*, Guest. Shall we do it now?" He turned toward his uncle and whipped out Lancaster's sword from his scabbard but Lancaster was so surprised he tried to reach for the blade before he seemed to realize what was happening and staggered back, surrendering it.

The king's sword hung from the royal hip. Clearly, it wasn't good enough for his purposes.

Richard brandished Lancaster's sword. "Shall we dub you now?"

Crispin stared at the blade. The light from the candles ran like golden beads along its shiny length. So much time had passed. Not just in moments, but in years. Richard was no longer the young boy he had been. He was a young man, able to properly wield a sword, ready to go to war. It wouldn't be long before he didn't need a steward and declared his majority. It wouldn't be long at all.

Richard lowered the sword to his thigh. "But before we do so . . . there is *one* thing." He slowly raised the blade until its point aimed directly at Crispin's chest. "We want to hear you ask for it. Go on, Guest. Ask for your knighthood. And we will grant it."

Lancaster closed his eyes. The king's favorites standing on the other side of his throne looked distinctly uncomfortable, staring at their feet or hands.

Crispin said nothing. He would not drop his gaze from the king.

"Did you hear me, Guest? Your knighthood. And not only that! For what good is a title with no lands and wealth to back it up? Lands and title, that, too, will we restore. All of them. And you will be yourself again, eh? And all you need do is get down on your knees . . . and ask. Well, Guest?"

Crispin felt them all waiting for his reply. He felt their eyes on him, their anxiety as thick as smoke.

All you have to do is drop to your knees, Crispin. Just swallow your damned pride and do it! Have everything you want again. What the hell's the matter with you?

He looked at the floor. Was it only a week ago that Miles laid at his feet begging for mercy? Miles, the man who did not know the first thing about honor?

Crispin wanted to kick himself. *Jesu.* Honor. Gilbert was right. Honor had become the bane of Crispin's existence. It seemed he couldn't take a piss without considering the nobility of the effort. Was honor a lost art? Was Crispin a relic of his own past? If that were so, then perhaps being a courtier wasn't all it used to be.

But to feel the weight of a sword at his hip again; to tell the sheriff to go to Hell; to eat decent food and drink fine wine. What was it worth? A few moments on his knees? A few words that meant little? What was the price of a man's soul?

He flicked his gaze toward Lancaster. Had the duke sold his soul to discover his friends from his foes? He had surrendered the lives of honorable men, including Crispin's. Lancaster had viewed it as a tactical move. And maybe that's all it was. If Crispin had retained his knighthood and status, might he have resorted to the same "tactical" move one day to discover *his* enemies?

He knew he had to say something. Should he make a speech, or just sink to his knees? In the end, only one thing occurred to him.

His voice felt coarse and low. "'Fire is the test of gold; adversity of strong men.'"

Richard frowned. "What did you say? Do you think you've been tested? You, who committed high treason?" The pleasant façade gave way to Richard's ire. He clenched his teeth. "We give you back your life. All you have to do is beg. *Beg!*"

And in that one word, the decision was made. Crispin clamped his lips shut, and lifted his chin.

The silence that followed cut through the crowd with painful intensity.

Richard reddened. He threw down the sword. The weapon clanged at his feet and skidded down two steps. "You whoreson! And *that* is precisely why you shall *never* regain your knighthood. You stubborn, arrogant bastard! We will *never, ever* trust you. *Never.*" He panted and backed up to the throne. When the back of his knees hit the seat he fell into it. The feel of it under him seemed to have a calming effect and he wiped his disarrayed hair out of his face. He straightened his shoulders. "Yes, your own man, I see." He gave a hollow laugh and turned to de Vere. "A martyr to the last. Saint Crispin. No shoemaker you. You make armor of old tunics, and swords of your words. A shabby knight without holdings. Is that what you are? Sir Crispin of the Gutter? Then we so dub you." He spat. It hit Crispin's cheek. Crispin slowly raised his hand and wiped the royal spittle away. "Still," said Richard, voice calm but face red, "you do deserve some reward for your altruistic actions." De Vere handed him a pouch. The king took it and tossed it forward. It arced over the steps and landed with the loud clink of coins at Crispin's feet. He had no doubt that there was a fine sum within. "Payment in full," said Richard.

Crispin looked down at the bulging pouch. Gold. He was certain of it. Enough to buy a string of tinker shops and maybe an inn or two. Enough to set himself up well for the rest of his days. Enough in the Shambles sense, at any rate.

He raised his head and looked at the king. Richard wore a self-satisfied sneer, and he turned his face toward his favorites, who smiled in complicity at their monarch. What else could they do?

Indeed. Crispin looked at the money pouch again. He saw his future receding, saw a life of relative ease decaying to dust. *Sir Crispin of the Gutter, eh? For seven years it was so. Well, and why not?*

"I saved the life of the king not for gold, your Majesty," he said in a clear tenor. "But in recompense for my faults. And because . . . England needs a king."

Richard fixed his eyes on Crispin. The royal lips were pressed tightly together.

Crispin gave one last wistful look at the pouch, bowed low to Richard, and turned on his heel.

He heard Richard jump to his feet behind him and the commotion of men and women whispering.

"Guest! You dishonorable bastard! You dare turn your back on your king? Guest!" Crispin was tempted to look back like Lot's wife, but he had no desire to turn to a pillar of salt. "Don't ever show your face at court again, Guest! Do you hear me? *NEVER RETURN TO COURT!*"

Crispin walked unimpeded all the way through the great hall's arch before he dared draw a breath.

29

CRISPIN SAT ON THE spine of a roof next to his back window and hugged his knees. The last of the day's golden light had sunk westward an hour ago, swallowed by churning blue-gray rainclouds. His cloak kept him warm enough, but he wondered today if his boots would keep him from slipping down the slick tiles. He further wondered if he cared.

He had either done the most foolish thing in his life or the bravest. Even now he still wasn't certain which it was. At least this time Richard appeared to the world like a spoiled child and all the court witnessed it. Still, to have been a hairsbreadth from his knighthood. So close to a sword in his hand once more . . .

"Master Crispin! What by God's wounds are you doing out there? I've been searching all over for you!"

Jack leaned out the window. His pale face seemed paler in the dark, and little wonder. The last he saw of Crispin, he was being escorted by two guards to court, and for all the both of them knew, to the gallows.

"Come on out, Jack."

Jack climbed out onto the sill and with arms outstretched for balance, made his way across the peak and sat next to Crispin.

"What are you doing, Master, if a body may ask?"

"Looking at the city. I think I prefer it at night. It's not as dark as one thinks."

His gaze followed along the spiky silhouette of the cityscape, rising and falling against a pocked field of stars so sharp they pierced the veil of night in pinpricks of light.

Jack hugged his knees and rested his chin on them. "I spend many a night like this, Master. You can see candles lit all over the city. It's never completely asleep, is it? The city, I mean. I used to look at windows glowing with light, wishing— Ah well."

"Wishing what?"

"Well, that I was inside."

"Men like us, Jack. We're never inside."

Jack fell silent. It was companionable. Until he felt the boy twitching beside him. He cocked his head and Jack's mouth was taut with thinking.

"Well?" asked Crispin.

"How did Grayce hide her bow anyway? You searched that room at the King's Head."

"Not as thoroughly as I should have done. I must confess that I did not expect to find a bow and so I little searched for one. But I suspect it was under the table all along. That was where Livith retrieved her bow in our last encounter."

Jack nodded and said nothing more. After a while, Crispin felt the boy staring at him. When he turned, Jack's eyes glittered at him in the darkness. "I heard a fool rumor about you," said Jack. "It can't possibly be true, now can it?"

Crispin rubbed his sore shoulder. "Oh? What rumor was that?"

Jack straddled the roof to face Crispin. "Well, the way I heard it, the king offered you your knighthood again, and you threw it back in his face. But that would be a lie, now wouldn't it?"

"And do you honestly think that the king, a man with little interest in honor or just causes, would champion me and offer me knighthood?"

Crispin flinched and almost slipped off the roof with Jack's surprisingly vigorous clout. The lad seemed to have forgotten his subservience. Crispin rubbed the offended shoulder.

"You dunderpate! He did! He sarding did! You idiot! And you have to go and turn your nose up at it, because Christ knows you've got all the money in the world! What in hell did you do a sarding, stupid thing like that for?"

Crispin offered a lopsided grin. "You truly had to have seen it for yourself."

Jack burrowed into his knees and mantle, grumbling. "You always tell me I must better m'self, but when you've got the chance, that's another tale."

"I do want you to better yourself." Crispin listened to Jack muttering for a time and then chuckled. Jack had none of the advantages Crispin had had, but the boy was very much like Crispin nevertheless. He recognized something of himself in Jack when he was that age. It seemed so long ago now. Eighteen years. A lot can happen to a man in eighteen years. A lot of good . . . or a lot of bad.

Crispin stood and nudged Jack back toward the window. He helped Crispin's bad side. Once back in the small room, Crispin held his free hand up to the hearth and looked about at the single candle, one chair, and one stool. He considered for a moment, then walked to the coffer, opened it, and took out his writing things. He placed the wax slate and stylus on the table and gestured to the stool. "Jack, how would you like to learn to read and write?"

Jack stood by the hearth and swiveled his head toward Crispin. "Me? You going to teach *me*?"

"Yes. Why not?"

"I'm just a— I can't learn no reading or writing."

"Don't be a fool. Of course you can. Now sit down." Jack stood as he was, nailed to the spot. His face was somber and white. Crispin patted the stool as if encouraging some stray dog to approach. After a long moment, Jack seemed to surrender something and shuffled along the floor until he reached the table. Slowly, he lowered to the stool. "We'll start with Latin. Then French. English, of course. And if you are a quick study, even Greek. Then you can read Aristotle for yourself instead of my quoting him to you."

Jack's jaw hadn't closed since Crispin's pronouncement. "You can't mean it. I'm . . . I'm only a cutpurse."

"You want to be a cutpurse all your life? You're my servant. And my protégé, if you wish. Don't you want to be a Tracker, too? To that end, I think it time I pay you a wage—say one farthing for each job I get. How does that sound?"

Jack didn't move. His face grew solemn. More than that. His mouth curved downward in a sorrowful grimace and suddenly a single tear traveled from his reddening eye down his pale cheek. He raised his hand and slowly opened the laces of his tunic, reached in, and pulled out a pouch fashioned in smooth, oxblood leather. Obviously not Jack's pouch. He lifted it toward Crispin, hand trembling. "I don't know who to return it to," he whispered.

Crispin solemnly took it. "As this is your last—isn't it?"

"Oh aye, sir." He crossed himself. "You can be sure of that!"

"Then tomorrow we'll give it to Abbot Nicholas and you can make your confession to him. Start clean."

"Aye, Master."

"Wipe your face and come closer to the candle. Now this is how you write your name in English." Crispin sounded out each letter as he penned them. "J-A-C-K. And in Latin . . . I-A-C-O-B-U-S and in French . . . J-A-C-Q-U-E-S . . ."

Crispin handed Jack the stylus and allowed himself a smile. Here was something no king could confer or ever take away.

Author's Afterword

John of Gaunt, duke of Lancaster, was something of an imposing figure in his day. Even though the plot that ruined Crispin's life is my own fiction, there were, no doubt, many plots laid for and by the intimidating duke.

Born in Ghent (Gaunt), Flanders, in 1340, he began his fighting career early and married well to further his holdings. He married his third cousin Blanche of Lancaster, and when his father-in-law died, he inherited the title, becoming the earl of Lancaster, which made him the wealthiest man in England. Later, his father, Edward III, made him a "duke." He campaigned with his older brother Edward of Woodstock (the Black Prince) and fought many battles in the Hundred Years War and in aid to his ally Peter the Cruel of Castile, though many of his more successful battles were in backrooms rather then on a battlefields.

When Blanche died, he married Peter's daughter Constance, or Costanza, and laid claim to the throne of Castile. He took command of the troops when his brother Edward fell ill, and through backroom and bedroom dealings, gained control of England while his father, Edward III, declined in health. If Edward of Woodstock had died without an heir, John would certainly have become king. But it is the quirk of the line of succession that fouled that up. Edward might have been quite competent. He was certainly well-liked, but he died right before his father himself gave up the ghost and Richard was the next in line.

The "Good Parliament" of 1376 cut Gaunt down to size by stripping him and his cohorts of power, but it wasn't long until he rebounded, put his friends in place, and put together his own handpicked Parliament in 1377. At this time his nephew Richard II came to the throne with Gaunt more or less as steward. Gaunt again was the most powerful man in England. He made some decisions that did not always sit well with the people, but since he wasn't the king he let Richard take the brunt of it. He made darned sure, in fact, that he wasn't associated with any talk of taking the reins from Richard. If he had wanted to do it, he surely could have. One wonders why he did not chose to do so.

In his household, Lancaster had the court poet Geoffrey Chaucer as a loyal friend and servant. Was it because he liked the poet or liked his sister-in-law more? For the duke entertained Chaucer's sister-in-law Katherine Swynford as his mistress for over twenty-five years, and even married her a year after Constance died. Katherine wasn't his first mistress. When he was a young man he took one of his mother's ladies-in-waiting as a mistress, Marie de St. Hiliare, and had a daughter with her, named Blanche Plantagenet. All told, he had about fourteen children both legitimate and il-, with nine living into adulthood. His illegitimate children from Katherine Swynford were made legitimate by King Richard when John finally married her, but they were barred from inheriting the throne.

Meanwhile, King Richard II had a falling out with the duke's legitimate son Henry Bolingbroke and kicked him out of the country. But it was Lancaster who got the last laugh. By the end of the century, Richard was forced to abdicate and was then left to starve to death. Lancaster's son Henry seized the throne and thus the royal House of Lancaster began. Unfortunately, the venerable duke was in his grave by then.

But speaking of inheriting the throne, Gaunt's eldest son by Katherine Swynford, John, had a granddaughter, Margaret Beaufort, whose son became Henry VII and who took the throne from the last Plantagenet, Richard III. And Henry VII in turn married Elizabeth of

York (who was also related to John of Gaunt), thus ending the York and Lancaster feud known as the War of the Roses.

Last laugh indeed.

The assassination plot in this story was my fiction, but it was certainly a precursor of things to come. Richard's reign began with hopeful spirits for a young monarch, only to end in tragedy years later. Crispin may have disliked Richard now (and indeed, Crispin reflected that sentiment in the Latin he used to bless the Crown, translated as "May you rot in Hell, loathsome king") but it was only later in Richard's reign that the citizens of England began to feel the same way.

These events are far removed from the next chapter in Crispin's story as he encounters his new adventure. This time it is the serial murders of children, the mysteries of the Kabbalah, and a dangerous golem on the loose in *A Conspiracy of Parchment*.

And by the way, you can keep track of some of Crispin's thoughts by going to his blog at www.CrispinGuest.com.

Glossary

ARRAS a tapestry.

BASELARD a slim-bladed dagger.

CAMAIL, or AVENTAIL a netting of ring mail that shielded the neck.

CHEMISE shirt for both male and female, usually white. All-purpose, might also be used as a nightshirt.

COTEHARDIE (COAT) any variety of upper-body outerwear popular from the early Middle Ages to the Renaissance. For men, it was a coat reaching to the thighs or below the knee, with buttons all the way down the front and sometimes at the sleeves. Worn over a chemise. Sometimes the belt was worn at the hips and sometimes the belt moved up to the waist. This is what Crispin wears.

DEGRADED when knighthood is taken from a man, usually because of treason or other crimes against the crown.

FLETCHER a maker of arrows.

FLETCHING the feathered part of an arrow.

HOUPPELANDE Fourteenth-century upper-body outerwear with fashionably long sleeves that often touched the ground.

JETTY/JETTIED the part of the upper floor of a building that juts out over the street.

GIRDLE a belt.

GONFALON a banner ending in long streamers.

SENNIGHT a period of seven days, a week.

SHRIVE/SHRIVEN to make confession in the penitential sense.

STOTT an inferior horse.

SUMPTER a baggage horse.

TRAPPER a colorful covering on a horse as one might see at a tournament or in battle, presenting the knight's colors.

TUN a large cask for wine, beer, or whatnot.

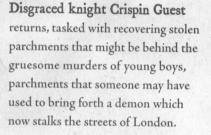